Cupid's Contract

S.N. Moor

Contents

To all the smutty social media groups that give women a place to find the word porn that tickles their fancy without fear of judgement. Who create a safe space and don't yuck someone's yum. You are the cliterati, a group of well read, smutty fuckers who always come through in a clutch. The ones, when someone asks for a rec on squid love, monster smut, feathers or three dicks, have books at the ready. You are amazing and should be appreciated!

Warnings

This is a reverse harem/why choose holiday romance. If you like it spicy, then welcome, welcome. Find a seat, grab your toys, grab a page holder in case you feel the need for the one handed read.

There is attempted sexual assault (not by the MMCs)

You will find DVP, TP, anal, throat grabbing, dom/sub, praise, kick ass female, a spunky, fun-loving bestfriend, and an unexpected ending. I don't want to spoil the ending, but if you need more explanation then click here.

"It's a Cupid party."

FUCK ME.

I glanced across my display of battery operated boyfriends, BOB for short, and they were all on life support. My favorite, the bright green one, with a large ripply shaft and little nubs on the end, was the worst off. My best friend, Lizzy, bought it for me when I was going through a monster smut kick. She thought it would make me feel like I was fucking a monster.

I guess I won't be using any of you tonight! I grabbed my phone off the dresser and flipped open the Let's Mingle app. At Christmas, I signed up for a one year subscription because I was drunk and the ad rhymed. Jingle, Jingle, Let's Mingle!

I'm a sucker for ads that rhyme. And gift with purchase. It could explain why I have a bar cabinet full of random liqueurs and fifty different martini glasses. Christmas is the best time of year to buy alcohol because of all the deals. Did I need all that liquor? No. But I was sad and wanted to be drunk. My favorite is the no stem martini glass with a pair of beady eyes at the bottom looking at you. Seriously, what was I thinking?

As soon as the app opens, the bubble beside my name turns green and my phone dings.

Eight new matches.

I quickly flipped through them all, but nothing catches my eye. I closed the app and dialed Lizzy, who picks up on the first ring.

"Bitch, you were supposed to call two hours ago!" She yelled into the phone, bass thumping loudly behind her.

I pulled the phone away from my ear for a second. "I'm calling now."

"Are you coming tonight?"

"I hope so." I looked longingly at Bob, Bob, Bob, and Bob.

"What? To the Valentine's party," she yelled again, before letting out a squeal. "Tony says you should totally come. He has a friend he wants you to meet."

I rolled my eyes. That was the entire reason I didn't want to go play third wheel at whatever club they were at. Not only did I think it was a stupid holiday created by jewelry companies to squeeze money out of men who were buying jewelry to apologize for not being present enough the rest of the year, but I didn't want to be set up.

I was old enough I should be in a stable, committed relationship, but that didn't really seem like it was in the future for me. The longest relationship I had was my last, which was fourteen months. I really thought we were going somewhere, and apparently he did too, with three other women. It's been six months since our official break up, so now I've become the natural pet project for most of my friends and Lizzy, being the biggest pusher of them all.

Her and Tony have been in a relationship for three months and one day. I knew this because we had to go out yesterday for her to find a special outfit for their three-month anniversary. We ended up at Le Rousso's, the local kink shop, because she wanted something extra spicy. When she caught me looking at their vibrator collection, she tried to buy me another one, which I declined, but am now regretting. She then insisted I come to this Valentine's party tonight.

I lied and said I had plans because I thought I did. I glared at my toys. Traitors!

"You know you don't have to set me up. I'm totally fine being single right now. I love the fact I'm getting to meet people."

"You were staring at a wall of dildos yesterday. How many people could you be meeting?" Fortunately, it seemed she had stepped outside because the music was quieter and she was no longer yelling.

"It's always good to have variety."

"Of men. Not dildo's."

"I beg to disagree."

"Girl. Come on. I know you're not doing anything tonight. You hate this holiday, so come and hang out with your friends and get wasted."

"It's a Valentine's party. You want me to go to a party celebrating the holiday I hate?"

She laughed. "When you say it like that, it does sound bad! I want you to come hang out with your BFF at a dance club and possibly go home with someone new. I'm just trying to help you get some. Isn't that what a wing lady is supposed to do?"

"Fine. I'll be there in a little bit. Text me the address."

"Wait. You need to dress up."

"Dress up?"

"Yes. It's a cupid party."

"What the fuck is a cupid party?"

She laughed that kind of laugh where you know you're fucked. The kind of laugh where your best friend just roped you into some crazy shit they knew you wouldn't like, so they made you agree to come before they told you all the details.

"Why am I still friends with you?"

"Because you love me, and your life would be boring as hell without me in it."

I shook my head, trying to figure a way out of this. "I don't have an outfit."

"Boo boo, do you think I would let you come unprepared? Go get the big red box from under your bed."

"You're shitting me."

"I shit you not."

I put the phone on speaker and walked hastily to the edge of my bed, dropped to my knees, and pulled the large box out.

"Hurry. Open it! You're going to love it."

"I doubt it."

"Stop, puss pants."

I untied the red velvet bow and cautiously lifted the lid off.

"What the fuck am I looking at?"

I lifted the white feather trimmed bra and matching panties, white sheer slip looking thing and a pair of red wings.

"Is this a fucking sex party?"

"No. No. No. Not really. But you have to dress up to get in."

"Like this?"

"Well, the men's match, but with no shirts on, obviously."

"Obviously."

I dropped the items back into the box and rubbed my face.

"You ok, boo?"

"Why didn't you tell me it was a Cupid party?"

"Because you'd say no," she paused for only a second. "Tony's friend is super hot and looking forward to meeting you."

"Yay," I said sarcastically.

"Get your ass over here!" The music in the background got louder, so she must have walked back inside.

"Fine. You owe me, though."

"You can repay me with your orgasms." She laughed out loud, the kind of laugh that you only do when you're drunk and realize you said something wildly inappropriate, but you don't care.

"Bye and please don't drink too much."

The line went dead.

I looked back at the box and picked the pieces up one at a time.

Here goes nothing.

Whammo Blammo

THIRTY MINUTES LATER I was waiting for my ride share to pull up, dressed in the skimpiest outfit I'd worn in several years, with an inconspicuously conspicuous beige trench coat draped around me with a pair of red angel wings in my hand and six inch red stilettos on.

The light blue, four-door sedan pulled up two minutes later with a woman as old as my grandmother driving, with her hair in rollers and a daisy patterned top on. I checked the license plate with the app on my phone and the driver's picture matched.

Betty.

Of all the people I could have gotten, it would be a Betty. I was certain I was going to have the scripture read to me on the entire car ride to the club.

I climbed in the back seat and she confirmed the address of the club. She flipped on her blinker and slowly pulled onto the road, casting several curious glances my way. This was going to be the most awkward twenty-minute ride of my life.

Lizzy sent me a picture of her and Tony. Her large white wings were highlighted against her light brown skin and dark hair and Tony was on her arm, chest exposed, loving life. She looked so happy and I loved that for her. I just didn't love she was in the dating stage where she tried to replicate her happiness in my life. She's already told me she was going to marry this guy, which seems a bit premature, but she's certain. And one thing about Lizzy is she always gets her way. I looked at the wings on the seat. Case in point. And the three times I've met Tony, he seemed over the moon with her too, so hopefully it worked out. She'd had some real assholes in the past, so I'd be ecstatic if she found her Prince Charming.

"Big plans tonight?" Betty asked with a deep southern accent, gripping the steering wheel.

"A party." Keep it simple.

She nodded and hummed. Yea Betty, I, too, would be wondering what kind of party I was going to.

"I did that once," she blurted, without reservation.

"Go to a party?"

She hesitated for a second, "Yes. A party."

You little wild child Betty, I teased to myself.

"Then the cops were called."

"Oh." My neck jerked back in surprise. Shit.

"Yea. They caught me snorting coke off a penis."

I choked. What the fuck, Betty? Not at all where I saw this story going.

"Sorry if that was too much. I just figured, you know. With you dressed like that... going to a party and all."

"No, no. All good." I pinched my arm to make sure I hadn't somehow hit my head and was passed out at my house. "What... happened?" Dare I ask... Yes, I dare. I very fucking much dare. Betty has surprised me and now I need to know more about her party.

She noticeably relaxed. "Well, I stopped going to parties. Scared me straight. I was rebelling against my father. He was our town's local preacher."

I swallowed hard and then looked around the car for hidden cameras. I felt like I was being punked right now. "So you never went to another party again because of the one?"

"Well, no. I wasn't allowed to."

"You weren't allowed to go to anymore parties? Can they do that?" I felt bad for Betty. One time getting caught snorting coke off a penis and bam! No more parties!

"Well, yea. I suppose they can." She shook her head like I had asked a stupid question, but there was clearly something I was missing. "Anyway, I settled down and found a real nice man who takes real good care of me now."

I looked around again, certain I'd missed the cameras on the first pass. I felt like there were large chunks... important chunks, missing from her story.

"Is it just you? It's not safe to be going to parties alone."

I couldn't help but feel parties was a code word for something else. "No. There's... I don't know how many people are there, but I would have to guess a lot. It's at a club. I'm meeting my best friend there with her boyfriend."

"Oh, that's trouble."

"What is?"

"You should never mix personal and business. That's what did me in."

I shook my head, not knowing where the story was going again. "How so?" But I couldn't stop. I had to know more.

"Well, Darlene thought it'd be fun to have me over for a party for her and her boyfriend. They had a couple other friends over, but it was Darlene's boyfriend's birthday and she wanted to do something real special for him."

"Seems nice."

She huffed, "I told her. I said, Darlene. Now listen. This ain't a good idea. But Darlene, she didn't listen. Put us two in a room together, turned the music on and, well, Darlene's boyfriend thought it was a different kind of present. I stripped for him and what not, had me about three beers too many and next thing you know." She hit the steering wheel. "You guessed it. Cock out, me on my knees snorting coke. Darlene's neighbors called the police on us and, apparently, Darlene's boyfriend had locked the door when

I wasn't looking. So they bust in, thinking I was a hooker. I mean, I guess I kind of was, but only the one time."

"Wow."

"Yea. Didn't speak to Darlene for a while after that. She was mad at me and I's mad at her."

"That was unfair to you."

"Heck yeah, it was. I was just trying to do my friend a favor and whammo blammo."

"Whammo blammo for sure." Note to self: don't get locked in a room with Tony and snort coke off his cock.

I stared out of the window, trying to process the twists and turns of that conversation, when we pulled up to the club a few minutes later. I stepped out of the car, but she called me back.

"Listen here. I've left that life behind me, but if you need me, you keep my number handy. I'll come get you. Us ladies of the night have to stick together." She nodded with a stone cold serious look on her face.

She thought I was a hooker. "Oh. I'm not a hooker."

"Me either," she winked.

Pink drinks are dangerous

I WATCHED BETTY TAKE off down the road and was beginning to second guess this whole thing. I looked at Betty's business card in my hand before I stuffed it in my little purse.

I felt so ridiculous right now. It had been a while since I dressed in anything that one could call sexy and paraded around in front of a bunch of strangers. My confidence was completely shot after my ex, but I kept reminding myself this was for Lizzy. I had to show her I was ok, even if I didn't fully believe it myself. Fake it, 'til you make it?

Valentine's Day was still four days away, but I already felt like it was suffocating me.

I glanced at the long line of people standing against the wall waiting to get in; some dressed in more clothes than me, but most in less. Which was saying a lot.

"Everlee!" I heard yelled from my left.

Lizzy was standing behind a rather large bouncer, waving at me. I looked to my right and saw the long line of people and then back to her.

"Come over here!" she yelled, bouncing up and down.

I walked over to her, and the bouncer looked me up and down, then moved the rope out of the way. I ignored the moans and groans from people still bouncing impatiently outside, no doubt cold from the winter air.

"What took you so long?"

"I had to get dressed and catch a ride. Not everyone lives down the street from the hot new club."

She batted her hand, ignoring me, and started untying the knot on my jacket.

"Well, if I knew you felt this way about me." I teased, shrugging the jacket off.

"Girl, you know I'd fuck you. I just didn't think you'd go for it."

I blew a breath from my nose and caught her smile, before she turned and handed my jacket to the attendant at the front desk, grabbing a ticket from them.

"Here. Don't lose this."

Ticket number sixty-nine, with a bar code on the bottom. I chuckled. What were the odds? Sixty-nine had been a running joke with us forever. We would set each other's thermostat to sixty-nine, may or may not have rounded a number or percentage to sixty-nine for work presentations, or gave an extra tip to round up to sixty-nine dollars. General immature shenanigans, but it always made us chuckle, and I loved it.

"Put your wings on and fix your tits."

"What's wrong with my tits?" I slipped the wings on and lifted my tits up.

"Nothing now." She patted the top of them like bongos. "Girl, you are fire."

"How much have you had to drink?"

"Enough." She winked, grabbing my hand and leading me through the club.

It was my first time at Club Vixen and it seemed like it could be a fun place. It was a new club in town and most of the decor was glossy black table tops and bar tops with light beams shooting around the room. There were several floor to ceiling cages set up with people dancing in them and a few others which had swings hanging inside. I don't know if the people in the cages were employees or others having fun, but the swings were calling my name. Give me a couple of drinks and I knew I'd be trying to sneak in.

A woman dressed in a black bra and matching underwear with black wings walked by carrying a tray of light pink shots. Lizzy grabbed two glasses and handed one to me.

"Free?"

"Yea. Your entry into the club covered all the costs."

"But I didn't pay."

"Tony did. He covered the party."

"Well, isn't that nice of him." I knocked my drink back and felt the burn ease down my throat and into my chest. "So where is this friend of his?"

She pointed across the room to a group of people standing in a corner, but with all the feathers and everyone wearing white, pink, or red, they all sort of looked the same. "He's super nice and cute, too."

"Will he make me come in the bathroom?" I laughed.

"Sorry," I said after I bumped into some guy walking past me.

Lizzy slapped my arm. "You dirty whore," she laughed.

"I thought it was a valid question. I need to feel my twat tingle. I need that big dick energy tonight."

Lizzy was still laughing when we got over to the group. I recognized a few of the people from various parties they'd had over the last couple of months, but really only knew Lizzy.

"Everlee, Derek. Derek, Everlee," she introduced.

"Hi," he smiled, holding his hand out for a handshake.

He was attractive. Dark tan skin, green eyes and dark hair trimmed short. He was wearing a pair of red silk boxers with hearts all over them and a set of red wings.

"Hey love," a man said, placing his hand on my back.

I turned and didn't recognize him. "Hi?" I said cautiously.

"Can I buy you a drink?"

"They're free dick wad. Keep moving. She's not interested," Lizzy interjected.

My head snapped in her direction. "A bit aggressive, don't you think?"

"I don't need some horn dog on my hoe."

"I'm your hoe now?" I smiled. "It's the drinks, sorry. You know how possessive I become."

"I'd hate to see what you'd do if a girl in here came up to Tony."

"Oh, they won't."

"They won't?" I asked, confused by her certainty.

"No. He's in white."

I looked around the group and saw most were in white, a few in pink, and a few others with red. "What don't I know, Lizzy?"

She smiled a wicked smile.

"Damn it, Lizzy, what did you not tell me?"

"You remember back when we were in college and we used to go to those stoplight parties?"

I closed my eyes slowly, letting everything click into place. "Let me guess. White off limits, pink maybe, and red is ready to bone?" I caught a shocked look on Derek's face and pulled my lips in apology for the assumption.

"Pretty much."

"Damn it Lizzy."

"You didn't tell her?" Tony asked, grabbing her arm, entering the conversation.

"You didn't tell Derek!" she snapped back.

I looked at Derek, whose lips pinched into a flat line, and he shook his head.

A woman in black walked by carrying another tray of drinks. I grabbed two off and knocked one back, and offered the second to Derek.

"No thanks. I don't drink." I couldn't hide the surprise on my face, and he quickly added, "I drink. Just not shots... or liquor... anymore."

"One time in Cabo, he had a few too many tequila shots," Tony added, providing context.

I knocked the other shot back before the conversation fell awkwardly quiet. I got the impression Derek was not super comfortable here and was probably lured out by Tony and Lizzy. Poor guy. I felt bad for him, but I needed to get my feathers flicked and my candy licked, and I was thinking he wouldn't be the one to do it. I know it made me sound whorish, but damn, it's been six months.

"Those shots are fantastic. They taste like those little sugary candy hearts," I said, licking the remnants off my top lip, trying to find another girl in black with a tray.

The room was packed with people dancing and lights jutting from side to side. It was almost mesmerizing to watch. I started to get a tingly feeling and looked up to the balcony above and found a pair of electric blue eyes watching me. The man had feathery dark hair, strong jawline with a sexy five o'clock shadow, and was wearing all black. He had those smoldering fuck me eyes I was hoping Derek was going to have, but Derek seemed like a good guy. The guy you'd want to meet your parents, but not the kind who could rock your world in bed. A soft fuck kind of guy. Not saying he'd be bad, but there would be that thing missing.

I couldn't pull my eyes away from the man and found myself not wanting to. I created a game in my head- a staring contest- one which he didn't know the rules of, so I would win. Was it stupid? Yes. But I liked games and right now I was loving this one. I felt my heart beating faster the longer we stared at one another. Was he playing with me, too? Testing me? Waiting for me to turn away?

I saw another man in a black suit, equally attractive, whisper something to him. His lips flattened and his face changed from amusement to frustration. His hands gripped the railing a little tighter before he turned to walk away.

"What are you looking at?" Lizzy asked, putting her cheek beside mine. "Oh, that's the owner's suite up there."

"Owner's suite?"

"Yea. Do you want to meet them?"

I looked at her, shocked. "No. Why? Do you know them?"

She laughed. "No. But Tony and Derek do. They helped design this place. I could talk to Tony."

"No. That's ok."

"Good. Tony said they were kind of weird."

"Weird?" Is it bad I was intrigued? I glanced back up to the balcony, but he was gone.

"Yea. He said there are four of them, but only one really talked to him. The others were... not standoffish... but I don't know."

"Maybe they were under a tight deadline to get the club opened and they each had their own roles," I defended, garnering an odd look from her.

"Anyway..." she laughed, turning us back around to the group. "We have this entire area." She waved her arm around to several seats and tables. "We are VIPs tonight, baby."

"Wooo!" I yelled, feeling the spirits of St. Valentine- rather St. Rum and St. Vodka- flowing through me.

"Want to go dance?" Lizzy asked our little group of four.

Both of the boys politely declined with the look of panic on their faces. "Let's go," I grabbed Lizzy's hand and dragged her to the packed dance floor. It had been a while since she and I went to a club and danced the night away. On the way there, I snatched us another shot off the passing tray and knocked it back.

"You should probably slow down," Lizzy warned softly.

"You've had at least as many as I have."

"Yes, but we all know I handle my liquor way better than you. I don't need you ending up in one of those swings tonight."

I squeezed both of her hands and twirled in a circle. "Do you think they'd let me?"

"No, and don't even think about it." She sounded like a parent talking to a child.

"You couldn't have Tony talk to them?"

"You're serious?" She stopped dancing for a second and then laughed. "You're one crazy bitch and I love it."

"Thanks."

"Anytime hooker."

"I won't snort coke off anyone's penis. I draw the line there." I shimmied my hips down and popped back up. "I guess technically that would be passed the line, so the line would be somewhere behind that. Or before that? And not the line of coke, obviously, because I'm not doing that."

"What in the fuck are you talking about?" she asked, thoroughly confused.

"Betty."

"Who's Betty?"

"She was my driver here. She's found Jesus now, but apparently she was not hookering for a friend and ended up doing blow of her BFF's boyfriend's dick." I laughed out loud as a thought hit me. "Do you think if she gave him head while there was coke on it, she could say she was blowing blow?"

Lizzy looked at me with a concerned smile on her face. "Let's go to the bar and get you some water."

"I'm fine." I was not fine. The room was spinning just a little, but I didn't need her babying me. I'll admit I probably had too many shots too quick together, but I wanted to have fun tonight. I may not have wanted to be here at first, but once I committed, I was all the way in. Which is why Rich hurt me so much. I was fucking committed. Planning out our future and babies and everything else. "Asshole."

"What?" Lizzy asked, pulling me across the club.

"Sorry. Inside thought slipped out." I leaned in and whispered, "Hey if my boob slipped out, would you tell me?"

"Yes. Yes, I would tell you." Lizzy pushed her way through the crowd to an open spot at the bar and flagged down a bartender. He was attractive with dark hair, dark eyes and a short trimmed beard that was perfectly etched along his jawbone, wearing black pants and a nipple piercing. That was it.

"Can I get a glass of water and a menu?"

"We don't have food here."

"Nothing?"

The man's lips flattened.

"Shit."

"She going to be ok?" He nodded in my direction.

"Yes. She-" I shook my head. "I'm going to be fine. Just keep those vixens-" I laughed out loud, realizing I didn't even mean to say that. "Sorry. I didn't mean... Nevermind. Just keep those delicious pink drinks away from me."

"That's my creation." He smiled pridefully.

"Well, you're going to hell sir, because those are delightful." I pointed my finger in the air.

He chuckled, "You're probably right, but not for that. They also pack a punch. How many?"

"Three."

"Four," Lizzy corrected.

"No." I counted back on my fingers. "Fuck. Yea. Four."

"I'll send someone out to get you some food."

"No, you don't have to."

"I think I do. If Callum found out my drink fucked up a lot of people, he'd kill me. So really, I'm doing it for myself, not you."

"Well, as long as you're being selfish." I winked. Was I hitting on the bartender? I mean, I'd tap that, but damn. I was horny and he was super fun to flirt with.

He waved someone over and whispered something in their ear before pulling his card out of his pocket.

"You're over there?" He pointed across the bar to the area where Tony and Derek were standing.

"Yea. How did you know?"

"I make it a point to keep an eye out on all the pretty ladies that could cause me trouble," he winked.

I couldn't help but smile.

I stopped and turned around when I saw him looking at something above my head. The man from earlier was looking down at us... me, again. In all my alcohol induced stupidity, I winked at him. His head tilted to the side like I'd broken him. Was he a robot? He huffed before he walked off. Not a robot.

I looked back at the bartender. "Who was that?"

"Who?"

"That man up there looking at us."

His face fell. "That was Callum."

"He didn't look too happy."

He looked down at the bar. "He's... an acquired taste. I have to go help some other patrons," he said before darting off, but then called back, "I'll bring you that food over though."

When he can't hear the word no, put him in his place.

LIZZY AND I WERE in a deep conversation about nipple piercings when I felt a tap on my shoulder. I turned around to find Callum, the mystery man from the second-floor balcony, standing behind the table with a bag of food in his hand. His intense stare focused on me, with a hint of something else. Annoyance? Curiosity?

"Thank you," I said, standing up to reach for the bag, but tripped over the shoes Lizzy had left on the ground. In my tipsy... yes, tipsy, not drunk state, I fell towards Callum. It was like I was in one of those fucking romcoms. Look at me clumsy bumsy, catch me if you can.

And he did. He not only caught me with one arm, but leaned me back like we had choreographed a sexy dance routine, eyes locked, staring at one another. My skin was on fire under his touch and under his gaze. He definitely had big dick energy with delicious fuck me eyes and I'm pretty sure my whole body was yelling pick me! Pick me!

"Everlee!" Lizzy shouted in shock. "Here," Lizzy said as she stepped forward to grab the bag out of his hand, breaking our trance.

With his other hand free, he used it to help me stand upright. I wobbled in place, staring at him, not because of the alcohol, but because he made my head spin. Holy shit! I'd be his valentine.

His eyes narrowed on mine. "You shouldn't drink so much," he commanded before turning around.

Before thinking, I sarcastically replied, "Yes, sir."

His head snapped around and there was a fire ignited in his eyes. I felt my breast swell and my stomach tighten as my breath hitched in my throat. Could I orgasm off a single look? Because fuck, I was close. Or was I masturbating in public and not realizing it? I looked down, relieved to find my hands hanging by my side.

When I looked back up, he was gone. Vanished. Like a ghost.

"Wow," Lizzy said.

"What?" I asked, hoping she hadn't seen me nearly melt into the floor.

"Nip, nip did you good."

"What?"

"I don't know his name, but the bartender bought you several gourmet sandwiches from Bo La Vie."

"Really?" I peeled the bag away from her and peeked inside. I pulled them out, carefully treating them like gold bars, and laid them on the table, looking at all my options.

I'd been dying to try the new restaurant, but could never get a reservation. The fact I even had to get a reservation to get into a gourmet sandwich shop irritated me, but now I was all too eager to try everything I could.

"Do you think nip nip would let me have a knife? I can cut these up and share."

"No. You don't need to share," Tony said.

Lizzy's eyebrows shot sky high. "Don't listen to him. That is a great idea."

I knew she wanted to go there as badly as I did and wouldn't let Tony stop her from trying the goods. I moved and swayed through the crowded dance floor and landed at the bar again. I waved my hand to get nip nip's attention. I really needed to learn his name. He walked over smiling, "I'm not serving you. You're cut off."

I pouted, "I wasn't coming over for a drink, but now I want one."

He looked over my head again and I turned to find Callum in his usual spot, watching me. "What's with him?"

"Who?"

"Callum," I said in a deep and spooky voice.

He laughed, then stopped. "What do you mean?"

"He's been standing up there most of the night watching... people." I didn't want to presume and say me, but I definitely felt his eyes on me.

"Oh. He's just... watching everyone. Big night."

"Yea?"

"This is our first big opening. We had a soft opening before, but tonight's the big night."

"So he's not always that uptight?"

He chuckled. "No, he is." He looked up at him again, then said nervously, "Well, I better get back to it."

"So you really wouldn't serve me if I wanted a drink?"

He pulled his lips. "Callum's orders."

I turned to cast daggers at Callum, but he was gone.

"Well, I didn't want one. Just a knife."

His neck snapped back in surprise.

I laughed. "For the sandwiches. Speaking of which, you really didn't have to get me food and from Bo La Vie, of all places. Although, I'm not hating it. I've been wanting to try that place out for a while and haven't been able to get in."

"Really?" He seemed shocked.

"Yea. Reservations are like a month out. How were you able to get food from there? Oh my gosh, do you want one? I can bring it over to you."

He laughed. "I know the owner and no, you and your friends enjoy."

"How much do I owe you?"

"Nothing, but you also aren't getting a knife." He winked. "Now I really have to go."

"What's your name?" I called after him, but he only smiled.

I walked back to the group. "No knife."

"I love you thought he would just give you a knife to walk across a crowded club with."

"Yea, I didn't really think that through."

I picked up a Wagyu sandwich with truffle and Gruyère and took a bite. I'm pretty sure if it wasn't for the thumping music, I would have thought I had died. It was the best thing I had ever put in my mouth and that included cock. And I loved cock. Unfortunately, chances weren't looking great since Derek left. I couldn't blame him. We didn't really seem to hit it off, and he was getting hit on every two seconds. For some reason, aside from the first guy, no one else tried to dance with me, which was a bit of a bummer.

"Lizzy. Try this," I waved my sandwich in front of her face.

"No. You have to try this. It's a grilled cheese, but..." she moaned.

We traded sandwiches, and both moaned in unison.

"Can I get some of that?" Tony asked.

"No," Lizzy and I both said at the same time.

We finished the sandwiches and decided to dance again. I felt a lot more stable and less drunk, but had a good buzz going. Part of me wanted to test a theory to see if Callum had really cut me off. There was something about him that made me want to push him. Was it because he seemed so stiff? I wanted to see him break?

I felt a prickly feeling on the back of my neck and turned to find Callum's eyes on me again. I turned to face him, to show him I knew he was watching me and if he was going to keep doing so, then I was going to give him something to watch. With my back to Lizzy's chest, I swayed my hips from side to side as our eyes locked again. I ran my hands over my body, over my chest, through my hair, and then down between my legs. I saw the fire in his eyes and felt alive. Electrified.

"You're doing your fuck me dance," Lizzy said in my ear. "Whose attention are you trying to get?"

"No one," I said, letting my hands drag over my breast.

"Liar liar, panties on fire."

I turned around and put both of my arms around Lizzy's neck and snaked down her body and then back up again.

"Well, whoever the poor bastard is, good luck to him. When was the last time you had a dick in you?"

I paused, "Lizzy."

"It was an honest question. Vibrators and dildos are great, but they got nothing on a good dick."

"Hey, ladies. I saw you two over here dancing and thought you needed some company."

I looked at him then looked up to see Callum was leaning forward on the railing watching us. I winked at Callum then put my arms around the man.

Break like a twig.

I don't know why he even cared. I didn't know him and before tonight had never seen him, but there was something about him that drew me in like a moth to a flame. He was gone when I looked up again.

Bye Felicia.

"I'm going to go sit down for a bit," Lizzy smiled. I gave her a kiss on the cheek to let her know I was ok. Our signal we'd been giving each other since we were in college. Her sitting down was her giving me space, but saying she didn't trust the guy. The kiss on the cheek was me acknowledging it and agreeing.

"That's hot. You can stay if you want," the man said and Lizzy just rolled her eyes and walked away. "What's your name?" the man asked, putting his hands on my lower back, bringing me closer to him. The smell of alcohol on his breath was pungent, and he had that loopy look in his eyes.

Inspired by Callum, I went with the obvious. "Felicia. You?" No way in h-e- double hockey sticks I was giving him my real name. He definitely seemed like a stage five creeper.

"Jordan. You want to get out of here?"

"Moving a little quick there, Jordan," I patted him on his chest.

"Not at all. You just look like a lady who knows what she wants," He gripped me tighter.

"I do know what I want."

"And I can give it to you." He put his leg between mine.

I pushed away from him. "I don't think you can, Jordan."

"Don't be a bitch."

"Jordan," I scolded. "That's not how you talk to a lady, and definitely not how you get her to go anywhere with you."

He huffed, "You didn't seem like much of a lady earlier, before I came over."

"Good bye Jordan," Lizzy was watching me like a hawk from her seat, so I quickly signed restroom. We had learned to use sign language in college, and it came in handy when we were at clubs or any loud event. She nodded, and I walked off the dance floor and followed the bright neon lights to the back corner of the club.

I went in and was shocked by the caliber of the stalls. Like most other things in the club, there was a lot of black, but it was more sophisticated, less goth. The ceiling was also painted black, with black beams running the length of the room. Along the wall were white pedestal sinks in front of oval mirrors in gold frames. It was like walking into a five-star hotel. Granted, this was their first night, so I'd have to check back in six months, or hell, even a month, but something told me it would probably be the same. They seemed to have a fine attention to detail.

A few minutes later, I walked out of the bathroom and my good friend Jordan was waiting in the dimly lit hall.

"Jordan," I huffed.

"I'm sorry. I shouldn't have said those things."

"Can you be more specific? There were several things."

He rolled his eyes. "The bitch part."

"And..." I prompted.

He looked at me, dumbfounded.

"And for assuming I was an easy piece of ass because I was having fun and dancing with my friend?"

He nodded. "Yes, that too."

"Thank you." I started walking by him, but he grabbed my arm.

"Let go!" I tried to jerk my arm away.

"I thought we made up. Aren't we supposed to kiss?" He pulled me in closer to him.

"No!" I said, pushing him away.

"Come on. Why are you playing so hard to get?"

"I'm not." I tried pulling my arm out of his grasp again, but his fingers only tightened.

"Come on, then." He swung me to the wall and pressed his body against mine, pinning me in place. He leaned in, putting his mouth on my neck with his forearm across my chest.

"Get. Off. Me." I jerked my knee between his legs and was fairly certain he was tasting his balls right now.

His forearm dropped as he slumped over, sucking wind.

I stepped from around him and started walking down the hall when he grabbed my wrist and jerked me backwards. "Wrong fucking move," he lashed out. "I get so tired of you women out here dancing like you do. Looking for attention. And then when you get it, you try to push it away. You asked for it, you're going to get it." He dragged me down the hall and into the ladies room.

Fuck.

I had tried to play nice with Jordan, but he seemed to need something more direct. When I was in college, there were a lot of girls getting attacked, so I took a self-defense class. I liked it so much I started karate and got my black belt. I lifted my arm and crashed it back down, breaking his grip on my wrist. I turned towards the door to get out, but he ran over and slammed it shut with his arms, pinning me to the door.

This motherfucker just doesn't give up. I brought my hands down on his arms, causing his elbows to bend and quickly used one hand to grab the back of his head, while my elbow crashed into the side of his cheek, swiping across his face. He grabbed his nose, which was bleeding down to his chest, yelling a mixture of expletives at me. I pushed him off and walked into the hall only to find Callum standing there, frozen, like I'd surprised him.

His intense gaze traveled from me to the door, which was bursting open with Jordan climbing out of it, still pushing forward. Asshole doesn't know when to take a hint.

A smile tugged on Callum's lips before he calmly walked towards me with his hand outstretched. I slipped mine into his and felt a heat, as he gently guided me behind him. He moved forward and grabbed Jordan by the throat, jacking him up on the wall so his feet were dangling. He leaned in and whispered something to him, so quiet I didn't even hear it, but the color drained from Jordan's face and his body went limp. After a moment later, Jordan fell to the ground just as someone else was walking up behind me.

I slid out of the way and saw another man dressed in black and recognized him as the one who was on the balcony earlier that had delivered information to Callum. He was even more beautiful close up. Sandy blonde locks and hints of tattoos protruding from under his black button-down shirt.

"Shit Callum. What did you do? It's our opening night."

"I did nothing, Knox. It was all her." He nodded in my direction and I felt there was a hint of pride in his tone.

Knox turned to look at me, and his eyes nearly popped out of his head. "I stand corrected, my lady." He gave a slight bow, and I smiled at him.

"Get him out of here and revoke his membership."

"What? Because of her? She better be glad I'm not pressing charges."

I lost my temper and marched over to him and grabbed him by the collar, pressing him against the wall. "Press charges, you asshole. I dare you. You fucking pussy. It's assholes like you that make it so fucking difficult for women to go out and enjoy themselves. It's amazing that all the other men and probably some women were able to not be a complete dick and want to assault a woman. You say it was my fault for dancing the way I was, but I say it's your fault. You were raised with a sense of entitlement and believing you can take whatever you want. News flash, you fucking can't." I raised my fist, and he flinched before I pushed off him.

"Take him," Callum demanded through set teeth.

Jordan batted his hand in the air before he was led down the hall by Knox.

"Come with me," Callum commanded, his tone a hair softer than before.

I followed him down the hall to a hidden door just past the ladies room. He pulled out a keycard on a retractable string and swiped it against the pad. The panel turned green, and buzzed before unlocking to let us in. He pushed the door open, inviting me in with his gesture. I got the impression he was a man of few words.

The lights flicked on in the room and I saw we were in another bathroom. Perhaps the employee restrooms, it wasn't completely finished.

"The door is going to lock behind us for privacy, but I will not touch you without your permission. You are safe." His words sounded rehearsed, like he'd used them before.

I nodded.

"I need to hear the words," his tone was soft, but final.

"Ok," I said.

He shrugged out of his jacket and pinched it on the upper corners, folding it in half and laying it on the couch. "Are you ok?" he asked, walking over to the sink. He rolled up his sleeves until the shirt was stretched around his forearm, exposing several tattoos which stopped just above his wrist.

He flipped the water on and let it run for a second before taking a rolled-up towel from a basket to the right of the sink and wetting it. I was entranced. The way he moved, the way his muscles flexed in his arm. The way his fingers expertly wrung out the cloth.

I felt my chest taking deeper breaths the longer I watched him.

"Do I have your permission to wipe the few scrapes on your face?"

I nodded.

"Everlee. I need your words."

"Yes, sir." I mumbled, curious to see if it would get the same result as before.

His eyes ignited again, but he maintained his calm. He cocked his head to the side as if he was testing something and responded quietly. "Good girl."

There it was. I forgot how to breathe for a second. That was the second time I said that to him. I had never... before... but. His hand gently grabbed my chin and tilted it up to look at him, our eyes yet again caught in a stare. They were mesmerizing in person, electric blue... and fuck. Sexy as hell. There were no other words to describe them. His other hand gently patted a scrape on my forehead. My heart was pounding a hole out of my chest, the same time butterflies were erupting in my stomach. What was happening to me? I was feeling lightheaded and woozy.

"My Cupid... in... armor."

Darkness swooped in like a raptor for its meal.

Don't push the intercom button when you're getting off in the shower.

THE SUN WAS SHINING down on my face as my cheek brushed the soft silk sheets.

Wait.

Where was I?

I slowly opened one eye and didn't recognize the room I was in.

Fuck. Where the hell was I?

I closed my eye and tried to remember the events from last night, but was having a hard time. Then slowly, it started coming back, piece by piece. The party, the dancing, the creep, the bathroom with Callum and then nothing.

My eyes shot open. I was in a loft space with a contemporary industrial feel. The room was large with brick walls, hardwood floors, exposed metal beams, and floor to ceiling windows trimmed in black metal. There was a chair in the room's corner and a dresser along the wall.

I rolled over and found an open shower that was as large as my entire apartment and another chair in the corner of the room with a man sitting in it.

I let out a mangled sound as I pulled the sheets up to my chin and rolled into a ball.

"Hey there. Sorry. I didn't mean to startle you. It's me, Emmett, from the club."

I shook my head, not able to place him. How much did I have to drink last night?

"Bartender." He lifted his shirt, showing his nipple ring.

I felt my body relax a little, even though I was still confused as fuck.

He held his hands up. "You're ok. You're safe. You're in Callum's room, but he slept on the couch. Your phone is beside you on the nightstand charging. Lizzy was worried about you, but Callum texted her and said you were fine and would call her this morning."

I glanced over my shoulder and saw my phone there just as he said, with a missed call and several unread text messages.

"I didn't mean to startle you. I was just worried about you, and Callum thought you'd freak out less if you saw a somewhat friendly face."

"Callum? Where am I? What happened?"

"I don't know all the details, but while Callum was cleaning you up last night, you passed out."

"I passed out?"

"Sometimes adrenaline spikes can do that."

"How did I end up here?"

His lips pulled. "Like I said, I don't know all the details. Callum is waiting for you downstairs. Breakfast is also cooked. I made pancakes, waffles, bacon, sausage, and eggs Benedict. Along with a tray of fresh fruit. I didn't know what you'd want."

"Thank... you?"

He smiled. "I'm glad you're ok. When I saw Knox walking by with that guy, I was worried about you. Then I found out you'd done that. Remind me never to cross you," he chuckled, standing up. "Feel free to use the shower to clean up. Also Callum bought some clothes he thought would fit you. They're on the chair over there." He pointed to another chair to my left.

How many chairs does one room need? I wondered.

"We'll be downstairs."

I nodded, still too stunned to speak. It was like my ears could hear all the words coming out of his mouth, but I was having a hard time processing everything.

He paused with his hand on the knob. "Would you like coffee or tea?"

"Coffee, please."

"You got it." He closed the door.

I stared at the ceiling, rubbing my face, and listened for any identifiable sound, but there was just silence. I rolled over and grabbed my phone to look at the messages.

1:06AM

Lizzy: Girl, where are you?

Lizzy: You better pick up.

Lizzy: I just saw douche McDouche being escorted out.

Lizzy: I went to the bathroom, but you weren't there.

Lizzy: I'm about to use the find a bitch app.

Everlee: This is Callum. Everlee is safe.

Everlee: There was an incident, and she's passed out.

Everlee: I'm taking her to my place to monitor her.

Lizzy: Callum?

Everlee: Tony knows me.

Lizzy: SHIT.

Lizzy: The owner.

Lizzy: Sorry for the shit.

Lizzy: Shit.

Lizzy: I'm drunk.

Lizzy: What's your address?

Everlee: It's late. You should get some rest. But you're welcome to come over tomorrow.
Everlee: 15087 N Pulgam Rd
Everlee: (555) 637-0928. That's my direct line if you need to contact me.

Lizzy: She's ok?
Lizzy: Like for real?

Everlee: Yes. He definitely got the worst of it. She's safe and will stay safe.

Lizzy: Thank you.
Lizzy: Tony also says you're legit.
Lizzy: He wants me to tell you legit was my word, not his.
Lizzy: Oh sorry. He didn't really want me to tell you that.
Lizzy: Ignore me.
Lizzy: But thank you.
Lizzy: Love what you've done with the place.
Lizzy: Shit.
Lizzy: Sorry.
Lizzy: Bye.

Everlee: If you need a ride home, please call me.

8:53AM
Lizzy: Are you still alive, hooker?
Lizzy: There was no coke off a dick, but it was close.
Lizzy: Shit. I assume you have your phone.

9:42AM
Everlee: Hey. I'm alive. I didn't pull a Betty.

Lizzy: Everlee! Oh my God!

Everlee: *Sorry. Just got up. Going to take a shower. Then going downstairs to get some answers.*

Lizzy: *Are you there?*
Lizzy: *At his house?*
Lizzy: *You are. Duh.*
Lizzy: *Is it nice?*

Everlee: *I'm only in the bedroom. I don't remember the rest.*

Lizzy: *Girlll. Tea time.*

Everlee: *Nothing happened.*

I lifted the sheets and saw I was wearing a t-shirt over my outfit from last night.

Everlee: *I'll text you in a little.*

Lizzy: *I'm coming over to pick you up. I need a shower and coffee first.*

Everlee: *See you soon. XXOX*

I put my phone down and threw the comforter off, then padded over to the shower. I stripped out of my clothes and put them in a neat pile on the floor before stepping into the oversized standing man bath and twisted the knob in the center. I stood to the corner, so the cold water wouldn't hit me while it warmed up. After a minute, the steam started fogging up the glass, so I stepped into the middle, where the water was pouring out of the rainfall shower head.

I did a complete circle and saw nine other jets, three on each wall. I ran my fingers over several buttons on the wall to find the one that looked like the jets. I had always seen them in movies, but never in real life and, of course, I had to try it out! I found one that looked like an upside-down

funnel which caused the lights to change in a rainbow colored pattern. I pushed another and music started playing.
I pushed a third, and water shot at me from all sides, and I
squealed in surprise.

The water was hitting all over my body, jets angled in
certain positions from mid-back to... oh, hello there.

No! I would not get off in his shower.

That's what my mind was saying, but my body was like a
raging hormonal teenager who'd been waiting for days now
to get off.

Herein lies the problem.

I stood there for a moment, letting the water massage me
and... my eyes rolled into the back of my head. Oh my God.
Why have I never done this before? I stepped closer to my
new favorite jet, and a moan escaped my lips. I pressed my
hand on the wall, ignoring the buttons, as the pressure was
building. Another moan escaped. "Fuck."

I adjusted my body again. My legs grew weak as my body
climbed, ached, needed. I stepped closer and a sound deep
inside of me echoed out. My moans were coming closer
and closer, my stomach tightening and then... ahhhh. The
angels were singing. My legs gave out, and I fell to the floor,
while the same jet that just got me off pelted me in the back
of the head. But I didn't care.

The door burst open and Callum stood there, eyes on fire,
looking completely feral. He ran into the room, grabbed a
towel and tossed it at me before racing into the shower fully
clothed. He pressed a button on the control panel in the
corner above my head and in an instant, the water, lights,
and sound were shut off.

I stared at him in disbelief. "What are you doing?" I shot
out when I finally regained control of my tongue.

He looked down at me, his white shirt now transparent
and clinging to his body like shrink wrap. He had muscles,
like a lot of them. Fully defined, touch them, feel them, lick
them, muscles that I wanted to run my hands over. Holy
fuck, he was gorgeous and a bit of a badass, it seemed. His

chest and arms were covered with tattoos that were now showing through his shirt.

His eyes locked with mine, but was interrupted by the bulge that was growing in his pants. My bottom lip scraped between my teeth as I contemplated how it would look if I sucked him off in the shower. I still didn't know what happened last night and for all I knew we fucked, and I didn't remember it, and looking at his body this morning... that would be a goddamned tragedy.

"What are you doing?" he snapped.

It was like a needle popped my vagina balloon, but it was fighting for anything to cover the hole to stop the air from escaping. *Horn dog.*

"What are you doing?" I retorted.

He stood up, taking his shirt off. Not in the overly sexy way you would hope, but the irritated it's clinging to me and I need to be free of these constraints kind of way.

"You..." he threw his shirt down. "Put a towel on."

"I put a towel on?" I was completely confused, lost in his body.

"No!" he snapped. "Put the towel on." He pointed to the one I was holding in my lap, realizing my breasts were on full display.

"Shit." I pulled the towel up.

"You..." he shook his head.

"What's so hard?" I added, "to say?" When a 'that's what she said' popped into my head, looking at the seam of his pants. I wanted to put my hands around that happy stick.

God. Lizzy was right. The real thing was better than all my BOB's and dildos. I was fucking horny for a meaty man stick, a schlonga dong dong. Fuck, call it cupid's arrow. I'd let it shoot inside of me.

Immature. As soon as the last words passed through my mind, I imagined cum. Lots of delicious Callum cum shooting inside me.

Fuck!

I needed to get control.

"You had your hand on the speaker button."

"The speak... er butt- oh fuck."

Balloon popped.

Total mortification.

I was drier than the Sahara desert.

"Did you hear..."

"Yes."

"Which is why you..."

"Yes."

My head fell into my hands.

I looked up a minute later, words still stuck in my throat.

He ran his hands through his hair, slicking it back, revealing more tattoos on the underside of his arm.

"Fuck," slipped out. He was a goddamn piece of art. A beautiful, sexy, tattooed piece of art.

He held his hand down to help me up.

Yes, please help me up from my post orgasm collapsed state on your shower floor.

I adjusted the towel, so it wrapped all the way around me.

"Do you mind if I change real quick?" he asked.

"No... no. Please."

He stepped out of the shower and walked over to his dresser and faced the windows. He slipped on a shirt then slipped off his pants.

Just his pants.

He was going commando.

Fuck. Shitballs. Mother ass.

His ass was perfect. Shit. I couldn't stop staring. It was so tight, and...

He looked over his shoulder. "You're moaning again."

My eyes grew wide, and I turned around. I would say I was sorry, but it'd be a lie. Because I wasn't. But I was beginning to wonder how many times I could embarrass myself in one morning.

I heard him slip on his pants and start walking to the door.

"Wait." I turned to him. He paused with his hand on the knob. "Did we? You and I? Last night?"

"What?" His brow furrowed and his eyes twinkled with mischief.

Was he playing with me? "You know?"

"I don't know what you're talking about."

"Did we?" I put my finger through the hole in my other hand.

"What is that?"

"Oh my! Did we have success? Shit. Sex. I don't... remember."

He dropped the knob from his hand and walked over to stand in front of me. My breath left my body. Like I literally could not breathe. He was standing so close to me I could feel the heat radiating off his chest. The back of his hand gently ran down my cheek. "One. You passed out. Two, I would never have sex with someone who can't consent. And three." His hand cupped my cheek while his fingers gently gripped the back of my neck. "If we had sex, there'd be no chance you'd forget it."

My head leaned into his hand as a breath puffed out.

The pad of his thumb traced along my lower lip, sending a fire deep into my core. I felt my clit start to throb.

But then he pulled away and walked to the door.

"Breakfast is ready, downstairs."

The door shut, and I was left standing in his room, completely immobilized.

He was trouble.

When and when not to moan

I WAS FOLLOWING THE voices through the hall and down the stairs fifteen minutes later. That was how long it took me to remember how to move and then get dressed. The louder the voices got, the more my cheeks flushed at the thought I'd be walking into a room of men who knew I'd just used Callum's shower to get myself off.

I stepped onto the last stair, which emptied into a large kitchen area. In front of me was an oversized island bar with eight seats around it and an impressive gourmet kitchen to its right. To the left was the dining room with the largest contemporary wooden table I'd ever seen, with enough seating for twenty people with two large chandeliers anchoring the ends. In the back right of the room was what I presumed to be the office. It had large floor to ceiling glass panels for walls with an oversized desk in it and to its left was a small sitting room. The rooms were tied together with whites, light grays, soft blues and wood tones.

"There's Ali!" Knox said, standing from a stool at the bar.

My head snapped back in surprise. I wasn't expecting to see him here. I knew Callum and Emmett were here because I'd seen them already, but now felt even more mortified, because Knox and some other guy I'd never seen were also here.

My lips pinched into a flat line and I waved meekly.

"Pull up a seat, Trouble," Emmett said, scooping some food onto a plate.

Callum stood by the far wall, ankles crossed and arms folded, watching me.

"Ignore him!" Knox bounded over, pulling out a stool for me.

"She seems capable of pulling up her own stool, Knox," the unknown man remarked.

"Shut up Jax. I'm just being polite."

Jax.

He was equally as handsome as the others, with light brown hair and chocolate brown bedroom eyes. He had a small scar on his cheek and another peeking out from the collar of his shirt that told me he'd been in his fair share of fights, but judging by his size, I'd have to bet he easily won. Anyone who would go up against him would have to be mad.

It was a group of some of the hottest men I'd ever laid eyes on. What would you call a group of hot men? Gaggle popped into my head, but that was for geese. Perhaps a brood of men? It was a stretch, but chickens were a brood, and they were a bunch of cocks. I'm going with a brood of men.

I sat in the chair and Knox pushed it under at the same time Emmett was sliding the plate across the oversized white granite bar. I picked up the fork and took a bite of the eggs Benedict and let out a moan.

Shit!

I looked around the room, panicked, and couldn't help be reminded they'd just heard me moaning not even thirty minutes ago for a completely different reason.

I saw a smirk playing on Callum's lips and felt a heat flush across my skin.

I put my hand over my mouth, "The eggs... they're so good."

"That's what she said," Knox chimed in.

"Real mature," Jax mumbled.

"Why are you such a grump this morning? We had an amazing night last night!" Knox retorted.

"Knox," Callum commanded, hushing him up.

The room grew awkwardly quiet and then Emmett chimed in, "You can moan anytime." He closed his eyes, shaking his head. "At my food. At my food is what I meant to say. You can moan anytime you're eating my food. Fuck!"

"Well, as fun as this breakfast is, I'm going to take off to the club," Jax said, excusing himself. "Everlee," he bowed his head before walking out of the room.

I quickly waved at him.

My phone buzzed, and I glanced at it. Lizzy.

Lizzy: Be there in ten minutes.

Lizzy: Unless you're getting boned, then five. I want to watch.

Lizzy: Mostly because damn. Callum. Girl.

Lizzy: Get. You. Some!

I was smiling while I read my texts.

"Everything ok?" Callum inquired, stepping off the wall and taking the seat Jax had just left. I had noticed he wasn't eating.

"Yea. Lizzy is on her way to get me. She said she'd be here in ten minutes."

"I could have taken you home, but I figured she'd feel better knowing she could get to you anytime she wanted."

"Thank you."

"Can you tell me what happened last night?"

He nodded, "I was cleaning you up and you passed out. Which I'd prefer if you didn't do again."

Again? Did that mean he thought we would see each other after Lizzy picked me up, or was he assuming I was a lush and would be frequenting his club? Did it matter?

I took another bite of eggs to stop my brain from over analyzing Callum's words.

"Once I determined it was more adrenaline related than alcohol," he gave a pointed glance at Emmett who held his hands up, "then I decided to bring you here."

"Why not take me back to my friend?"

His head cocked to the side. "You all had been drinking. If by some chance it wasn't adrenaline related, I wanted to watch over you to make sure you were ok. I didn't want to put that responsibility on your friend."

"So you watched over me last night?"

He nodded.

A flutter tickled my stomach. He watched me sleep. Oh, no! What if I snored or said something inappropriate?

Like moaning while getting yourself off in his shower. My subconscious reminded.

"You didn't snore or anything like that," he smiled.

I shrugged, brushing it off like it hadn't just been a concern. I took the last bite of eggs and savored it because it was hands down the best I'd ever had.

"Well, thank you. You didn't have to."

He cocked his head to the side, but didn't speak, and we just stared at each other. I noticed we did that a lot and I don't know why. What was it about him that drew me to him? Why did he stare back at me?

The doorbell rang.

"I'll get it!" Knox jumped up from the seat. He reminded me of a Labrador dog. Eager to serve and please and generally just a jovial guy. Quite the opposite of the cool and calculating Callum, and even different from the playful yet super skilled in the kitchen, Emmett. I still hadn't figured out Jax yet, and probably never would, since this would likely be the last time I'd be here.

"This is the kitchen," Knox waved his arm out talking to someone behind him.

Lizzy walked into view seconds later with her mouth on the floor. She made quick eye contact with me and mouthed 'OMG'. I smiled, climbing off the stool and walked my plate around to the sink.

"If you tell me where your dishwasher is, I can put this in real quick."

Emmett chuckled, "No dishwasher here. Just these hands."

"You wash Callum's dishes?" I asked, confused.

"Well, all the dishes."

"You live here?"

He laughed, "Did you think I came just to cook you breakfast?"

My lips flattened and my cheeks blushed red. "You know... I really had no idea. This morning has been... a lot."

Callum stood up and walked over to Lizzy, holding his hand out to shake. "Nice to meet you, Lizzy."

"Thanks for taking care of my girl," she said, her knees getting weak briefly.

"No problem at all."

"Are you ready to leave?" I chimed in, interrupting Lizzy's probable panty explosion.

"No. I mean yea, sure. You?"

I turned to Callum. "Thanks again. Emmett. Knox." I nodded in their direction.

"No, you don't. I'm a hugger," Knox said, smiling and holding his arms out. I walked into them and they wrapped around me, holding me tight. He was such a good hugger, and he smelled fantastic. The start of a moan escaped before I caught myself.

He whispered in my ear, "Next time, don't stop it."

I felt a full body flush as my stomach tightened and clit throbbed. Panty slasher! The theme to Mortal Kombat played in my mind as a sword wielding Knox slashed through my panties, cutting them to shreds before he claimed me. His words echoed in my mind on repeat.

I placed my hand on his chest and gently pushed him away as his eyes locked with mine and a smirk crossed his lips.

I stepped out of his hug and walked over to Lizzy, who was trying to decipher my face. "See you later, Trouble." Emmett waved from the kitchen.

"I'll walk you out," Callum offered.

"Thanks again for last night," I said when we got to the door.

I felt Lizzy's head snap in my direction, but I didn't look at her.

I stretched up for a hug and Callum's hand grazed across my lower back just under the lip of my shirt, setting fire to my skin. He sucked in a breath. Or maybe it was me. I felt my breasts pressed against his hard chest and held it for a moment.

"Take care," he mumbled.

I turned away, but not far enough to cause his hand to drop from my back and I found myself frozen there, not wanting to break this contact between us. I wanted to feel his hand there and everywhere. I wanted to taste his lips on mine. I wanted to feel his hard, chiseled body pressed against mine, feel his gigantic cock in my hand, in my mouth, in my throbbing pussy. I wanted it all.

I looked from him to Lizzy and felt like this game we'd been playing with the eye contact had now moved into physical contact and he was waiting to see if I'd break it first. I didn't want to and if we weren't standing at his front door with one foot out and Lizzy staring at me wondering what in the fuck I was doing, I'd likely move in closer to him and reach my hand down his pants before taking his lips into a passionate kiss that would most definitely make me moan.

But Lizzy was here, and we were leaving. I stepped out of his touch and regretted it the moment I felt his hand drop. I stepped through the door and didn't look back.

When you need that dick and all your boyfriends are charged up.

THE ENTIRE CAR RIDE back to my apartment was Lizzy rambling about how nice and huge their house was and how it was because he was compensating for something. I didn't tell her he wasn't because that would lead to the embarrassing story of me in the shower and him bursting in. Though I never saw his dreamsicle, I could tell it would be huge because of the bulge in his pants.

I replayed that scene over in my head and wished I had the balls to have taken him, or at least tried to. He would be divine in bed.

"You ok?" she asked, pulling to a stop in front of my apartment building.

"Yes."

"Was there something you didn't tell me? Like how you rode that man candy's cock-a-doodle-doo?"

"No. I did not have sex with them."

"Them?" She looked at me.

"Him. I mean him."

"You want to have sex with them all, don't you?" She rubbed her chin. "I bet they'd be down. Fuck. Imagine your first time getting that donkey dick back in you. It's with a threesome... shit a foursome."

"Jax was there earlier, but he left." Why did I add his name to the list? It's not like she needed any more encouragement.

"Four?" Her hands clasped together under her chin. "Please, please, please. If you ever loved me or valued our friendship, you'd jump on that dick train and ride it," she growled. "Ride it so fucking hard." She turned in her seat. "And then, of course, you'd come back and tell me everything. Every little detail to the ounces of cum you suck down or squeeze out."

"Oh my God. Gross." I smacked her arm.

"What? I need to know these things."

"No, you don't."

Her eyebrows raised, but she didn't say anything else.

"Bye. And thank you for picking me up."

She smiled and stretched. "I'm feeling we should go to the club tonight."

"What? Are you crazy?"

"Maybe for that dick," she said in a deep voice, enunciating every word.

"You have a dick."

"I do and I love that dick very much, but a girl can hope and dream her BFF gets four fabulous dicks as well."

"Bye." I closed the door.

"Wait!" she yelled. She bent her head down so she could see me outside of the passenger window. "Valentine's is in a couple of days."

"So?"

"Do you want a bouquet of Vixen dicks?"

I batted my hand and turned towards my building.

I heard her cackling as she drove off.

I flipped open the app on my phone and scanned it over the reader to get in. Digital keys were so great.

I got to my apartment and sat on the couch, replaying everything that had happened. What a crazy fourteen hours. I stood up from the couch some time later and walked into my bedroom and saw the large red box still lying on my bed.

Shit!

I left my outfit at Callum's house. I stopped. I assumed it was Callum's, but it could have been Emmett's... or Knox's... maybe Jax? I had no clue.

Well, I guess I won't see that again.

But I really liked it and who knows how much Lizzy paid for it, and if she knew I'd left it, she'd drive me back just so I could see them again. She'd probably leave me there to make sure they'd have to drive me home.

Would it be weird to show up at their house and ask for it back? Maybe I should go to Vixen and ask Emmett and then schedule another pick up time? No. That seemed like a lot of extra work, because he would probably just tell me to run over to the house to get it. I rubbed my hand over my face.

Damn it!

What was I going to do? Why was I fighting against this so hard?

Because I wanted that donkey dick, damn it!

I looked over at my shelf of boyfriends and saw monster dick had the green light.

Hello friend, I smiled. It was probably no Callum, whatever his last name was, but it would have to do. It was the biggest one I had. I slipped out of the clothes Callum had bought for me, which until this very second I hadn't realized he had clothes for me. Like, how? Why did he have clothes that fit me? Was there another woman living there I didn't see? Did he keep an assortment of sizes and styles for women they bring home? What if they were like some kind of weird sex cult and they were trying to initiate me in? Was I upset that they could be, or that they could be, and I didn't get the nod for the invite? Was Jax the leader and when he left, he was signaling a no go?

I hit my head.

What in the fuck did I drink last night and why was I thinking about these random things?

No. They were not a sex cult, and if they were, Callum would definitely be the leader.

Callum and his big dick energy.

Yes. That was the thoughts I needed to be thinking of.

I laid on the bed and grabbed my monster dick, turning it on to adjust the vibration and let him play on my clit for a minute, before I slowly glided him in. I stretched around him as he moved inside of me, hitting on all the delicious spots.

Flashbacks of last night replayed in my head. Callum on the balcony. Callum's hands gripped on the rail. Callum's chest in the shower. Callum's bare ass.

My orgasm was coming, building higher and higher as the memories played on repeat. My back arched off the bed as my hand traveled over my breasts and down my body. Rubbing. Imagining it was Callum's.

My breath shuddered as I hit my climax. My body pulsed and throbbed around the green goblin. I pulled him out, turned him off and laid on the bed for a minute, letting my body relax.

My phone buzzed, and I rolled over to look at it.

Lizzy.

Lizzy : You use the green machine?

Everlee : What?

Lizzy: Girl, we both know, that I know, you went home and got you some.

Lizzy: And that your favorite is the one I bought you.

Everlee: OMG.

Lizzy: *You just finished, didn't you?*
Lizzy: *Still in bed?*
Lizzy: HAHAHAHAHA

Everlee Your a sick fuck.

Lizzy: *You're.*

Everlee: One handed typing. ;)

Lizzy: YASSS QUEEN.
I tossed my phone on my bed and laid there just staring at my ceiling for a moment.
I decided to jump in the shower. I wasn't a two shower a day kind of girl, but after the interrupted shower this morning and all my dirty thoughts, I needed something to just wash away the night and the morning.
I trotted into my bathroom and looked at my shower tub combo and was suddenly missing the luxury of Callum's. I didn't need all the lights or music, but the rainfall was nice. *And the jets...* My subconscious reminded.
I flipped the water on and then looked at myself in the mirror, seeing a minor scrape above my eyebrow and was reminded of the dickface from last night. Why do guys have to be like that? I was having a great time with Lizzy and then he had to come over and ruin it and then make me feel like it was my fault because he had self-control issues. But I guess that's the problem today.
I remember going to school and at the beginning of every year, we would have a kickoff meeting reviewing rules segmented by girls and boys. Boys... two rules. No cleats and no ripped shirts. Girls. Well, pull up a chair and pack a lunch because the list was extensive. No tight pants, no short shorts, no shorts above the knee, no tank tops, no this, no that. It was especially frustrating when going into the stores to buy clothes and almost every piece

was something that couldn't be worn at school, so I was stuck having to wear pants every day. Ninety degrees or twenty degrees didn't matter, because it was the girl's job to remove temptation from boys instead of boys learning how to control themselves.

I sighed. This was an argument or pet peeve of mine that popped up far too frequently. I stuck my tongue out in the mirror, then climbed into the shower, taking my time since I had nothing to do today.

I dried my hair and put on a light layer of make-up and then sat on my couch flipping through Netflix.

After a Valentine's Day themed romcom, I flipped open my work laptop and checked my emails. I usually did it later at night, but now seemed like a good time since I needed to keep my mind busy. I could not get thoughts of Callum out of my head.

"Shit." I clicked open the link that said Valentine's dinner reminder. It was a customer event from one of our biggest clients. They had apparently rented out a ballroom or something and invited my entire firm plus one to dinner on Wednesday. I forgot I'd RSVP'd several weeks ago and I guess part of me hoped I'd be able to find a date before then, but the other part tried not to think about it and completely failed.

My first thought was Lizzy, which was stupid. She used to be my date for these sorts of things, so much so that for a long time my boss thought we were dating. Could I get sick between now and then? I'd have to start building the story tomorrow. Go in fine, because I didn't want them thinking I was just hung over from the weekend, but at around one or two, get a little mopey, a sniffle here or there. Tuesday, go in and talk about the awful nights sleep I had and then leave early. BOOM! Plan locked in place!

My phone dinged.

I looked at it, expecting a text from Lizzy, but instead found my restaurant app confirming a reservation to Bo La Vie for tomorrow night at eight, for four people.

I stared at the app confused since I hadn't made a reservation, but then noticed it said Thank you Emmett for making your reservation! In special notes, it read. To foods that make you moan with a winky face.

I threw my phone down and then picked it up again.

"Asshole!" I laughed.

That wonderful, handsome asshole.

I don't know why he made a reservation for me, but I was beyond ecstatic. I called Lizzy and told her the good news and invited her and Tony to come with. She said she'd be there, but Tony wouldn't be able to make it. He had dinner with a customer to talk about some project he was about to start, which probably meant Derek, too. I had hesitated a minute before calling her, because naturally Tony would probably expect me to want to invite Derek. I mean, I hope not after last night, but it was still weird ground. Another reason on the list of many, why I didn't like them setting me up. When things don't work out, it's just awkward for a bit.

I didn't know what to do with the extra two seats and thought about modifying the reservation for only two, but didn't know if Emmett would join or wanted to join. Was this his way of asking me out? *In a really weird way.* My subconscious chimed.

Ok. So probably not Emmett asking me out, but who would use the other two seats? Maybe he was just giving me the option? Why was I over thinking this? I squealed.

I ran into my closet and flipped through all of my clothes, trying to find the perfect outfit for tomorrow night. This would probably be the last time I'd be able to eat here for a while because I definitely wasn't going to make a reservation for a month out.

Scratch that. After the sandwiches I tasted last night, I would probably make it for a year out... I'm just not that patient of a person. Maybe I could get in really tight with Emmett and he would tell me who his friend is that can give me the hook up.

Yes. All the plans were coming together.

When they kiss you like that...

THE CAR DROPPED ME off at the front of Lizzy's condo. We decided on her place since it was closer to Bo La Vie.

"Thanks." I tipped the driver, but she was no Betty. I regretted not calling her because I felt a connection with her.

I climbed out, pulled my dress down, then walked up the short flight of stairs.

Before I could knock, Lizzy threw the door open. "Hey, girl, hey!"

I smiled, stepping inside from the cool weather.

"I'm so excited! I've been looking over their menu all day."

"Me too!" My face pulled. "I didn't realize how much it cost." I quickly added, "I don't have a problem with the cost, but I have a problem that Emmett probably spent a small fortune on those sandwiches we ate. I feel like I should pay him back."

"Yes, *you* probably should." She laughed.

"I should?"

"Shit. You were volunteering."

"Lizzy," I scolded.

She sighed, "Fine. You talk to him and I will contribute." She handed me a martini when we walked into her kitchen. "A little pre-game action."

"What are you getting?"

"Girl. I have no idea. I stared at that damn menu all day and everything looked fantastic. I think I'm just going to take whatever the server suggests or the special... I don't know. I saw a sampler, but that's only like three."

"What is a girl to do?"

"Indeed!"

We finished up our drinks and debated on calling a car. We didn't mind the walk, and it was only a few blocks away, but the temperatures were dropping. In the end, we decided to walk, in part because of time, but I really think it was because Lizzy wanted to go by Vixen.

Ten minutes later, we were walking down the sidewalk, core shaking, with our hands bundled near our faces. When we looked at the weather, we didn't consider the wind chill factor. The wind was whipping, and we were freezing, but we were too far down the road to turn back or admit defeat. Nope. We were both stubborn as shit and would suffer so we could talk about how we defeated the great frost that never was.

We had the idea to stop in Vixen for just a second to get warm, but the front doors were closed. "Should have looked at the hours," I mumbled through chattering teeth.

"Note to self, Thursday through Sunday only."

I looked down the road and saw the sign for Bo La Vie sticking off the side of a building in white and black font with round bulbs around the sign. Very classic.

"So close, yet so far away." My eyes were watering through the wind.

As we were coming to the road that led to the back of Vixen, a car pulled to a stop in front of us. After a second, the window rolled down.

"Everlee?"

"Jax."

"Jax?" Lizzy asked.

"Get in the car. Both of you." He jumped out of the driver's side and opened the back door, not waiting for an answer. We slid in and relished the warmth of the car. He climbed back in and turned around with a scowl on his face. "What are you both doing? I thought you had reservations at Bo tonight."

"We did... we do," I quickly corrected, nervous under his gaze. It wasn't as intense as Callum's, but it was close. "We were walking there."

"In this weather? Are you mad?"

"Apparently." I cut my eyes to Lizzy.

"Hi. I'm Lizzy. BFF of Everlee and apparent bad decision maker."

He smiled. "How about a lift? I was headed there anyway."

"You were?" Lizzy asked, bumping elbows with me.

"Yes. We're having a team meeting there tonight."

"What a kawinky-dink," Lizzy teased.

Jax slowly turned around and pulled down the road. "I can drop you two at the front door, then park."

"No!" Lizzy and I both jumped in.

"You don't need to do that," I added.

"Plus, this way you get to walk in with two beautiful ladies, one on each arm," Lizzy said.

"That is true." His gaze fixed on me in the rear-view mirror.

It had only been a day and a half since I'd seen Callum, but he was on my mind every hour of that day and a half. My poor BOB's were getting the most use they'd had since... ever. Callum was a thirst I needed to quench and Jax was quickly moving up that list, too.

We were parked at Bo's less than five minutes later.

Jax opened the car door for us and Lizzy was gushing about him being a gentleman. He offered us each an elbow, making a joke he looked better with us on his arms and I appreciated it. I felt like a million dollars when I was around him. Callum too. Maybe that's what was adding to my thirst.

It had been so long since I felt the slightest bit confident, but they... they all made me feel that way with just a look.

A doorman was waiting for us when we arrived. "Good evening Mr. McCall." He looked at each of us with a furrowed brow. "Will they be dining with you?"

"No, I was escorting them in. They have a reservation at eight."

"Yes. Ms. Everlee."

"That's me." I held up my hand.

"Shall we wait for the others?"

"No. Lizzy jumped in. My boyfriend couldn't make it and Everlee doesn't have one."

I shot her a glance.

And she shrugged, before winking.

The doorman, again confused, this time by Lizzy's random statement about my love life, or lack thereof, directed us to the hostess stand.

"Good evening, Mr. McCall," the woman said when we arrived, nearly melting in her spot. The man did know how to wear a pea coat. That was for sure.

"Good evening, Eliza."

Such the charmer.

"The rest of your group is here at their table." She directed her arm to the second level.

My eyes traveled up and standing on the edge, hands gripped around the rail, was Callum, wearing a button-down blue shirt, under a black jacket and a pair of faded jeans. Holy fuck. And those eyes... my God. The blue shirt made them pop even more and right now they were penetrating into the depths of my soul. My jaw fell open as my breathing changed.

"Damn," Lizzy moaned, looking at him too.

"Your table is this way, Ms. Everlee."

"Enjoy your meal, ladies." Jax waved to us as he started his ascent up the wide spiral staircase.

Once we were seated, I looked around the restaurant. The floors were a beautiful hand-scraped wood, and the colors were very simple, black and white, with large chandeliers. It reminded me a lot of Callum's house. On the far side of the room was a glass panel running the full length of the wall, and behind it was the open kitchen where they were making and preparing the food. There were about twenty large round tables spread throughout the main floor, with several tables on the border for couples. Because we had the reservation for four, they sat us near the center of the room. I looked to the second balcony, wondering how many other tables were up there, and caught those familiar blue eyes resting on me. If I didn't find him so incredibly sexy, it would be creepy, but I don't know if there was anything about him that could be creepy.

I wiggled my fingers at him with a small wave, and he sent back a wink. My legs reflexively clenched together, because of the things he did to me. It was just a wink, but fuckin' aye it was the best goddamned wink.

It was a wink filled with a promise of sex. Lots of amazing rock your world sex. Sex that makes you forget your name and where you are. The kind of sex-

"Everlee?" Lizzy asked, concerned.

"Yea?"

"Your cheeks are flush and you're panting."

"Sorry." I blinked hard and returned to my menu, but not before I saw the hint of a smile playing on Callum's lips. It's like he knew the effect he had on me and he enjoyed watching it.

The head server was over a minute later introducing himself, with two others behind him. Three servers? The younger one, named Sven, began taking the extra place settings off the table while the second server, named Isla, filled our water glasses. "The owner has prepared a special menu for you both tonight. He called them bite flights to make you..." he looked around uncomfortably and dropped his voice, "moan."

My eyes shot open wide, and I looked around the restaurant. I knew he had to be hiding somewhere. The sneaky bastard.

"Ooh I do love a good moan," Lizzy said.

I looked up to the second level and found him standing there with a cheeky grin.

I scowled playfully and pointed my finger.

"He also wanted me to tell you, your meal is on the house tonight."

I looked back up at Emmett, and he blew a kiss, smiling. I mouthed the word thank you, and he winked back. What was it with those boys and their winking?

"You will have fifteen total plates, with a drink pairing for each. Each drink has been carefully selected and paired with your bite flight and will be approximately two ounces. Once complete with the starters and main course, you will have a flight of desserts served with a coffee."

"Wow. I have no words other than I'm so excited to try anything and everything."

The servers all smiled and dipped away.

Lizzy grabbed my hand and whispered. "You said you didn't sleep with anyone."

I chuckled. "I didn't."

"Then why... all this? A special menu? Comping our dinner? This would have to be almost a grand for tonight."

"I don't know."

If Emmett was the owner here, then why was he bartending at Vixen?

"We need to find out more about these boys." I nodded to the second balcony and saw the four of them were deep in conversation, pointing at something on the table. Likely a drawing of some sort. I realized this was the first time I'd caught Callum not looking at me. It was intoxicating to watch him. The way the heel of his foot was propped on the chair leg while his hands gripped and rubbed into his thigh. The way his jaw moved when he spoke or how the light reflected off pieces of his hair.

The server returned with the first tray and a printed menu of all the things we'd be trying tonight. In front of me was a small salad in a glass twice the size of a shot glass, paired with a white wine. I picked up the small fork and carefully stabbed it into the glass, capturing all the ingredients for the one perfect bite. I placed it in my mouth and my eyes nearly rolled into the back of my head. When I opened my eyes again, I saw Emmett and Callum watching me. Emmett had a huge smile spread across his face and he turned to say something to Callum, who nodded, smiling. I had a feeling it was about me and I was dying to know what it was.

Callum caught me and signed, 'Eat your food and stop watching us'.

How did he know I knew ASL?

I signed back, 'Thank Emmett for us', followed by my command for him to stop watching us.

He smiled, and I watched his lips move towards Emmett, who snarled at me when he sat back down, causing me to chuckle. Then Callum signed back, 'Maybe I enjoy watching you.'

'Maybe I like watching you too.'

With that, I turned away before I could see his response. I felt like I was in high school passing secret notes to a crush, only I was signing in the middle of a very expensive restaurant.

"So, he signs too?"

"Apparently."

The servers brought us our second dish. Another salad with a sort of balsamic glaze. I'm pretty sure I was in heaven right now. How was this my life?

"You have it bad," Lizzy said.

"What? No."

"I'm not faulting you because damn. The only problem is, who do you choose? All four of them seem to be smitten with you and all of them are hot as hell."

"Do I have to choose?"

Lizzy's eyes grew wide. "I like your style. I always said a man could never hold you down, maybe four can."

I laughed. "Well, I think we're putting the cart in front of the horse. I'm not dating any of them."

"This sure feels like a date."

"I'm here with you."

"Yea, but no."

"What?"

"You can't keep your eyes off them. We've hardly spoken. Which don't get me wrong. I'm not hating it because I love that you're getting the attention you deserve. Like you said, you're not even dating them and look how they treat you. Imagine if you were dating them." She wiped an invisible tear from her eye. "It would be magical."

"I love you. You know that?"

"I love you too, sis."

That's what we were. We were sisters from different misters. When we met, we immediately hit it off and were inseparable. During our freshman year of high school, her parents got divorced, and she took it hard. Even harder when her dad started dating again so soon. She lived with me for a while until her parents finally put their foot down and made her go home. But she was always there for me. My ride or die.

We finished all the starters and several sandwiches. I'd lost count on which tray we were on, but my bladder was about to explode. I'd had so much to drink and even though they weren't big glasses, I felt obligated to drink it all at one time to make sure the pairings all went together. So that being said, I was feeling a little tipsy.

Emmett seemed to have everything planned perfectly except the one detail. I was most definitely a lightweight. I would tease the guys when we went out on dates, saying I was a cheap date because I was good to go after one, maybe two drinks.

"I'll be back."

She nodded, tipping back the most recent drink. An Argentinian wine.

When I walked out of the bathroom, Callum was standing there. "We need to stop meeting like this, in dimly lit halls outside of restrooms." I gave my dress an extra tug.

He smiled, "There isn't anyone inside?" He pointed to the restroom.

"No."

A smile played on his lips as he stepped toward me and I instinctively took a step back.

"You aren't going to beat me up if we end up in there, are you?" His words were smooth like velvet.

My heart was beating out of my chest. "No," I managed to get out.

He took another step forward. "Are you having a good time?"

"Mmhmm."

His hand came up to my face, the pad of his thumb pulled my bottom lip down. "Use your words, Everlee."

"Yes."

He pressed his body against mine and I could barely breathe. "Yes, what Everlee?" his words were low and silky.

"Yes, sir."

"Good girl." My stomach was somersaulting on itself as butterflies erupted and my entire body tingled.

All the tension in my jaw released as it dropped to the floor. He called me a good girl, and I liked it. Not liked it, but fucking loved it. Did I have a praise kink I was unaware of?

"I haven't been able to get you off my mind," he admitted, pressing his cheek to mine, inhaling pieces of me.

"Same. I..." It was so hard to focus right now, he was making my head spin. "I haven't stopped thinking about you."

"This is a problem for me, though."

"Why?"

"Because I don't do girlfriends."

"So?" I whispered as his hand moved to the back of my neck.

"You deserve more than what I can give you." His lips found their place under my jaw and my neck dipped to the side, giving him more access as a moan escaped my lips, but I didn't care. Not one fucking bit. His lips slid down my throat. "I love when you moan."

"I'm sorry. I..." My breath hitched as his tongue gently licked my collarbone before his lips kissed it away.

"Don't be sorry. It makes me..."

His hand grabbed onto my hip, squeezing roughly like he was fighting with himself.

"Makes you what?" I asked, turning into him, inhaling his scent.

He chuckled a low laugh. "I can't tell you."

My lips found his neck. "Please."

"God, you are fucking intoxicating." His lips started climbing up my cheek, and I couldn't wait. This game we'd been playing to see which one would give in first. It was going to be me. I needed to feel his lips on mine now. I needed to feel him inside me. I needed... him. Every part, every inch.

I pushed the door open, grabbed a handful of his shirt and pulled him into the bathroom, pressing his back against the door. Without hesitation, his lips crashed unforgivingly onto mine. His tongue pushing its way in. It was a fucking dream. My panties were soaked as I moved against his body, wanting to feel him on every part of me. I felt the bulge in his pants and knew he wanted it to. I grabbed his belt, but he stopped me, pushing me away.

I stood in front of him, head swimming. "What's wrong?"

He closed his eyes and ran his fingers through his hair. "I shouldn't have done that."

"Done what? Kiss me? I wanted it."

He shook his head. "There are rules and I just..." He opened the door and walked out. I followed him, thoroughly confused and flustered.

"I don't understand."

"You aren't supposed to."

"I thought you wanted..."

He stepped forward, his hand resting on my face. "I do. So fucking much. More than I have ever wanted anyone before. But I can't..."

"I-" I stopped myself, staring at him incredulously. "I need to go. Lizzy is waiting for me."

"I'm sorry."

I stopped walking down the hall and turned back towards him and whispered. "What did you think was going to happen when you look at me like you do all the time and then follow me to the bathroom?"

"I wasn't trying to fuck you in it, if that's what you think. I respect you more than that."

"Are you saying I don't respect myself?"

"No. I'm not saying that at all."

"Then what?"

He shook his head. "You deserve more than what I can give you."

I rolled my eyes, then poked my finger in his chest. "That's fucking bullshit and you know it."

I turned to walk back to the table.

Lizzy watched me walk up and her eyes grew wide.

I sat down and took a deep breath. I would not let him ruin this fantastic evening.

"You want to talk about it?" she asked.

"Not yet."

She nodded, "This one is probably my favorite. It's so cheesy."

I smiled, thankful she knew me so well. She knew when to press and when to just let me be. I took a bite of the sandwich. "This one is good and almost as cheesy as you."

"Everlee's got jokes."

The rest of dinner passed with jokes and us talking about Lizzy's future wedding. It was a pleasant distraction from Callum. I had to fight the urge to look at the second balcony and failed a few times. Fortunately, those times he wasn't looking, but I could tell he was agitated.

We took the last bite of dessert and both slumped back in our seats. A moment later, shadows descended on the table and we looked up to find Emmett, Jax, Knox and Callum standing around us. Most of the restaurant had cleared out, so it was just us and the remaining staff.

"Well, how was it?" Emmett asked, beaming.

"It was phenomenal. Fantastic," Lizzy sighed.

"It was absolutely outstanding. I didn't know you were the owner."

Emmett smiled. "It's my passion project, and these boys helped me get it off the ground."

"Well, thank God they did, because wow."

Knox stepped forward. "He's been talking about it all day. He wouldn't shut up."

"Well, really... it was amazing. Words can't describe. And you really didn't need to do this."

"It was nothing, love," Emmett said. "The look on your face when you eat. If I could frame it and look at it every day. That is what brings me joy... and-"

"Don't say it."

He smiled, "Is there anything else you want? Need?"

"Gosh no." Maybe a dick. Anyone's dick at this point.

"Can I get a picture?" Lizzy blurted. "With all of us?"

"Yea. Of course," Emmett and Knox answered at the same time.

Emmett called our server over to take the picture. Lizzy put me in the middle of all the guys, while she stood on the outside of Jax. I was between Emmett and Knox in the front, with Callum was behind me to my right and Jax beside him. Emmett and Knox slipped their arms around me, hand resting on my waist and then a second later, Jax and Callum slipped their arms in, resting their hands on my hips. All their hands on me sent a fire to my core.

Lizzy, being Lizzy and having planned this perfectly, got one pic and then asked for a second with just me and the boys. I rolled my eyes when I realized what she was doing.

Once the pictures were taken, their hands were reluctant to drop, and I didn't want them too, but they did because if not, it would just get awkward.

Jax stepped forward. "If it's ok with you both, I'm going to take you home Lizzy and Callum will take you home, Everlee."

Before I could say anything, Lizzy agreed to it for both of us.

I looked at Callum and couldn't read his face.

"Perfect," Emmett said.

I leaned over and gave him a hug then a kiss on the cheek. He tickled my side when I pulled away and made me giggle.

"What about me?" Knox whined.

"You didn't do anything," Jax reprimanded.

"I helped with... something. I'm sure."

I smiled, leaning over to plant a kiss on his cheek.

"Are we ready now?" Jax asked.

"Yes, we are," Lizzy answered again, looping her arm in Jax's.

We walked to the front, and the doorman gave Jax and Emmett a set of keys.

"See you boys at home," Jax said. "Good night Everlee." He leaned down and gave me a kiss just off the side of my lips that left my head spinning. He hadn't been overly affectionate, but that kiss, while it wasn't on the lips, felt... intimate.

We watched the others hop in their cars the valets had pulled up and I waited for them to hand Callum his keys, but they didn't.

Once the others had taken off, he looked hesitantly at me. "Are you ready?"

I nodded, and he scowled at me. I wasn't going to give him the words he wanted.

He huffed then pushed the door open, holding it for me. A cool gust of wind blew my dress up, and I quickly pushed it down.

There was a black Audi Q7 parked in the front with a man waiting in the cold by the back door. "This is us."

He has a driver. Of course he does.

I climbed in first, sliding over for him.

This was going to be an interesting ride.

Rules were meant to be broken

I GAVE THE DRIVER my address, and he plugged it into the GPS.

Twenty-two minutes with traffic.

He made a turn at the stoplight, beating the yellow light, causing my hand to brace on the center of the seat and Callum's to do the same.

His pinky brushed mine, and he apologized.

"What exactly are you sorry for?" I mumbled out.

I felt his gaze land on me, but I didn't give him the satisfaction of looking at him. I couldn't, if I wanted to stay mad at him and I don't really even know why I was mad. Was it because I couldn't get him off my mind? Because I wanted him to take me in that bathroom even though I usually found that disgusting? Was it because I let myself get attached and dream up some world where I thought he wanted me too? I rolled my eyes, getting irritated with myself.

"Everlee," he whispered, grabbing my hand.

I pulled it out of his grasp and looked at him. "I know you have your rules, and I don't want you to break them."

"I've gotten permission."

My head snapped in shock. "Permission?" From who? A girlfriend? Wife? I didn't see any signs of a woman at his house. Maybe it wasn't his house... Surely he didn't have to ask permission from the boys. Unless... they were together. No, that's not possible, is it? No. I shook my head. At the bathroom, the way he looked at me...

He sighed, "Everlee." His eyes softened, like he was struggling with something. "Brady. Can you pull over here?" he snapped.

"What?"

"I need to talk to you. I need you to understand, and I don't need to feel pressured to explain everything in the remaining thirteen minutes I have with you," he said, looking at the maps on display at the front.

There was a pain, an ache, in his voice, which made me want to reach up and touch his face and tell him everything was going to be ok, but I had to hold the course.

Brady parked the car and climbed out, standing on the sidewalk.

"He's getting out?" I asked, looking at him standing with his hands clasped in front of him with his black pea coat and beanie on.

"He's giving us privacy."

"What's going on?"

"That's what I'm trying to tell you. I don't... I don't usually have these conversations. This is Jax's department."

"He has conversations with girls for you."

He chuckled and reached up to cup my cheek, his thumb swiping across my cheekbone.

"Not quite."

"So, then?"

"If I gave you an NDA to sign, would that weird you out?"

"An NDA?"

"Non-Disclosure-"

"I know what an NDA is. I was just surprised you asked me to sign one. I barely know you."

"That's for good reason."

"Who are you?" My gaze narrowed on his face.

"I'm Callum," he smirked.

"No shit. I mean-"

He was chuckling and as our eyes met, the air changed around us. His gaze became intense, sexual, needing. "You are a temptation like nothing I've ever experienced," he whispered, leaning forward. There was something in his voice that caused my stomach to tighten. No man's words had ever turned me on the way his have. There was something about the power he commanded that was like lighter fluid for the sexual flame burning within me. Screw the lighter fluid like a whole container of gasoline.

I tilted my lips up towards his, eager to feel them on me again, but he held there, an inch away, his eyes watching me.

"The first time was a mistake, and I was weak. I can't do it again."

"Kissing me was a mistake?" My breath was heady and my head was swirling.

"God, no. Well, technically yes," he chuckled, "But not in the way you think."

He pulled a small packet of papers from inside his coat. "Please sign this so I don't have to be so guarded with you. So I can kiss you, fuck you, and make you moan all night."

A puff of air escaped my lips, and my clit started throbbing. It was like someone had turned on the faucet in my panties. Fucking hell.

I nodded. "Got a pen?"

He chuckled, reaching into his inside pocket.

"You had me at kiss and sold it with fuck."

"You have a very dirty mouth." He watched me sign my name and continued. "One that I want to punish."

I bit my bottom lip and let my teeth slowly scrape over them. "So, what do you need to tell me?"

He batted the paper on the ground, swooped over, wrapped his hand around the back of my neck and pulled me towards him. "That can wait," he mumbled before his lips crashed onto mine, taking them in an unapologetically hard kiss. The kind of kiss that you need on a very basic level. The kind of kiss that you need because your life depends on it.

A moan escaped my lips, and I felt him smile before he leaned forward more, pushing me back. His hand tightly gripped my hip like it was his lifeline, while mine greedily stroked up his chest. I needed him. Needed to feel him, needed to taste him, needed everything about him.

"I'm going to make you moan my name," he whispered against my lips.

I looked at him, smiling. "I doubt it."

His eyes twinkled with mischief. "Game on." His hands simultaneously lifted my dress at the same time he shimmied down my body.

Oh my God. He was going to eat me out in the back of his car with people walking on the sidewalk not even ten feet away. I briefly had the wherewithal to tilt my head up and see the windows were tinted. I didn't know how dark, but-

He slid my panties aside and his tongue plunged into my wet depths.

"Fuck me!" I exclaimed, pressing the palm of my hand to the window behind me.

"I plan to," he said before diving back in.

Holy shit, he was skilled in the art of cunnilingus. Cunnilingus? Of all the words I could use- shit. So. Fucking. Good.

I felt like I was about to explode in his mouth. The pressure was building up, my stomach was tingling, and I was fairly certain I was seeing stars. I moaned out his name, which only made him swirl and pulse his tongue faster. "Callum."

He slipped in two fingers while his tongue played with my clit, sucking it into his mouth.

"Oh, fuck."

"We're really going to need to work on that mouth," he said before running his tongue up my slick folds. "You taste so good. I could live the rest of my life down here."

My body was grinding, moving on its own, the closer I got and his words put me on a bullet train.

I moaned again and again and again.

So much for winning that. He was playing to win and I could appreciate that. Over and over again.

His fingers curled and hit that magic spot, and without warning, my world exploded. Hearts and arrow and little flying Cupids swirled around my head. The moan that escaped my lips was unlike anything I'd ever heard. It was deep, from the depths of a well that had never been explored before. I felt my pussy clinching around his fingers as his thrusts slowed.

He looked up at me, face still between my legs, his eyes pure sex and fire. What have I gotten myself into? He crawled up my body and found my lips, and I could still taste myself on his tongue. His kiss was soft, passionate.

I was fucked.

Literally and figuratively.

I grabbed for the hem of his waist, but he put his hand on mine. "Not right now. This wasn't for me. Well, not entirely." He winked, sitting us up. He pulled his phone out and sent a text. Moments later, Brady was walking back to the car.

"Do you need to go home right now?" he asked before Brady got back in.

I shook my head, still unable to form words.

Brady sat in the chair and I freaked out for a second, wondering if he knew what had just happened. There was no way he didn't know, was there? I watched him, but he showed no sign of it, if he did.

"Brady. Can you take us to Rosemary Park?"

I looked at him quizzically.

"Can you ice skate?"

I nodded. "But I'm not really in the outfit for it."

"It's ok. They have stuff we can buy there."

"Callum."

He kissed the end of my nose. "Rule 1. What I say goes."

I laughed. "Hate to break it to you. But I'm a rule breaker."

"I've gathered as much."

"Rule 1. You can tell me what you want to happen and we'll discuss it."

A smile tugged on his lips. "We'll see."

I'd take the small victory for now. I think some part of me knew going into this he needed to be in control, and maybe that's what drew me to him. That dominant big dick energy. DBDE!

We were at the park ten minutes later and it was packed. I had seen flyers floating around for it, but dismissed them since it was all Valentine's Day themed. I had no desire to go... before. I still didn't believe in the holiday, but that didn't mean I couldn't appreciate the benefits.

Brady dropped us off at the main entrance, but before we got out of the car, Callum grabbed my hand. "There is still a lot we need to discuss, but for now, we'll enjoy each other's company." He kissed my head and opened his door, not waiting for a response. Brady was opening my door a second later, and I stepped out to Callum's waiting hand.

Damn, he looked fine as sin. That's what he was... a sin. I had a gut feeling I was going to get hurt, but right now, I didn't care.

We walked up to the glass walled building that was sitting right in front of the rink and when we opened the door, a thick hot air hit us right in the face. It was loud, from young couples in love to tired parents chasing children around who had to put their hands on everything.

Callum raised up on his tippy toes and lifted his arm as a child was tearing through the shop across the aisle. He was laughing when the child's mother came racing by to catch him, apologizing.

"It's fine." He smiled before grabbing my hand, looking at me. "Let's get you some appropriate wear." He walked over to a rack which had a limited supply of pants, shirts, and jackets.

He held up a pair of thick, gray, water resistant pants, a thermal black shirt and a teal, gray, and white jacket. "What are your thoughts on this?"

I glanced at the price tag and felt my muscles clench. The markup was atrocious! "I don't really need the jacket. I'm sure I'll be fine without it."

He laughed and leaned down so his lips were brushing my ear. "I will not have you freeze to death before I fuck your pretty little pussy."

My head snapped in his direction as I tried to figure out how badly I wanted to be arrested for fucking him in the middle of the store. "When you say things like that, I could strip down right now and still be hot."

His eyes glared playfully. "You wouldn't."

I grabbed the top of the zipper on the side of my dress and started inching it down, not taking my eyes off his. His lips parted and I could see the vein in his neck throbbing.

He placed his hand on mine and turned abruptly to the teenage employee walking by. "Excuse me, she needs a room to try these on."

Half paying attention, she nodded to the corner of the building where a makeshift changing room had been created.

"Thank you." He grabbed my wrist and nearly pulled me across the store, weaving through all the shelves and scattered, hats, gloves, light-up wands and bouncy balls that were strewn all over the floor. He knocked on the door and when no one answered, pushed it open, glanced behind him and pushed us both into the room.

I squealed out laughing, and he quickly put his hand over my mouth. "Don't make a peep." He locked the door and looked at me with a wicked grin.

I grabbed his hand and started to speak, but in one motion he was on his knees with my panties around my ankles. How was he so fast?

"Callum," I whispered.

"Not a sound... or a moan." His eyes twinkled.

"You know I can-"

I couldn't finish speaking as he lifted one leg, tossing it over his shoulder, and buried his face in my still glistening pussy. It hadn't even been thirty minutes.

He slowly licked from back to front before slipping his tongue in. His eyes darted up to meet mine and my God. I bit my bottom lip, trying to hold back the moan that was begging to escape. It wasn't like anyone would hear me anyway since it was so loud in here, but something inside of me wanted to obey him.

He slipped two fingers in and swirled them around in a circle as my stomach clenched. My fingers ran through his hair and I grabbed tightly, holding him there while I rocked on his face. He slipped in another finger, stretching me and I felt my knees buckle.

"Callum," I moaned out quietly.

He stopped, pulling out his fingers, and looked at me. It took a second before my eyes focused on his. "Rule one."

I shook my head back and forth. He couldn't be serious.

He was lifting my panties back up. "You better get changed quickly."

"You. Are you?"

He wiped his fingers across his lips before kissing me on the forehead. He unlocked the door, poked his head out, and walked out.

I was standing there like a high diver on the edge of the platform and he just walked away. Fuck rule one. I make my own rules. I slipped out of my dress, trying to ignore the light brushing of my panties across my throbbing clit, then got an idea. Before putting on my new outfit, I slipped them off and put them to the side. I balled them back up and put them in my pocket, saving them for the right time later. I folded my dress over my arm and walked out of the dressing room to a waiting Callum who was bent over in a seat, I'm sure working on getting his erection down.

I cast a sideways glance at him and headed to the register with the tags in hand. I heard him chuckling behind me before he slipped his arm around my hips. There was another teenager working the register who seemed to have smoked weed prior to his shift, because he could give two shits about the chaos happening around him on top of the fact his eye were red and his fingertips were orange with Cheetos dust on them.

He looked up from the register a second or two after the total appeared and dragged out the total of three hundred and twelve dollars. I dove into my little purse, but before I could pull out my card, Callum was handing his over.

"I can get it," I said.

"I know, but I wanted you to come. So my treat."

I stared at him in disbelief, not missing his word choice and the obvious pause on the word come. A new game seemed to be afoot, so I readjusted my imaginary top hat and pipe and nodded. "Thank you. I wanted to come."

His lips pulled to the side and the guy at the register said in a monotone deadpan, "Yay. You both wanted to come."

Callum and I both looked at each other and snickered.

"You can get your skates around the corner," he mumbled, pointing at a wall before handing me the receipt.

"Could I get a bag?"

The guy's brows pinched into the most dramatic v, so I held up my dress.

"We don't sell those here."

I shook my head. "I know. This is what I was wearing."

"Why did you bring it with you?" he asked, his head tilting back, seemingly too heavy for him, because he was struggling to keep his balance.

I closed my eyes, trying to maintain my patience. "I just bought these clothes and changed."

"Oh, right." He nodded emphatically, staring at us.

"So, can I get a bag?" I pressed.

"Right…" He handed me a bag, and we walked around the corner to wait in line for a pair of skates.

I waited until he was talking to the attendant pulling skates and reached in my pocket with the receipt in hand, grabbed my panties and then stuffed them both in Callum's pocket. "Here's the receipt for your purchase."

He nodded, completely unaware of my extra gift. "What size?"

"Eight," I told the kid behind the counter.

He handed us our skates, then pointed to a screen. "We limit the number of people on the rink. When it's your turn, your number will be called. It's not too bad of a wait right now. Here's your ticket."

I peeked over Callum's arm to see what number we were and how long we had to wait and snorted when it said we were number sixty-nine. "My favorite," I mumbled.

"Nice," the kid behind the counter said.

"Eww," I retorted before we stepped away. I looked up at the screen and saw they were on sixty-seven. "Shame we don't have more time."

"We could leave," he suggested.

"Nooo," I droned playfully. "I really, really wanted to come." I bent over and put on my skates.

"You should have followed rule number one."

"I told you... I'm a rule breaker."

"That's fine, but there will be consequences, and that's probably the easiest rule."

"How many rules are there?"

He smiled. "Sixty-nine."

I snarled my upper lip at him.

SIXTY-NINE. The computer voice called out.

He stood up and stuck his hand in his pocket, no doubt feeling it was extra full. His eyes opened wide in surprise as he chortled, "You will pay for that."

"I hope so." I walked through the door at the same time he slapped my ass.

Old Fashioned's and Contracts

We skated around the rink about three laps before Callum grabbed my hand and informed me we were going home. We had managed to return our skates, grab my bag, and put on our shoes in record time. My dress shoes with my skating outfit really seemed to work for me, because I was getting a lot of turned heads. Or maybe it was the look of sexual fire in Callum's eyes or the fact he was just hot as fuck.

Brady was waiting for us, standing by the back door of the sleek car with his hand on the handle when we walked out. Callum guided me in first.

"Was the ice skating enjoyable?"

"Very," I said, smiling.

His eyes shifted in the rearview to look at Callum. "Where to, sir?"

"Home."

"I have to work tomorrow," I whined, not wanting the night to end. I checked my watch and choked, since it was almost eleven and I had a feeling the night was just starting.

Screw it. I was going to relive my college years and go into work with only three hours of sleep. How bad could it be?

Callum looked at me. "Me too."

I cocked my head to the side, staring at him.

"I can have Brady take you home now, later, or first thing tomorrow morning."

"Tomorrow morning? Awfully presumptuous of you, isn't it?"

"You say presumptuous, I say hopeful."

I looked between Brady and Callum, and my resolve weakened. I wanted to see where this was going, plus he left me horny as shit when he walked out on me in the dressing room and I'm fairly certain the things he's done to me tonight have him equally as horny. I wasn't going to get any sleep tonight or probably be able to walk tomorrow, but I had a feeling it'd be well worth it. "Your house is fine and he can take me home tomorrow morning."

Brady nodded without speaking and turned out of the pickup lane.

The car ride was silent. More silent than I would have expected, given our earlier conversation. The look on his face caught me off guard. Gone was the sexual fire and in its place was trepidation.

I glanced at the NDA still on the floor and handed it to him, but thought I should actually read what I signed. I knew it was very irresponsible of me, but in the moment I didn't care. I wasn't thinking with my head, just my greedy little kumquat.

I read through the agreement and it read like a standard NDA with only a few words jumping out like the fact it mentioned a relationship with any or all the men. They were all covered under this one document? Is that what we had to talk about? Is that what was making him nervous? My head was spinning with thought after thought. While he hasn't come out to say they were some kind of group, he'd been dropping hints whether or not he realized it. Getting permission... the fact they all seemed to live there...

I scooted over to sit beside him and ran my hand along his leg. He looked at me and the paper in my hand and smiled. "I'm glad you finally read it."

"Yea, probably not the best decision I made."

His brows furrowed.

I quickly added, "Signing without reading first." His hand rested on my leg before he looked out of the window again. I could tell we were getting close to his house. Their house? Because the landscape was changing from buildings to trees. They were still in the city, just on the very edge of it. Having a house the size they did would be impossible to find in the city.

I leaned against him, soaking in whatever time I had left. I was not prepared for this shift in mood, and questions about what to expect the rest of the night were dancing around in my head, leaving my stomach in knots.

We pulled up to the house and Brady moved around to open the door, but Callum stopped him, offering to do it instead.

He grabbed my hand and guided me up the stairs.

"Are you ok?" I asked quietly.

He looked at me thoughtfully. "I'm... uncertain."

"Uncertain?"

He sighed, "I can't seem to control myself around you, and it's putting me in a weird spot."

"A weird spot?"

Before he could answer, he was opening the door, and a voice yelled out from another room. I recognized it immediately as Knox, with his bountiful energy. "How did it go? Did she say-" He slid into the room and stopped talking when he saw me.

"Oh. Hello there." A smile stretched across his face as his tone changed to mock innocence. "How was your evening?" he asked, grabbing my hand and planting a kiss on the top of it.

He was so easy to smile at. "Good. Yours?"

"I've been waiting here on pins and needles to see what'd you say."

"Say?"

His confused eyes darted to Callum, who held up his hand just as the other guys were walking into the room. "I haven't talked to her yet."

I was getting the impression there was a lot more going on here. A group play situation, perhaps. I'd read it in my smut books, but the fact I was actually living it, experiencing it. Possibly... probably... I didn't know how I felt about it. Excited? Nervous? Curious?

The ladies in the book just seemed to know what to do and while I wouldn't necessarily call myself sexually vanilla, I wasn't experienced in group play or whatever you called it. It wasn't an orgy, was it? Maybe I'd have to get my books and do some research if this was happening. Googling it was not an option, because I'd end up on some site, get horny, masturbate and forget to do actual research. Although isn't that what happened when reading my books, too? The good ol' one handed read. Should be a hashtag created. Maybe there already was. I needed to get back to the conversation with the boys and out of my head. I could be going down an unnecessary rabbit hole for no reason.

"Everlee?" Callum asked.

"What? Huh?" Shit. Pay attention.

"Do you want something to drink?"

"Old Fashioned."

Knox squealed. "Can we keep her?"

Jax glanced at him disapprovingly. "She's not a pet."

Knox grabbed my hand and spun me around, dipping me backwards, his face an inch from mine. "I know, but one can hope." His eyes danced with an unexpected heat, leaving me breathless and causing my cheeks to blush. He stood me back up, leaving me dizzy and wanting. Wanting to feel his lips on mine, but I banished the thought. For now. If I was misreading the situation, then I didn't want to come off the wrong way to Callum.

The guys walked towards the kitchen, so I followed. We all took a stool around the bar, watching Emmett fix a drink for everyone.

"Is everyone getting the same thing?" I asked, trying to break the awkward tension in the room.

"It's our house drink."

Of course it is.

Emmett handed it to me, and I tilted it back, taking a sip. Fuck me, that was good. Probably the best old-fashioned I'd ever had. "This is magical."

Emmett beamed. "It's the cherries. Luxardo all the way."

I scooped it out with my finger, sucked it into my mouth, and bit into it. Oh my God.

Was it possible to have an orgasm from eating food? A cherry specifically?

I must have moaned because all the men's lust filled eyes were on me with mouths parted. I felt like they were lions and I was a piece of meat in the middle of their safari and the feelings moving through me were not fear, but excitement. It was such a turn on to know I had this effect on them.

Shit.

I looked at each of them and my body felt electric. Heat was pulsing through my veins, my stomach was clenching and my needy little cunt was aching to be touched, kissed, and fucked.

They must have read me like I was reading them because the entire atmosphere changed.

"It was a really good cherry." I stifled a laugh.

"Get her another!" Knox cheered and Emmett jokingly slid the whole jar towards me.

I laughed, which seemed to bring us all back from the edge, for now.

"So lay it on me."

Callum looked at Jax.

Callum started to speak, but I jumped in, "From Jax. Doesn't he usually handle this sort of thing for you?"

All eyes were on Callum with a mixture of shock and awe. I gathered people didn't interrupt him while he was speaking. While his eyes gave nothing away, his tone did. He was frustrated and his words were clipped, "Yes. Jax does handle the terms of the arrangement."

Arrangement? Curiosity was killing me. I was a cat walking la-ti-da into a den of lions. I just hoped it didn't get me killed. Fucked to death, I was ok with. It had been a while since I felt an actual dick in me and Lizzy would be ecstatic to hear it was four. What would she say when I told her about this? She'd lose her mind.

I felt a pang of... what? It wasn't guilt, or remorse, but I just realized I signed an NDA. I couldn't tell her about this. How was I going to keep this from her? There was no way. She was my best friend. She'd know something was up. We shared everything. I chuckled at my current predicament and realized we didn't share *everything*.

"Let's finish our drinks and then we'll talk," Jax directed.

I'd gathered Callum was the alpha of the group, which would make sense. He seemed the one in control over everything with his rules, coupled with the way everyone looked at him to make decisions. He also naturally took the seat at the end of the bar, and I realized he was sitting at the head of the table at Bo's tonight discussing whatever it was they were looking at. At least part of their night was talking about me, since he had to get permission from them to take me out. Although I was getting the feeling that having him go down on me twice was not part of the agreement.

Jax would be his beta. The one the others looked to when Callum wasn't around, the one who handled the negotiations. Negotiations? I got the feeling the arrangement I would be presented was a take it or leave it sort of thing, but a girl could try.

I didn't know where Emmett and Knox ranked, if they ranked at all. Emmett sort of had his own thing with Bo's, and I wasn't quite sure what Knox did. He seemed the faithful, obedient server, but I had a feeling he was much more complex than that. He had dealt with dickhead from the club without question. I got the impression he was efficient in that sort of thing, perhaps ex-military. Was his fun-going personality a facade?

He saw me looking at him and winked, then blew a kiss.

There was no way it was pretend. It didn't mean he couldn't be both, just uncommon, I guess. I laughed since I was basing all of this off the books I'd read. I had no experience with any of this stuff, but I knew everyone served a role in this relationship. Is that what it was? A relationship?

I finished the last of my drink and my stomach tightened into a ball of nerves as everyone looked at me, a mixture of glances. Emmett's was weary, Knox's was hopeful and Callum's... his was guarded. Was he angry with me?

This was not at all how I expected this night to go...

Jax called my name. "Are you ready?"

I looked around the room one more time. "Yes."

"I'll be in my room," Callum stated without emotion. He reached into his pocket and pulled out the NDA and another document, and handed them to Jax. He then reached into his other pocket and pulled out my panties, and the room looked between us.

"You can keep those." I winked and was happy to see a smile tugging at his lips. He wasn't mad at me, but uncertain. His words replaying in my mind. He was nervous I couldn't handle the arrangement, but little did he know I had already talked myself into while we were sitting around the bar silently. I wanted all these men, if that's what it ended up being. I know it was what I was hoping at this point. Four men that were probably the hottest I had ever seen. Muscles, tattoos, and those eyes.

Callum tucked them back into his pocket and turned to leave the room, followed by Emmett and Knox.

"We'll go into the office." Jax pointed at the large glass paneled room off the kitchen.

I nodded, too nervous to speak.

I prefer penii not penises

THE OFFICE WAS AS impressive as the rest of the house. Three of the walls were floor to ceiling glass panels and on the far side of the room were dark wood shelves with a mixture of books and other modern decor on it. In the center of the room was a large desk with a single chair behind it and, in front of it, four dark brown leather chairs.

"Please take a seat," he offered, then took the seat beside me. I'd expected him to sit across the desk, a show of authority and control, but Jax knew I was no threat and he felt I knew my place. He was making it more intimate, making me feel more comfortable, and I appreciated that.

He flipped the NDA open and looked at it. I got the feeling he was confirming my signature on it before we started talking. Trust but verify, I suppose.

"So I'm going to assume you have put a few things together about us, but potentially have some questions. I usually have a whole discussion planned, but you seem to have mixed things up a bit."

"Sorry." I fidgeted with my hands.

"Don't be sorry. It's nice to see Callum let his guard down, even though it bothers him."

"Why?"

"He needs structure. Control."

"I got that impression, based on some things he's said and done."

"I have to ask... only because it will change the tone of the conversation. Have you had sex?"

"I'm not a virgin."

He chuckled, "Sorry. I meant with Callum."

"Oh." I hit my forehead and wiped my hand down my face. "No. Not yet."

A smile flickered on his face, but then he shook his head. I presume, trying to focus himself. "Let's get this over with, then. I don't want to be the one standing in the way of what Callum wants."

I sucked in a breath.

"What theories have you drawn so far?"

I hesitated because if I was wrong, I would feel super embarrassed.

"Don't be shy. You can't say anything I haven't heard."

I swallowed the lump in my throat. "That you all... share?"

A smile flickered across his face. "Anything else?"

"Callum seems to be in charge, followed by you. I haven't figured out Emmett and Knox's role yet."

He nodded, not adding any other information. "Anything else?"

My eyes bulged out of my head. Was there something else? I'm sure there was, but I couldn't think of it right now, so I shook my head.

His hand reached across the space and grabbed mine, flipping it over and rubbing my palm. It was affectionate, but also sexy. I didn't think he was interested, but the way he acted tonight before dinner and then now... His thumbs brushed across my wrist and paused. "We are a group, a unit. Call it what you want. We share."

He swiped this thumb across my wrist, turning me on. Was the wrist an erogenous zone, because it was making my heartbeat quicken... or maybe it was the idea of having all four men to myself. Four cocks in this aching pussy.

"How does that make you feel?"

Excited. Scared. Like a little horn toad ready to get her freak on. Is this why Callum felt uncertain? Because he didn't think I'd be ready for this? How could I not be? These men are fucking gorgeous and they wanted me. Me!

I must have looked like a deer in headlights, because he chuckled. "You don't have to answer right now."

"I..." I started, then stopped. "What else aren't you telling me?"

He nodded and dropped my hands.

This was it. The awkward elephant in the room. The one in the corner, sipping on her tea with a lace umbrella over her head, legs crossed, waiting with bated breath.

"This isn't a long-term relationship sort of deal. We have found it's better to only do it a few times at most, that way no one gets too emotionally attached."

It felt like a gut punch. Did Callum think I'd turn it down because I'd want more than a bang? A *world changing, mind-altering bang*. One that would likely break me for all future sexual encounters. One that would be the epitome of all sexual relations for the rest of my life and one I could never talk about? I'd bang them and then have to be let out into the world, searching for the same feeling, the same height of satisfaction. It would turn me mad with lust, cycling through guy after guy, looking for what I can't have. Send me into shady sex clubs. *Not all sex clubs are shady.* I agreed with myself, but how would a non-shady sex club benefit my internal monologue about me turning into a sex crazed spinster who would be broken after my encounters with them? Encounters, because I would try to push it to the very limit. He said a few. Not one or two, but a few. Few meant a small number of, but it was not an exact number and left open for interruption of the word small. Small could be three... it could also mean three hundred. *If you were comparing it to three thousand.* Relative.

I had to bring myself back from the brink of the cliff I was racing towards. I heard his unspoken words. Instead of stating the obvious, he tried to smooth it over, but what he really meant was so the females didn't get attached. Why wouldn't they? Having four desirable men to sexually ravage your body. Hell, I'm attached right now and have only had Callum tongue fuck me in the back of a car and in a makeshift changing room. Imagine what he could do if given enough space. Add in the others and actual dicks...

The elephant was now swiping hundred-dollar bills in the air with a gold chain around her neck.

"And if I want more than that?"

His lips pinched in a hard line.

"I see." Nothing.

He leaned in close, his leg brushing the inside of mine as his hand rested on the space between my neck and cheek. "I'd love to fuck those pretty little lips of yours," he said as his thumb pad traced over my bottom lip, pulling it down. He leaned in closer. "I, too, want to make you moan over my cock."

I felt my breath hitch at his words, but then he pulled back.

"Here's a document you can review. If you agree to this arrangement, you will need to sign this and then also mark the things you would like to do, not like to do and maybe like to do."

I looked over the document, and random things caught my attention like anal, edging, and double penetration. I fought the urge to look down. It's not like I have x-ray vision and could see my v-hole, to actually visualize two penii entering me. I call it penii even though I know it's not a word because I feel like it should be a word. Penises sounds too sussy.

He stood up. "Take a day or so to think about it." He chuckled, "Actually, take until the fourteenth. If you say yes, I can promise it will be a Valentine's Day you'll never forget."

I stood and walked out of the room, looking over my shoulder briefly to see him staring at my ass. As I left the room, my eye contact never broke from his. He was standing there in taut perfection. Goddamn, he, too, was hot as fuck. I was going to hell.

"Just say sir and I'll give you the goddamned world on a platter"

I ONLY GLANCED AT the contract one time before I got to Callum's room. I knocked, but the door was cracked, so I poked my head in.

Mother Shitballs!

He was in the shower, music on, looking up at the rainfall, hands pressed against his face and his... I had to lean against the door frame to hold me up. His beautiful, beautiful cock. Hanging there begging to be touched. To make it come alive. And his tattoos. They were all over his torso, running down his hips, wrapping around his back. I forgot about them, because the businessman the world sees is collared, button up shirts and suits, but underneath it all is this tattooed, dark, sexy man beast.

I couldn't control myself. His dick was like a siren song calling me.

I shut the door quietly, tossed the contract on the floor, then slipped out of my shoes and dress. I know this was most definitely breaking the rules, but fuck them. I'm a rule breaker. It's up to him to stop me and I prayed to all the gods and goddesses he doesn't, because I needed to feel that thing inside of me. I needed to get fucked. I hoped it would take away whatever madness was making me want to agree to these terms. I know I'll want more. That was the only thing holding me back. I'm going to love it and want more. But I won't be able to have it. That was the part I'll have to come to terms with.

I slipped into the shower behind him and reached my hands around his hips, then ran them down his legs. He tensed for a moment, then relaxed. When he turned towards me, he towered over me, while his bright blue eyes stared at me.

"I didn't think you'd come."

"I haven't yet."

A deep throaty laughed bounced around the walls.

I couldn't stand it any longer. I slowly dropped to my knees, his cock already standing at attention. My goodness, it was huge. I slowly wrapped my hand around the base of it and looked up at him. The water poured down on him, running down his chest. He looked impossibly sexy right now, all muscles and tattoos.

I pressed my lips to the tip of his cock.

"Everlee," he nearly moaned through set teeth.

"Hmm?" I ran my tongue along the underside and took just his head in my mouth and swirled my tongue around it.

"I know we don't have the green light. You didn't sign the contract."

Is that why he looked the way he did when I walked in? I took him in my mouth, letting him hit the back of my throat, then pulled out slowly.

"Is that a problem?" I took him in my mouth again.

His words shuddered in the slightest. "It's not following... the rules," he breathed out.

I took him back in again and swirled my tongue around his head then pulled him out. "I'm a rule breaker." I took him in again and again, running my hand down the length of his shaft each time. "I can stop." I lined my lips up again, but this time he pressed into my mouth, his hands getting tangled in my hair, and I smile.

He thrusted three times, hitting the back of my throat, making my eyes water. I tried to relax it to take him further, but then he pulled out. He swooped down and lifted me to standing before he forced me back against the shower wall. The cold of the glass stung my hot skin, but only for a second. His mouth took mine, his tongue forcing its way in while his hands grabbed my breasts. "Fucking perfect."

His lips trailed down my jaw to my neck, where he bit and sucked, causing my knees to buckle briefly and a moan to escape my lips.

"I'm going to make you moan so much you won't be able to speak tomorrow and I'm going to fuck you so hard, you won't be able to walk."

I felt myself dripping as another moan escaped from my lips.

"Good girl," he mumbled against my neck. His tongue swiped the water away before he sucked the skin into his mouth again.

"Fuck me," I pant, instead of plea.

"I plan to."

I lifted his chin, taking his mouth on mine as I hooked my leg around him. I felt his hard cock pressing right at my entrance, so I tilted my hips forward.

"No, no, no. We're not going to rush this. I shouldn't even be doing this, but you're like a drug I can't say no to. The boys are going to be pissed they aren't here, so I'm going to enjoy this as much as I can to help with the aftermath."

My body rocked against his, feeling the length of his cock as it slid up and down and brushed against my clit. I grabbed his shoulders and rocked my hips harder and faster.

"You don't listen, do you?" He pulled away, leaving me wanting. "Do you have any hard no's?"

"What?" I shook my head. "I don't know."

He tilted his head to the side. "Give me a safe word."

"Safe word?"

"Oh, baby." He brushed a kiss on my nose.

He started to explain, but I cut him off. "Shit. I know what a safe word is. You... this... my head is just discombobulated."

"Discombobulated?" He smiled.

I pushed against his rock-hard chest, but he grabbed my wrist, pinning me to him. "Safe word."

My head was spinning. "Cupid."

He chuckled. "Cupid?"

I nodded. "Sorry. It's that time of year."

"Don't apologize," he said, leaning down to take my mouth in his. This time it was softer and more passionate. I moaned into his mouth as his body pressed against mine and his cock rocked against my needy little clit.

"Your moaning is going to be the death of us all."

"Do you think..."

He pulled away, looking at me.

"Do you think they want to watch? Would you get in less trouble?" I felt a tightness start in my chest and pulse down my body. I couldn't believe I just asked that.

"Are you ok with that?"

"I'm not against... the sharing." Was this the wrong time to be having this conversation?

"But?"

"My problem is..." I couldn't help smile with embarrassment. "The time limit set in place." Feeling more confident, the words rushed out. "I haven't even had you all yet, but I know once I do, I'll want more."

His lips met mine in a harsh, but brief, kiss. "You're mine tonight, but they can watch if it's what you want."

"How?"

"How do you want them to watch?"

"What are my options?"

He smiled, the kind of smile that told you, you were in over your head, but you knew no matter what was said you wouldn't care.

"We have the shower camera and intercom here. They can come into the room, or..." He paused, studying my face.

"I've already signed the NDA and will sign the other contract tomorrow once I change a few things."

His laughter boomed. "Of course you would change something." He stepped towards me, running his hand down my torso, rubbing his finger over my clit. "You're so wet."

I moaned again. I never realized how much I moaned. If I were asked, I would have said no, but knowing how it affects these men, I'm acutely aware every time I do it. Perhaps it's the fact I haven't had a man's hands on me in months and they were just stored up in their own little moan bank.

"The other option is a voyeur room." He read the confusion on my face and continued. "It's like a regular bedroom, but there's two-way glass on the wall they can look through. Lights are set low so you can't see them, but they can see us."

My eyes lit up.

"You like that?"

I nodded, biting my lip. He pressed his fingers into me, nearly lifting me off the ground, pulsing them in and out a few times. I threw my arms around his neck, to help hold me up as my legs grew weaker the closer I got to climax.

"You aren't coming yet. Have you ever been edged?"

"I don't think so."

"I told you I was going to punish you for breaking the rules and now even worse for making me break the rules. You won't come until I let you come. I'm going to get you close and then stop. Over and over again until you can't fucking stand it. Then I'm going to fuck you so hard until you come around my cock that you're going to see stars, and then I'm going to fuck you some more."

I stared at him in shock. Needy, lustful shock and I couldn't wait.

He walked over to the intercom on the wall and pressed a button. "Voyeur room. Now."

Jax chimed in with a modicum of concern. "Did she sign?"

"Not yet. She wants to negotiate timing."

"Callum," he warned.

"We'll discuss later. If you want to watch me edge her, then fuck her, and listen to her moan, then meet me there in two minutes."

He flicked the shower off and scooped me up in his arms, not waiting for an answer. I squealed in delight.

"How many rooms do you have?" I asked, tracing my finger around the tattoos on his chest.

He smiled.

The cool bite of air outside of the hot steamy shower caused goosebumps to spread over my skin. He swung his door open, and I freaked out, clutching to him.

He looked down at me with a quizzical brow. "You're concerned about someone in this house seeing me carry your naked ass into a room where they are about to watch me kiss, lick, and fuck you?"

I threw my head back dramatically, then popped it back up quickly. "What are you going to do to me again?" I let my finger glide between his pecs.

"You have no idea, love. Just remember your safe word. You say it and I will stop immediately."

My body felt electrified right now. Every hair stood on end, every nerve responsive and wanting. My heart was nearly pounding out of my chest. We passed several doors, then went up a small flight of stairs to another short hallway. He stopped in front of the first door on the left.

He bent down to grab the handle with his hand that was supporting my ass, and a moment later, we walked into a dimly lit room. It was huge, probably the size of two rooms in one, and in the middle was a large circular bed with red satin sheets. Three of the walls were draped with decorative black curtains, with several dressers placed around the room.

He tossed me on the center of the bed and I stared at the wall to my left, which was made of large glass panels. The fear and hesitation I had was quickly replaced with excitement. I'd never done anything like this before, nor had I ever thought I would, but right now... I had to pinch myself to make sure I was awake because this didn't feel real.

"Are you ok?" Callum asked, walking back over to me. Damn, he looked delicious. I wanted to lick and suck every tattoo on his body and then climb on top of his cock and ride him until I came and then came again. *While his friends watch*, my subconscious added.

"Yes. Just waiting for you."

His quiet laugh hid the deep growl from within his chest. But I heard it. I felt it.

He slowly crawled onto the bed, mounting me with his cock laying on my stomach. He grabbed my wrists and lifted them above my head, pinning them to the pillow behind me. He leaned down and whispered, "Remember your safe word."

I decided to test the waters because I was beginning to like the way it felt to see the fire in his eyes when I said the two magic words. "Yes, Sir."

His eyes caught mine and he did not disappoint.

"Say it," he commanded softly.

"Cupid," I whispered.

"Good girl." He grabbed something above my head and a second later, a soft fur was tickling my wrist. I tilted my head back and confirmed... pink fuzzy handcuffs.

He slid down my body, taking my left breast in his mouth, while his other hand teased and squeezed the right, rubbing the sensitive bud between his fingers. A heat shot through my core, straight to my clit, making my body light up like fireworks. My back arched off the bed, pressing my breast further into his mouth. "Moan for us," he softly commanded.

The word us threw me for a loop for a minute and then I remember. They're watching me. My head fell to the side, looking at the darkened glass, wondering if they could see me, because I couldn't see them.

"Do you want to see them?" Callum asked, reading my mind.

I looked back at him, asking myself how far I was willing to go down this rabbit hole when the word escaped my lips. "Yes."

A second later, they were there.

My guys.

Well, my future guys, because looking at them all sitting there with their cocks in their hand watching me caused the flurry of butterflies in my stomach to go crazy.

"Everlee," Jax said, slowing stroking himself.

"Hey Ali," Knox said, hand paused.

"Trouble," Emmett said, and I couldn't help but smile.

Callum took two fingers and guided my chin back to him. "Shall we?"

"Please."

He smirked and quickly turned me on the bed, the satin making me slide around like water. He aimed my pussy right at the men. I couldn't see much, but I could tell their posture had changed. Changed for me. I could feel their eyes raking across my body, lusting after it.

Callum backed off the bed, pulling me with him so my ass was on the edge and his knees were on the ground. "Shall I make her come this way, boys?"

"No," they all say in unison.

I popped my head up and stuck my tongue out at them, eliciting a laugh from the group. My eyes are still glued on them when Callum swiped his tongue across my clit, causing another moan to escape.

"She tastes so fucking good." He hooked my legs over his shoulders and his arms around my legs, holding me to his face. He licked and swirled his tongue around my needy little cunt like it was his last meal. The moans continued as I inched closer and closer to release. I rotated my shoulders so my handcuffed hands latched onto his hair, holding him in place, while I fucked his face.

"She's getting close," I hear someone say.

Callum pulled back, my hips still thrusting like a dog without balls humping the air. My body and my mind now catching up with the fact Callum pulled away just enough so that I couldn't even feel his breath on me, because that's where I was.

One breath and I'd come so fucking hard. This was hours in the making, since he left me wanting in that changing room. My hands eagerly tried to find my clit to finish what he started, but it took a second too long to figure it out with the handcuffs. Callum caught me and threw them over my head again.

"You will learn to follow the rules," he growled.

"Rules were meant to be broken," I snap back.

"And so were you," he threatens. "If you try to come again without my permission, the punishment will be a lot worse than the edging."

I suck on my bottom lip, causing him to let out a groan.

"I want to feel that pretty little mouth around my cock again. I want to feel it hit the back of your throat and I want you to moan around it."

He stood up, helping me off the bed, and I dropped to my knees faster than I ever had before. Something about his words sent me over the edge and made me feel things I've never felt. "That's it, good girl." He stroked my hair and I nearly melted into a puddle on the floor.

I positioned my hands around his cock. It was awkward with the cuffs, but I made it work. I ran my tongue along the length of his shaft before I swirled it around his head, sucking it in like a lollipop. I heard him gasp at the same time his hands tangled in my hair.

The sounds he made and the way his body moved for me, because of me, made me want more. I repeated the same steps over and over again, teasing him. If he wanted to edge me, I could edge him right back.

"Shit, Everlee."

I couldn't take any more. I took his full cock in my mouth and relaxed my throat so he could get as deep as possible. His legs gave the lightest shudder as I heard a moan escape his lips. I caught the boys out of the corner of my eye, and they gave me fire. I bobbed on Callum harder and faster and watched their hands move faster. I had the power of sucking four dicks at once. I could make them all come together.

I started to moan.

"Not yet!" Callum pulled himself out of my mouth and tossed me back on the bed.

He climbed down my body like a man on a mission and thrusted his tongue into me. "Fuck!" I screamed out. My legs clutched to his ears like a pair of earmuffs while my ass lifted off the ground and with it, Callum. I sat up and realized I was vertically fucking his face. The boys, right in front of me, their eyes were wide in amazement. I wanted to lean back but if I did, I knew we would topple back to the bed. "I'm about to come," I cried out.

We crashed back to the bed, and I thought he was going to pull away again, but he commanded me to come and that's all I need. He sucked my clit as he inserted two fingers. My body was moving, writhing in pain and lust. I was so close I felt like I was going to explode, like I was going to burst at the seams. He added a third finger and I felt myself stretch around him, the pressure almost too much. His moves were precise, but quick. He pulled a finger out, curved the two remaining and found that magical spot. I cried out. The sound came from deep within, a guttural groan. I struggled to find anything to grab, my toes and my fingers curled, the muscles in my body tight. "Oh, God!"

"I'm your God right now."

My eyes locked with his, my chest still heaved as my body is rode the waves, lost in a state of euphoria. Seconds turned to hours turned to days. I'm lost. When my body came down from the biggest and best orgasm I've ever had, I felt a tingling in my toes and fingers and a throbbing in my core.

I couldn't even catch my breath before I heard the click of the locks on the handcuffs. With my hands free, I rolled over and found him sheathing his cock in a rubber. "I'm going to fuck you now." He crawled onto the bed and over me, murmuring against my neck, "I'm going to make you come so hard again that you'll be seeing stars."

Even though I just had the absolute best orgasm of my life, I needed more. I wanted more. I needed to feel his cock seated deep inside me. My body was already moving again on its own like a sex crazed animal in heat. *This is what six months without a dick will do to you.*

If I couldn't get them to agree to give me more time, then this was it, and I needed to make it count.

"I need your dick in me now." I sat up and looked at him.

"Ask nicely," he toyed.

"Please put your dick in me and fuck me like there is no tomorrow, so I may cream all over it. I want my cum running down your cock to your ballsack. I want your dick so far in me I can taste it in my mouth. I want-"

"Fuck Everlee. Just say Sir and I'll give you the goddamned world on a platter."

"Sir."

The blunt end of his cock pressed against my soaking wet folds and I shifted, but I didn't have to wait. He plunged inside of me so hard and so fast that the sound which passed through my lips was unlike anything I'd ever heard. My body was alive. I wanted to sing out in jubilation as every fiber of my being was electrified.

He stilled for a second, letting my body adjust to the size of his girth. He was much larger than monster BOB which was my biggest. The pressure was intense, but he was my

God right now. My body shuddered with delight. He pulled out slowly, then slammed in again, holding himself there. He moved in rhythm now, harder and faster.

"I've missed dick," I mumbled out by accident.

Fortunately, I don't think he heard through the sounds of his own grunts and groans. In one swift motion, he flipped us over, his cock still pressed into me. Straddling him now, I sank further onto him, our chests heaving. I took this moment to appreciate the sight of him laying underneath me, my palms pressed into his chest and the way his eyes sparkled.

"You're so fucking beautiful," he said, grabbing my legs.

I slowly rocked, gyrating my hips back and forth. "Oh, my..."

His hands clamp to my thighs. "You're so tight. You feel so good wrapped around me."

I slowly popped my body off and slid back onto him, causing him to let out a low moan. "Now who's moaning?" I tease.

A second later, the bed rotated, catching me off guard.

"We want to see your face while you fuck him," Jax said through the intercom. His hand was pressed against the wall, which I had to assume was the control for the bed.

I felt like a queen right now. I sat back on Callum's cock and ran my hands over my breasts as I rocked my hips back and forth, putting on a show for the others.

"Touch yourself," Knox chimed.

I watched him stroke himself through the glass.

I slid my hand down, finding my clit, and began to rub. It was still hypersensitive from my last orgasm, but I don't care. My body needed it. I needed it. They needed it.

I circled faster and faster as my hips moved with the same speed. My free hand grabbed my breast, pinching my nipple as I bounced on him. Callum's hips started thrusting up, causing me to crash back on him. I pressed my hands to his chest for support, raising off him just enough so he could fuck me from underneath. I moaned again and again. He leaned up and took my breast in his mouth, swirling his tongue over my nipple.

"Oh... my..." My body was getting close again. It was like that deep wave you knew was going to take you over the edge of the fucking world. "I'm about to... come... again."

He flipped us over and rams into me harder and faster than before. The look on his face is pure fire. Lust. Need. I cried out as he picked up even more speed, the sound of sex bounced off the walls as his balls slapped hard against my ass.

I latched my arms around his neck and hooked my ankles around his back. I watched the way his eyes flickered and noticed the wrinkle that appeared on his forehead. I listened to the sounds he made, the grunts and groans, the feel of his biceps in my hands. If this was all I had, I needed to remember it. I would remember it.

My legs inched up higher, giving him more access. His fingers find my clit, and he began working it, but it only took two circles before I was screaming out his name. I felt the pressure inside of me build just before he came. There was a low groan that ripped through him and vibrated my very core. I leaned up, pressing my lips to his in the most passionate post-coital kiss I'd ever experienced. I felt his chest on mine, his heartbeat pounding against mine as our breathing slowed.

"Everlee. You're worth every rule I've broken tonight."

All I could do was smile since my tongue refused to make words. I felt like one of those things at car dealerships, their arms and legs just a bunch of mush being blown around. I looked over at the window and saw the boys sitting there not moving, part of me feeling guilty they weren't here with me, but the other part knowing my body would literally not be able to function with four of them. It would be too much coming off a six-month hiatus.

Callum kissed my forehead, bringing me back to him.

"Let's get you washed up."

I don't know how much time had passed. My body was spent and my head was woozy from that in-between state of awake and asleep. The place where you feel like you're on a merry-go-round that's descending further and further into the dark abyss. That's where I was.

I was still vaguely aware of what was going on around me, but I was happy. Satisfied. I couldn't remember the last time I felt this satiated. I felt like a limp noodle. A happy limp noodle that had just been thrown against the wall to see if it was done and yes, I was done.

I felt my body rocking back and forth, heard the opening and closing of doors, but I didn't open my eyes until I felt myself being submerged in warm water.

I opened my eyes and saw Callum standing there in all his naked glory, smiling down at me. "You rest. We're going to take care of you."

We're...

The smell of lavender and lemon grass wafted up as I continued to sink further into the tub. I felt a pair of hands on my feet, another on my shoulders, and a third lathering up a washcloth. I wondered where the fourth person was, but my question was answered when I felt him slide into the tub behind me, holding me against his chest, so I didn't sink under the water.

I heard him giving soft commands to wash and rub and then I was gone.

I will not masturbate at work

THE SMELL OF COFFEE and bacon wafting through the air woke me up. Confused, I opened my eyes and quickly remembered I was at Callum's house, or their house. I didn't know what to call it.

It was early. The sun was barely beginning to peek out from behind the veil of darkness. I rolled over and found Callum sitting up in the bed, tattooed chest exposed, with his e-reader in his hand, wearing a pair of glasses. Just behind his ear, I noticed a hint of silver weaved through his dark locks. How was it possible he could get any hotter? I lifted the covers just enough to see he was wearing a pair of tight black boxers that fit low on his hips, exposing the forkalicious v that was like an arrow, directing needy cunts like mine to the man candy below.

"Good Morning." He smiled.

"Yes," I mumbled, still drowsy, before realizing it was a statement, not a question. "Good Morning," I corrected, rolling on my stomach, looking at him.

"How do you feel?" He sat his e-reader on the nightstand beside him, along with his glasses.

"Good." I wanted to scream fucking great, but I felt that was too much energy for this early in the morning. "Did you all wash me last night?"

He chuckled. "I hope that wasn't a problem. They wanted to take care of you."

"It's ok." I smiled, closing my eyes for a second.

"There's coffee, if you want it, on the table beside you, and Emmett is fixing some breakfast downstairs."

"How does it feel?" I mumbled into the pillow before rolling to sit up.

"How does what feel?" His words were guarded.

"To have a fantastic cock. Shit. I mean cook. To have a fantastic cook at your beck and call?"

He smiled as he rolled over on his side, letting his finger lazily stroke across my collarbone. "The cock... pretty fantastic and the cook isn't so bad either."

His breath smelled minty fresh, which reminded me that mine did not. I rolled out of bed because if I didn't put space between us, I was going to be crawling on top of him and sinking onto that delicious cock in about six point nine seconds, and I didn't want his last thoughts of me to be stinky breath McGee. "You're dangerous," I mumbled.

I looked down and noticed I was wearing a pair of his boxers and one of his t-shirts.

"I'd say the same thing about you," he said, admiring the way I looked in his clothes, before he rolled out of bed and reached towards the sky.

Holy shit, he was sexy.

He looked over his shoulder with a wicked gleam in his eye. I hurriedly turned away. Devil! He was the devil in a beautiful man's body. I could already feel myself getting moist at just the sight of him. "Where are my clothes from last night?" I asked, looking around the room and changing the conversation.

"I had Brady pick you up some this morning." He pointed to the bench at the end of the bed.

"This morning?" I looked at my phone, ignoring the three missed text messages and one missed call from Lizzy. "It's just past six in the morning."

"We know a place." He offered nothing else as he walked across the room to his dresser, slipping on a pair of black joggers and a gray shirt that fit more like a schmedium the way it hugged his biceps and pecs.

Glory be. I was screwed.

I slipped on the very cute black leggings and gray sweater dress with a pair of black flats. Everything fit perfectly, which should have been concerning, but it seemed to fit Callum's attention to detail persona.

"I'll meet you downstairs when you're ready." He nodded. "Also, there's an extra toothbrush and brush in the bathroom if you need it."

"Do you do this for all the women who stay the night?" I teased.

"We rarely allow that." He closed the door behind him and I was stuck in the middle of the room with my jaw on the ground. What did it mean that I've stayed the night twice, and we weren't anything official?

I was getting ahead of myself. I brushed my teeth, washed my face and combed my hair, then made my way downstairs to a full kitchen. All the men were sitting around the oversized bar sipping coffee, reading the paper, and doodling when I walked in.

"Good morning," they all said in near unison.

A blush crept onto my face. Why was I being so shy around them now, especially after what happened last night?

"Do you like pancakes, eggs, sausage and cheese?" Emmett asked, both of his palms pressed onto the counter, causing his biceps to flex.

I nodded, unable to form words with my mouth or tear my gaze away.

"Good. I made you the Emmett special."

"It's so good," Knox exaggerated.

"It's ok," Jax teased.

"It's like heaven in your mouth," Callum noted.

My eyes shot over to him. He was watching me with his usual intense gaze. "Heaven in my mouth was last night." I heard someone blow out a low breath, chuckling. I had to assume it was Knox, but I didn't tear my gaze away from Callum to find out. "I can't wait to try it." The stool at the end of the bar creaked a little under my weight, it was cold and hard, very different from Callum's bed. Once settled, Emmett slid a plate over to me.

"It's like a sausage, egg and cheese biscuit, only it's on pancakes."

My mouth started salivating the closer I brought it to my mouth. The smells were tantalizing and when I took a bite, a moan escaped. Shit! Every damn time!

I cautiously looked up and saw all the men's hungry gazes on me. I wanted them. I wanted this. I just wanted it for longer than they wanted to give me and I had to be ok with that.

Could I?

A few nights of damn near guaranteed mind blowing sex only to walk away from it and never experience it again? I had to talk to Lizzy about it, but needed to figure out a way that didn't violate the NDA. Stupid NDA.

"I have a question."

"Yes, buttercup?" Knox said with his devilishly charming grin.

"Why the safe word last night?"

"Yes, Callum, why the safe word?" Knox turned his entire body to look at him.

Callum shot a glance at Knox, who turned back to face me, pulling his lips.

I couldn't help but smile before I looked back at Callum, who wasn't speaking.

Jax entered the conversation. "Because he had plans for other things, but he lost control."

"I didn't!" Callum interjected, like losing control was a bad thing.

Jax looked at him coolly over his shoulder, clearly not as nervous speaking his mind as Knox was. "It's ok to lose control every once in a while."

Callum rolled his eyes.

"What else were you planning on doing?"

All the boys looked at one another before Jax answered for the group. "We'll save it for when you sign the papers. We don't want to ruin the surprise."

The kitchen fell into silence as we all thought about what that meant. They obviously knew what was planned, and I had no idea. I was vanilla, and I was getting the impression they were some sort of delicious dark chocolate. While nervous, I definitely wanted a taste.

I finished up my sandwich and pulled Jax aside before I left. In the craziness of last night, I had misplaced the form I needed to mark and sign, but I also clarified what I could and could not say about last night. I told him Lizzy knew me better than anyone and had a sixth sense about my sex life. She would know I had sex and would put two and two together and come up with Callum and how denying it would only create a dog with bone that she'd go after until she got to the bottom of it. He agreed that if it came up, I could discuss how we slept together, but gave me strict guidelines. No mention of group play, the room, the rest of them or the contract, or the fact there was an NDA to begin with. All things concerned, Callum and I slept together once and it will probably never happen again.

I understood why the NDA. They had a kink that few people understood and they didn't want it getting out and staining their reputation in the business world. Which speaking of, I was curious how many pots they had their hands in. I knew of at least Vixen and Bo's, but I felt like there were more. All upscale, with a certain class to it, and they were planning on something else.

I got home and toyed with taking a shower, but part of me didn't want to wash off the remaining lavender scent on my skin. I wanted to hold on to as much of last night as I could. When I got to work, I texted Lizzy back, telling her I was safe, which resulted in an immediate call.

I was chuckling when I answered the phone. "Hello?"

"Where the hell have you been?"

"Good Morning to you too."

"No. No. Nope. Spill."

"What are you talking about?" I tried to play coy as best I could.

"Hooker, please. I know you were hoing it up last night with Mr. Fancy Pants."

"How would you know something like that?"

"The looks you two were casting. How you came back all hot and bothered from the bathroom. How he demanded he was taking you home."

I was silent a moment, which only further excited her. I could nearly feel her bouncing through the phone. "Can you do lunch today?"

"Hell to the fuckin' yea, I can. Where are you taking me?"

"Meet you at the salad place at the corner of Third street, say noon?"

"Yasss Queen! I'm so happy your pussy got pummeled last night. Ciao Chica!" She hung up before I could say anything else. I was still smiling when I opened my laptop. I flipped through a few emails, but was having a terrible time concentrating.

I pulled out the contract from my bag and looked at it and started checking the boxes of yes, no, or maybe. I still wasn't sure I was going to sign it and do this, but I could be prepared just in case. *Just do the damn thing! You know you are. Why are you even pretending?*

What if I could make it so good for them, they changed the rules for me? This wouldn't be a few times thing, but long term? I started picturing what it would be like and a reel of sex movies started flickering through my mind. Sex in the kitchen. Sex in the voyeur room. Sex in the shower, bathtub, balcony- I'm sure they had a balcony. Sex at Vixen. We would just be having lots of sex all the time everywhere.

What would it be like to date club owners? They'd be gone every Thursday through Sunday night with half-dressed women throwing themselves at them, because come on, who wouldn't? Would they eventually find one they wanted more than me? What would my future look like? I had always planned on getting married and having kids, because that's what society told me I had to do. But with them that didn't seem to be an option because I couldn't marry four of them and kids. I laughed. How would you explain that? Whose would it be? Could you imagine little Sammy or Julie going into school and telling everyone they have four daddies and one mommy? During parent-teacher conferences, five of us show up. On emergency contacts, only the mother and father could be listed. Whose name would go there?

My head collapsed onto my desk.

"Are you ok?"My assistant walked into the room.

"Yes." I looked up and realized what was on my desk and quickly shifted papers on top of it like I was cleaning up. "What's up?"

"A group of us are going out to lunch. You haven't left your office all morning, so I wanted to see if I needed to pick you up something."

"What?" The time glaring at me on the corner of my computer told me it was almost lunchtime. Holy cow! "Sorry. No. All good. I have lunch plans."

"With a special someone?" Her eyebrows pumped up and down.

"No," I chuckled.

"Oh. You seem..." she was struggling with the words to say, then just spit them out. "You're glowing, so I thought that..."

She thought I got laid! Well, I did. But freakin' aye! Do I have a billboard attached to my chest that says ask me about my pussy?

She started to walk out, but then tapped on the door frame. "Oh. Angelica from Meyers wants to know who to put as your plus one for tomorrow's dinner."

Shit. I completely forgot about the customer dinner. "Let me get back to you?"

"Sure. She just requested it by four this afternoon."

Shit! Shit! Shit! I had a perfect plan to flake out on the dinner, which started yesterday and I completely forgot. There was no way they'd buy I was sick now... especially after my new sex glow. I grumbled as I pulled the contract out from the stack of papers.

"It's all your fault." I pointed accusatorially at the paper.

Then an idea hit me. Maybe Callum would go with me.

I picked up my phone and dialed him up, thankful he'd dropped his number to me this morning in case I had questions about the contract.

He answered on the third ring. "Everlee? Are you ok?" His voice was tense.

"Yes. Yes. I'm fine, but need a favor." I bit the inside of my cheek as nerves were getting the better of me.

"Anything."

"I need you to be my date at a dinner tomorrow."

"On Valentine's Day?" His words were hesitant.

"Yeaaa... for a customer meeting at work."

"Oh."

I could tell by the way he spoke he was going to say he couldn't because it broke some rule. They didn't date, just had really great sex. "Listen, I know the rules and everything. I just committed a while ago to attend this event because it's one of our biggest customers. I thought by the time V- day rolled around, I'd be in a relationship, but I'm not. With no prospects. I can't bring Lizzy, because she's been my plus one so many times they think I'm an 'in the closet lesbian', which who knows maybe I am which is why

I haven't found a man and I had this plan to start faking an illness yesterday, but I completely forgot because I was so excited about dinner at Bo's and now this morning they see my new just been fucked glow, so there's no way I can pull off being sick." I took a deep breath once the word vomit stopped.

"That's a lot to unpack."

"Sorry."

"Do you think you're a lesbian? I mean, this could really change things?"

"Callum," I scolded.

"I'm kidding. I knew you weren't after the way you sucked my cock last night."

A puff of air escaped my lips.

"You like that, do you? Do you want me to tell you I'm sitting at my desk at Vixen with my pants pulled down and my hard cock in my hand, pumping it, thinking of your perfect little pussy?"

I clenched my thighs together. "Callum," I warned.

"How I can't wait until you're sliding onto it again? How I can't wait to watch the others with you? Taking you in every hole you have at the same time."

"Callum," I breathed out, pinching my eyelids together and gripping the edge of my desk. *I will not masturbate at work. I will not masturbate at work.*

"How-"

"Jesus Fuck Callum. When I see you I'm going to-"

"Come all over me?"

I disconnected the call. I couldn't take anymore. My skin was hot, my heart was racing and I'm fairly certain it looked like I pissed myself with the probable moisture that had leaked through my skirt. My fault for not wearing underwear today, but this skirt was one of those kinds you can't wear underwear with.

My phone chimed with a dick pic and my knees buckled.

Everlee: What the fuck are you trying to do to me, Callum?

He sent back a wink face emoji.

Callum: That was my way of saying I'd go with you tomor-row night. I just need to figure out how to break it to the boys.

Everlee: Would it help if I signed my contract?

Three dots appeared, then disappeared. Then appeared again. I stared at my phone, waiting for a response, but the dots kept coming, then going, coming, then going. Curios-ity and anticipation were killing me.

My phone dinged, and I looked at it, only to find Lizzy asking where I was. Shit! *Leaving now. Be there in three!*

I grabbed the list off my desk and stuffed it into my purse. I didn't need to leave that lying around, only to have someone accidentally pick it up. No thank you!

I was walking into the salad shop a few minutes later and found Lizzy in the corner by the front door with her arms crossed. "You better have a good reason you left me waiting."

"It was five minutes," I said, looking at my phone. I tried to hide the disappointment that Callum still hadn't responded yet. I shoved my phone in my pocket and gave Lizzy a hug.

She grabbed me by the shoulders, looked me up and down, pinched my cheeks and smelled my hair. I'm sure people in the salad shop were wondering what in the hell was going on.

She pointed her finger in my chest, just above my breast and said, "You've been laid."

"What?" I grabbed her arm. "Do you want to yell that a little louder so everyone else can hear?"

She took in a big breath.

"Don't you dare."

"Or what?" she teased, her eyebrows raising to her fore-head. "Everyone should know you got a piece of ass." She grabbed my wrist, pulling them down, bringing our face an inch apart. "How was he? Oh my God. I bet he was amazing. He looks like he would be."

"I never said we did."

"Hooker, please. You and I both know you got your little kitty kitty taken care of last night. So spill."

Thank God Jax allowed me this one thing, because she'd be impossible. I'd have to avoid her for a week or more for her not to pick up on it. "It was amazing."

"Yes!" she yelled, thrusting her fist into the air, garnering several curious glances. She chuckled meekly, "My favorite author just released her book a week early! Yeaaa." She pumped her fist in the air again.

People turned back to what they were doing and her gaze landed on me. "Can you believe them? Authors releasing books early is exciting!"

"But yours didn't. Your feelings are hurt over something you just made up." I laughed at her. She was complete chaos, and I loved it. She always was. We were and still are inseparable. In school, we were known as the dynamic duo and teachers knew we could never be in class together. One year in tenth, they accidentally put us in the same chemistry class and so, of course, we partnered up. Almost set the school on fire. To be fair, the gas line was faulty. At least that was the story we were sticking to.

We ordered our salads and found a table in the corner. "So," she asked.

I rolled my eyes, both excited and not excited to tell her. I didn't want her getting her hopes up about this relationship since it wouldn't last very long. Maybe it's just what I needed. The hump I needed to get over to get back out there. Literal and figurative hump.

But this hump was going to break me for all future humps. Gahh!

She cleared her throat, bringing me back.

"So after we left, he was planning on taking me home, but then we got to talking, then he..."

Lizzy had a fork of salad in her mouth, frozen. She motioned for me to continue with her other hand.

My eyes got big and my head bobbled from side to side.

And then her eyes got big with understanding. "In the back seat of his car? Where was the driver? You didn't do it in front of him, did you?"

Her question about the driver told me there was no way I could tell her about the situation with the other three guys... even if I was allowed to. She had joked about it before, but that's when it was only a joke and not for real. "He was standing outside on the sidewalk." My mouth pulled to the side as my stomach tightened, remembering the start of my crazy night.

"Callum was just like yo dude park right here while I have my dessert? Go wait outside in the frigid cold?"

"Not quite like that, but kind of."

"So you." She propped her arm on the table, leaning across and whispered, "Got your little boom boom yum yummed, parked on the side of the street with the driver just chilling outside, waiting, and people walking by?"

I nodded, taking a bite of food, knowing it wouldn't hide the blush from my cheeks.

"Kinky."

She plopped back in her seat and took another bite of food. "Continue," she said in a very diplomatic voice, waving her hand like the Queen would.

I was smiling so much my cheeks were hurting. "So then he surprised me and took me ice skating."

My phone dinged.

Callum.

Callum: Where are you?

Everlee: Salad Shop eating lunch.

I answered without thinking. I put my phone back in my lap. I wasn't mad at him, but I was a little irritated about the whole bubble incident earlier.

"But you weren't in the clothes for that."

I shook my head so I could focus on Lizzy. "I know... so he bought me some and then..." My head face planted into my palm.

"No," Lizzy said, grabbing her salad bowl up under her chin and stuffing her mouth full like a kid would do with a bowl of popcorn at a movie theatre.

I nodded. "Again, in the changing room."

Her fork dropped in her bowl and she stared at me wide eyed.

"But he didn't let me finish."

"That bastard."

"Right," I laughed. "So I took my panties off and, when he wasn't paying attention, stuffed them in his pocket."

"Oh my God. Who are you Queen and what have you done with my shyish Everlee?"

"I'm not shy."

"Well, you also did more exhibitionistic things last night than you ever have before."

If she only knew. But she couldn't. A flashback of me riding Callum's cock on the bed with the others watching as I played with my clit had me blushing again.

"Girl, do we need to get you a fan, because damn?" She started fanning me.

"Stop."

"So then. Please tell me you got to tickle the pickle after all that. You needed it, after all."

"What's that supposed to mean?"

She batted her hand. "Girl, you know. Now stop procrastinating and get to the good part."

"After skating, he took me home where we... you know..."

"That's it? That's all I get?"

"Fine. He had another snack in the shower."

Lizzy smacked the table loudly. "Three!" She lowered her voice, "Three times? I'm going to call him the Cookie Monster... shit. Nom, nom, nom is the name of the game with him. Shit!" she repeated.

"Well, we went back and forth and then we went to the bedroom." Where three other guys watched.

"Let me guess? Nom Nom?"

"Yes, and then bang bang." I shook my head again. It always sounded stupid when I tried to come up with cutesy little names for things.

"Big?"

"Huge. I'm so sore today."

"Wow," she breathed, looking into the air.

"But then after, he ran us a bath and washed me."

Lizzy's head hit the table dramatically. I'm sure from all the outbursts and movements she's been making, fellow patrons were likely concerned for my safety.

"Everything ok over here?" a voice boomed behind me at the same time I felt a hand brush across my shoulder.

Lizzy tilted her head up, so her chin was resting on the table and once she saw who it was, cursed out a string of expletives and then sat up.

I looked up to find Callum's gaze on me.

"What are you doing here?"

"Everlee? Don't ask the man that. Offer to pull up a chair for him."

Poor Lizzy. She was already invested in my relationship with a man I'd only be with for a few more days, likely. The pain at that realization stung real bad.

His brow furrowed as he studied my face. "Are you ok?" His knuckles brushed across my cheek.

I heard a loud sigh from Lizzy, who looked like she'd been love struck with Cupid's arrow.

"I'm good." My lips flattened. We both knew I wasn't doing a good job of hiding anything and he could probably make two guesses to figure out what's wrong.

"I didn't mean to interrupt your lunch. I just wanted to say hello."

I stared at him, causing him to wink back at me.

"You aren't interrupting. We're just getting caught up on girl chat."

"I'm sure that's what you're doing." His eyes twinkled knowingly.

I just pumped my eyebrows with an 'I told you so' glance.

"I'm going to grab a bite to eat, but I'd like to talk to you for a minute before you go back to work."

"I'm sure you would... nom nom nom..." Lizzy mumbled.

My eyes shot daggers at her. She shrugged her shoulders defiantly and mouthed, "What? I'm sorry. Not really."

I don't know if Callum heard her, but if he did, he didn't react. I'm sure I'd hear some snarky comment later, and the thought of that filled me with more excitement and trepidation than I wanted.

"Man can wear a suit. Who would have thought a businessman like him would have a little freak to him?" Lizzy said when he walked away.

I wanted to tell her about all the tattoos and everything else, but I couldn't. Tattoos may not be an issue, but I wanted to keep that to myself. He worked hard on maintaining his image outside of his house, and I didn't want to spoil it. If he revealed that to her, then so be it.

Never try to go toe to toe with a dom in a salad shop

AFTER WE FINISHED LUNCH, which was pretty much over the moment Callum walked away from the table because of Lizzy's inability to focus, coupled with the fact she was pushing me towards him, I walked over to his booth and stood beside it.

He looked up at me and winked.

"May I sit, sir?" I whispered so only he could hear me.

His eyes flashed with blue flames. I loved I could get that reaction out of him. "You may." He patted the seat beside him as he slid over.

He grabbed my hand. "You don't need to do that in public."

"Maybe I wanted to." I mouthed sir.

He leaned closer to me, so his lips were brushing against my ear. "Careful or I'll bend you across this table and fuck you in front of everyone."

"Maybe that's what I want." Who was I right now? I was a little nymph who, after getting some nom nom wanted more of that dom dom.

Lizzy, I sighed. Her influence on me was problematic because even thinking the thoughts, I felt silly. When she says it, I'm all like yea nom noms and magic sticks when I say it, it's like the brakes screeching on a car.

"Oh, really?"

Shit. I was in trouble. Never go toe to toe with a dom in a salad shop.

"Turn your body towards me some," he commanded, stepping into his role with ease.

I hesitated, not for fear of being caught, but for fear of liking what was about to happen and losing control.

His finger lightly directed my chin towards him. "Use your words Everlee," His tone was quiet, but intense.

"Yes, Sir."

Thank God he had a booth in the back corner and the next set of people was one booth away. Six feet, if I was lucky.

"Good girl." He took a bite of his salad. "Now stay still."

I nodded, and he cast a glance at me, so I corrected. "Yes, Sir." Why was this so hot right now? My body was electrified. It felt like lightning was shooting all over it.

His left hand fell on my leg by my knee and squeezed gently. I ran my teeth across my bottom lips to stop the moan that was going to escape. We both knew it was going to happen, but they had to be limited. The only problem with putting a dam on the moans was when it was released, it was going to be one loud fucking moan. Like a break the glass kind of moan. Like a get the cops called on you kind of moan. And that could not happen.

His fingers slipped up my leg, and I knew what was at the end of that rainbow, so I watched his face intently, waiting for him to find the pot of gold. His hand slipped under my skirt as he took a bite of salad. When he got a little further up, he found the surprise and his eyes shot to mine, at the same time his fork clamored to the table.

His lips parted and his breathing changed.

Got'em! I exulted in glee.

"Everlee," He hissed through his teeth.

"Yes... Sir."

"Why the fuck aren't you wearing any panties?"

I bit my bottom lip, and he grabbed under my jaw, holding me there for a second, his eyes frantically looking between mine. "Goddamn you." His mouth crashed to mine, his tongue pushing its way in, dancing with mine. His kiss was fire. Like his life depended on it. He pulled away, his electric gaze on me. "We're going. Now," he said, nearly pushing me out of the seat.

"Where are we going?" I stood there dazed, both by his reaction and his kiss.

He grabbed my hand and pulled me outside, his movements frantic, hurried.

Brady was standing outside of the car and opened the back door for us as Callum stomped towards it. He was a man on a mission and I was it.

Brady closed the door and waited outside, taking a few steps back.

"Take your shirt off now before I rip it off," his voice was husky. Deep. The passion, the heat, tore through me like an earthquake ripped through the ground.

Without hesitation, I pulled it over my head at the same time he pulled his pants down, freeing his already hard cock. He reached into his pocket and cursed.

"I'm clean and on the pill," I said before he had any time to change his mind. I needed him inside of me now.

He stared at me for a moment, "Me, too. Clean." He said before he lifted me up to slide onto his cock as my skirt rode up to my hips. "You feel so fucking good," he moaned, unhooking my bra with one flick of his fingers. The clasp was in the front, so all he had to do was push the bra and it slid down my arms. Before I could get it completely free of my wrists, he took both of his hands and cupped my breasts, squeezing them before taking one in his mouth.

He was rough, uncontrollable. His teeth scraped over my pebbled nipple as he sucked, like his life depended on it.

I gyrated on his lap, while my hands were still pinned behind me in make shift handcuffs because of my bra.

"I'm going to get into so much fucking trouble for this."

"Then let's make sure it's worth it," I murmured back against his neck before I bit it. His cock twitched inside of me.

"Fuck Everlee." His palms ran down my back, pressing me towards him before his hands grabbed my hips and lifted, before he held me down as he grinded into me. He was so deep, causing an ache within, but it felt fantastic. "Where's your contract?"

"Now?"

"Yes. Now."

I shook my bra off my wrists and dug into my purse as he continued to grind into me. "It's not signed yet."

"Show it to me." I flicked it open with one hand and held it up.

He quickly scanned the page as a devious smile played on his lips. "Of course you'd be perfect." He nodded, indicating I could toss it on the ground.

"Do you remember your safe word?"

I nodded.

"Words Everlee." His teeth bit my neck, sucking my skin in making my back arch.

"Cupid."

His mouth closed on mine again, his tongue mimicking his body.

"You feel so good."

"So do you, baby."

He brought his finger in front, rubbing my clit. I leaned back so he could have more access. "So fucking wet." He put his finger in his mouth, sucking me off of him. I'm pretty sure my eyes rolled into the back of my head. Never in my entire life had someone made me feel like a queen the way he did. The level of want and need he had for me is... I had no words.

He rubbed my slickness off the base of his cock, but this time, instead of licking it off, he moved his hand around to my back and brushed his finger over my hole. Oh fuck. I knew what was about to happen. He wanted to see my contract to see if I'd marked anal and I put yes. I'd done it once in college, but haven't done it since then. *Looks like you're about to get your freak on.* My subconscious sang. She seemed to have permanently taken the shape of the elephant, which was smooshed in the front passenger's seat wearing a bedazzled sleeveless jean jacket with a pair of vintage golden trimmed opera glasses aimed straight at my butthole.

His mouth took mine, this time more gentle. He slowly pushed his finger in, and I let out a moan inside his mouth and he swallowed it down. He pushed his finger in again, his other hand gripped on my hip. A squeak came out, and he pulled away. "That's new."

"Shut up and fuck me." I rocked my hips forward.

"Yes, Ma'am."

I let my head fall back in pure bliss. He was now using his finger in my ass to guide us, rock us. He picked up speed, his other hand moving from my hip to my clit.

"Ooh huh huh," I bellowed. It was like these sounds were stored in some untouchable place, untouchable it seemed from anyone but Callum. He was a magician, an explorer, a pirate searching for his lost treasure, and he found it. Every. Fucking. Time.

He rocked and moved faster and faster, and my moans were getting louder.

"If you're not quieter, the cops are going to get called."

"Let them come. They'll bring the handcuffs."

His mouth took mine as he pounded and rocked harder and harder. There was no way the car wasn't moving, and we were parked on a very busy downtown street in the middle of the afternoon, but I didn't care. The only thing that existed right now was his cock.

"I'm..." I stuttered.

"Come with me," he commanded.

Two thrusts later, his mouth on mine, I unleashed another groan from deep within as my orgasm tore through me. My body continued to grind slower and slower each time, riding every ounce of that feeling I could. He took each breast in his mouth, giving them a quick suck and a nibble before he reached into the door handle and pulled out some wet wipes.

"Just in case you need a good anal sesh in the back of your car?"

He looked at me, throwing the wipe in my face.

I giggled, then grabbed it and climbed off him so I could clean the cum dripping out of me. "You know. This would have been a great time to have a condom. I don't have panties, so now I get to walk around the rest of the afternoon with your cum leaking out of me."

"Maybe I wanted to mark you as mine."

I felt the sting in his words, because while he was kidding. I would never be his or even theirs. "Yours for a few group fucks." I tried not to sound bitter or upset.

"It was supposed to be only two fucks, period. So you're capped out."

I felt my heart racing as disappointment weaved through my veins like a snake in the grass.

"But I don't think the boys would allow that, which is why I'm going to get in a lot of trouble."

"Was it worth it?" I asked.

"Every goddamned second." He looked around at the people passing by on the sidewalk. "I'd do it again if I didn't think we'd get in more trouble."

I slowly unbuttoned his shirt.

"What are you doing?"

"Don't worry." I leaned over and kissed his chest. "I missed seeing this." I ran my palm over his pecs. "And these." I traced my fingers over several of his tattoos. "Such a man of mystery. So guarded. Hidden from the world."

He kissed my forehead and reached for the wet wipe I held in my hand to add to the one in his fist. He stuffed them in a small trash can in the back of the car. He bent down and handed me my bra and I clipped it back together, then pulled my shirt back down.

"You want these?" he asked, holding up my panties from last night. "I washed them for you."

"You washed them or had someone else wash them?"

His head snapped back in defense. "I washed them. In the sink with lavender soap."

"You hand washed my panties?"

He playfully tapped my nose. "I'm not completely helpless."

"Hmmpf."

"Hmmpf?" he mocked, tickling my side.

I squealed in delight. "Thank you." I grabbed them and stuffed them in my bag.

"You aren't going to put them on?"

"Doesn't really go with my outfit."

He rubbed his chin, admiring me.

I bent down and picked up the contract off the ground and dug through my purse to find a pen.

"Use mine." He held a pen in front of my face.

I pressed the paper to the seat and signed, the ink gliding along the paper like silk. There went my heart. I knew it. This was going to wreck me, but my horny little cunt won the argument. Head and heart were no match for big dick energy McGee and his beautiful tattoos and his band of merry-men. Down the rabbit hole, I go.

"I'm keeping this pen. It's a good fucking pen."

"I can't wait until tomorrow night."

"For the dinner?"

"That, but mostly because we'll get to punish your filthy mouth."

Cliterati for the win

THE REST OF THE workday was a bust. I couldn't get my thoughts off what happened after lunch and the threat? No. Promise? Callum made. Tomorrow was the night I got my world rocked by four hotter than hell men. I felt like I should jump on my smutty social media book groups and look for recs on fivesomes. Those smutty fuckers always delivered. Give me a rec on monster love. Boom. Boom. Boom. Need a rec on mermaid love, a three headed Cyclops, a God, or a book where one character has tentacles and the other has feathers? You'll get twenty recommendations in less than five minutes.

They. Are. Fantastic!

They are my Cliterati. An elite group of highly read females (and males) who can give you your true heart's desire. They're like a Rolodex of sex. A Sexodex. A Rolosex. I was getting too excited. Although my chair would argue I've been in this state all day.

I grabbed my phone and flipped through several groups, copying and pasting the same request.

Book Recs Needed: Fivesome. FMMMM. Quick reads, less than 250 pages. Must be spicy! Research needed stat!

Sent.

I looked at the post and hoped I put the F in the right spot. Placement was very important.

I smiled when I saw I already had six notifications across the three different groups.

See.

Amazing.

My phone buzzed.

Lizzy.

Lizzy : How was it after I left?

I started typing, then stopped. Erased it and started over. Erased it again. I didn't know what to tell her. I wanted to tell her everything and nothing.

My phone was ringing, and I laughed when I saw it was a video call.

I pressed the green button and before I could even get to my door to close it, she yelled, "You had sex with him again! At lunch?"

"Geez Lizzy." I propped my hand on my door and shook my head at my assistant, who I was fairly certain heard every word. "No," I said, for added measure, before I shut the door.

I walked back to my desk and propped the phone up on the stand.

"You lie like a rug. Spill."

"You know it's a freakish gift you have."

She smelled the air. "I can smell sex on you a mile and a half away."

"Weirdo."

"So you boinked again."

"Yes, we boinked."

"Tea girl."

"Well, I just went over to talk to him. A friendly conversation." *About a sex contract for him and his buddies.* "And I must have had a look in my eye or something. Because he told me to sit beside him. He started running his hand up my leg and found out I wasn't wearing any panties."

"You hussy."

"The skirt..."

"Both are valid."

"Anyway, when I say his eyes lit up... it was like fire. Pure, unadulterated lust. He nearly pushed me out of the seat and said we were leaving. He pulled me into his car. He was feral. Wild. It was erotic."

"So you ba-doinka-doinked in the back of his car. Poor driver man. I hope he gets paid well."

"It was amazing."

"Told you... you needed the dicky dick up in you."

"You were right."

"I know."

"I do have to go, though. I'm at work."

She mocked my words back to me. "Real quick. I meant to ask earlier. Are we still going dress shopping tonight?"

"We didn't have plans to go shopping."

"I know. But I figured if I phrased it that way, you couldn't say no, because the guilt of forgetting a date with your BFF would be too much to handle." She threw the back of her palm across her forehead and sighed dramatically.

"You're too much."

"But seriously. You're going out to a gala tomorrow night with McStudmuffin. You know your man is going to look fine as hell. He can wear the newspaper and..." she moaned out. "You have nothing in your wardrobe close to the level he's going to bring tomorrow."

I thought about it for a minute and knew she was right and the other part wanted to be a present delivered by Cupid himself to my men.

"You know I'm right."

"Yes. We can go," I added quickly, "But it can't be a late night. I have to get some work done because I've been absolutely useless today." It was a lie. I had to get home and read my smut to prepare for tomorrow night.

"What time do you want to meet?"

"I have a meeting at four, but I can leave after that. Hopefully forty-five after."

"Or fifteen til? You crack me up. I'll do some research. Is it themed?"

"Likely. I don't know."

"Find out."

"Love you boo."

"Ditto and text me back. You're going to look fire," She drew out the word fire, singing it, while the call was disconnected.

I sat there for a minute, staring at my phone. Guilt was slowly creeping in. She was so happy for me because she thought I potentially found someone to fill the hole Dick had left. He always went by Rich, short for Richard, but times have changed and I decided to go the other route.

I popped my head out of my office and gave my assistant the name of my plus one and inquired about the dress code. Black tie. Simple. General.

I quickly texted Lizzy back, then Callum, then checked the recs and was happy to see I had fifty notifications and a few repeated recs. Tonight was going to be a good night. Bottle of wine, my reader and some take out sushi.

I flipped my phone face down so it wouldn't tempt me anymore and got to work.

Finally.

It was only seven after two. Not my best day, admittedly.

I crushed the next two hours, knocking out several reports, put together a bid for another client, answered twenty-seven emails and deleted over sixty and prepared for the meeting. Maybe I should have sex in the back of a car on my lunch break more often.

I was riding the elevator down at forty-three after. Crushing it!

Lizzy was downstairs waiting for me with her car parked out front. "I know this will be the first time in a while you've been in a car without having an orgasm, but let me remind you how us common unsexed folk have to live. I'm also not opening your door for you," she cackled, running around the front of her car.

"It's so hard to find good help these days."

"Don't I know it?"

"So where to?"

"There is one shop I want to hit first. I'm fairly certain they will have what you need and we can be done."

"Is it La Belle?"

"Oui."

"Their dresses are so expensive."

"But totally gorge!"

I couldn't argue there.

"Can't you write it off as a work expense?"

I let out a sound somewhere between a snort and a laugh. "No. I can't. Are you mad?"

She shrugged. "A girl had to ask."

We were at La Belle, forty-five minutes later. Traffic getting out of downtown was a nightmare, but we kept busy talking about her and Tony. I felt most of our conversations lately had been centered on me and I wanted to share the love. We talked about Lizzy's infatuation with a Valentine's Day proposal. She said Tony was acting cagey, and they were going to a very nice restaurant, even though he wouldn't tell her where. Lizzy said she was joking that he was going to propose, even though it had only been a couple months because he's been dropping hints over the last week or so. I told her I didn't think it was a good idea, but she reassured me that if he did, she'd have a super long engagement, which we both knew was a lie.

Her goal in life since middle school was to find a man, settle down, get married, and have a dozen kids. I thought that was my goal too, until Vixen happened. Now, I don't know what I want.

"Welcome ladies."

"We had an appointment at five- thirty. Apologies for being a couple minutes late. Traffic."

"No worries at all. You're the last appointment of the night, so there's no need to rush," she laughed. "Well, we close at six thirty... so only rush enough for that. Champagne?" she asked the same time a light brown-skinned male with a shaved head wearing some sort of block pattern suit walked around the corner carrying a tray.

"Yes, please."

We each took a glass.

The man sat the tray down, pulled on his jacket and held out his hand. "I'm Andre. What can I help you with this evening?"

"My friend here needs a dazzling drop dead gorgeous dress for a gala tomorrow night."

"My friend here loves spending someone else's money." I shot her a nasty side glance.

He nodded, "Yes. We've had several people stopping in here over the last several months getting fitted." He looked me up and down and I felt self-conscious.

"We don't want any of those dresses. She needs to stand out," Lizzy said, her hands flying away from her body like stars... or jazz hands.

"You have a nice figure and may get lucky with the sizing, so alterations won't have to be completed."

"Thank you."

"Do you have a color in mind?"

"She wants red."

Andre looked at me and I nodded. "Sure, let's start there."

"Fire," Lizzy whispered, this time with definite jazz hands.

We went to the red section of the store and on the end of one of the aisles was a display of dresses that were absolutely stunning. It was a red sequin dress with an ombre to black at the bottom, with a daring neckline plunge, and a mermaid train.

Lizzy was smacking my arm repeatedly. "Could you imagine?"

"It is beautiful."

"These just came in, so no one at your gala will be wearing this."

Lizzy took my champagne. "Go try it on."

Andre flipped through, finding my size, and walked me to a dressing room.

"Let me know if you need help!" Lizzy shouted from outside the cloth curtain.

I slipped my clothes off and pulled the dress on, pulling the zipper up the side. I turned around and looked over my shoulder at my back. It was a low scoop on the back as well, resting just above my hips. I shifted my girls around a bit and liked the way they looked in this dress. I could get those sticky cup things and push them up a bit more, but I liked the natural look. Plus, after the party, the cups may impede my sexual escapades.

"What's taking so long?" Lizzy whined.

"I'm coming out. I wanted to look at it first."

I pulled the curtain back, and Lizzy's mouth dropped.

"Fire," she said simply.

Andre came over to inspect the fitting. "Honey, you in this dress may just turn me straight."

"It may turn me into a lesbian," Lizzy added.

"Stop." I looked in the mirror again, rubbing my hands down the dress. It was stunning. "Ok. We'll take it."

Andre's brows rose in shock. "You have been my easiest fitting of the year," he chuckled. "But if you know, you know, and honey, you should know. Whoever you're going with tomorrow night better appreciate you because you are... completely gorge."

We got in the car fifteen minutes later and Lizzy turned her full body and grabbed my arm with a smile plastered across her face. "I can't believe you spent that much on a dress."

"You brought me there!" I defended. "Plus, it was probably going to be one of the cheapest."

"Keep telling yourself that," she teased. "But seriously, you should have spent a mill on that. It looks amazeballs on you and he's going to looosseee his mindddd. Maybe he'll propose to you too, because why wouldn't he?"

I laughed. "He's not proposing to me. I don't know if he is the settling down kind. I think he's just going to be fun for a while."

"What? No. He is smitten with you."

"No. I think I'm just new."

She rolled her eyes. "There is new, and then there is what you two have. I'm pretty sure my hair was standing on end when he came around you."

I blushed. I was trying to lay the groundwork for this being a fun short-term thing, but it appeared this was going to be a harder sell than I initially thought. She had to be misreading things because it wasn't just the two of us. Sure, right now it was, but it also wasn't. The others were there, and I wanted them too. I wanted to experience all of them and I would tomorrow night. Ideas flittered through my mind at all the wild and crazy things I was going to experience. I'd had a threesome once in college too, but a fivesome. I felt a wave of excitement travel from my chest, past my stomach, to my clit, which was now throbbing.

Divert! Divert! Divert! I yelled at myself like a submarine blast echoing through the tight metal chambers. Tonight was going to be research and planning and tomorrow we would implement said plan into action.

Bring on the magic sticks! Nope. Beef whistles? Crevice crawlers? One eyed yogurt slingers? I sighed. I tried to channel my inner Lizzy, but I couldn't do it.

She dropped me out in front of my apartment building, giving me a quick hug and a hopeful smile. I gathered the bag, threw it over my arm, and hiked up the stairs. I hung the dress in the living room and walked into my closet, kicked off my shoes, slipped into my jam jams, grabbed my e-reader, and waited for my sushi to be delivered.

Tomato Tomato

THEY CLOSED THE OFFICE at lunch today so we could all go home and get ready for this evening. Usually theses big events were on the weekend, but our client wanted to make it a Valentine's Day gala. There were talks around the office the company was flying in a chef from France, apparently one of the most sought after in the world.

Last night, I had skimmed through two books and found the key smut sections very enlightening, so I had a good idea of what I needed to do so I didn't embarrass myself. And! And! I didn't masturbate while reading. Goodness knows I wanted to because dammmmnnn, but I was letting it all build up for tonight. Although I was pretty sure I was going to be sexually ruined without any help from me, but I was proud of myself. Small victories.

Dinner started at six, but we were expected to show up at five for hors d'oeuvre and champagne. I would try not to mispronounce hors d'oeuvre, but ever since that Christmas movie where the wealthy had to go home and visit their less than wealthy family and are offered 'whores do vrey' which ended up being spray cheese on crackers, I can't say it any other way.

Callum texted and said he'd pick me up at four fifteen. He wanted to make sure we didn't get stuck in traffic and didn't want to be late. I could appreciate that, but it meant we would likely get there thirty minutes early, and thirty minutes stuck in the car with a man god was going to be trouble for me.

I finished getting ready, opting for light makeup with a hint of shimmer and a simple updo with hanging curls. I wanted to get my hair off my neck, but not make it overly complicated for the post party shindig tonight.

Nerves were starting to take grip the longer I had to wait. I glanced at my phone. Three minutes.

My phone buzzed.

Lizzy.

Lizzy : *Girl. You better be getting ready to send me a pic!*

Everlee: Yep! You caught me.

Lizzy: You weren't going to? After the countless hours I spent with you shopping?

Everlee: You mean the fifteen minutes?

Lizzy: Tomato Tomato.

I chuckled because I read it the same way and was confused for half a second until I read it again the way she would have said it.

I sat my phone on the table, set the timer, and gave her a few model poses. I checked the photos and then sent them to her.

Lizzy: Did you wax? Shave? You aren't on your period, are you? Oh, that would be horrible.

Everlee: No. Yes. No. And the worst.

Lizzy: Get you some thundersword, girl.

Everlee: Thundersword?

Lizzy: Yes. Sexcaliber, Yankee Doodle.

Everlee: Where do you even come up with these things?

Lizzy: Fine. Cock. Boring. Go get you some cock.

Everlee: I plan on it.

Lizzy: Yea girl!

Everlee: I won't have my phone, but I will text you tomorrow when I get home.

Lizzy: I'll do a drive by tonight, pretend to be a pizza girl or something to check on you.

Everlee: No, you won't. Plus, they'd recognize you.

Lizzy: Right. And they probably order some high end fancy schmancy pizza. Get it flown in from Italy or wherever.
There was a knock on my door.

Everlee: He's here. Gotta go. Love you boo.

Lizzy: Love you too. Have fun and use lots and lots of protection and lube.

Everlee: Geez.

Lizzy: Bye, love.
I put my phone on the charger and made my way to the door. I looked through the peephole and saw him standing there and felt my stomach tightened. I only saw a small glimpse of him and nearly came. How was I going to last the whole night and, more importantly, how was I going to walk away from this?

I opened the door and his eyes raked over me as his lips parted. "Fuck me... you're... shit... Do we have to go to this dinner?"

I blushed. I'd never made a man speechless before, but I felt his words. I knew I looked good in this dress, but his reaction was enough to drive me crazy with desire.

Maybe I should have practiced the old one handed read last night, because I was going to have to walk around most of the night with my legs clenched together.

"You look very handsome as well. And yes. We have to." Handsome was an understatement, but I felt if I told him what I really thought we'd never make it to the party and we had to, at least for a bit. He was all six foot something God in a white button down, with a deep red vest that matched my dress almost perfectly, and a black jacket with black pants. Very basic, but at the same time not basic at all. His hair was slicked back, his beard shaved to the perfect five o'clock shadow, and his blue eyes were like fiery crystals.

"Let me send a pic to the boys. They were so upset they couldn't come tonight, but," his head bobbled from side to side. "It would be kind of hard if you asked for a plus four."

"That's why you don't date or have this arrangement long term?"

His face fell. "It just gets complicated. We try to avoid that."

"By sexually ruining girls for any other man. You are effectively creating spinsters, you know?"

He laughed and held out his hand. "Let's go. We don't want to be late."

I grabbed his hand, and he followed me down the stairs. I heard him curse under his breath when he saw the back of my dress. "Are you trying to send me to an early grave woman?"

I looked over my shoulder and winked.

He grabbed my wrist and pinned me against the wall, his lips taking mine. I moaned into his mouth just before he pushed away. "I can't wait until you're moaning around my cock tonight, while Emmett and Knox are fucking you at the same time."

I flushed about as red as my dress, then leaned in, letting my lips touch his ear. "What about Jax?" I tried not to show my cringing face. I was horrible at dirty talk and that wasn't even dirty. I was trying to be sexy, but I think it just came out as a question with my voice in an awkwardly low octave. But his dirty talk... there was something about it that was so raw, so filthy, so perfect.

"Don't you worry, red, he'll be there too." He smirked, glancing at his watch. "What's the minimum time we have to stay?"

I smiled before continuing down the stairs.

Brady was waiting outside with his hand on the car handle, ready for us. His eyes grew wide as he saw me walk out of the door. He helped me in the car and whispered, "You look amazing, Ms. Everlee."

"Thank you, Brady."

By the time Callum got in the car, his phone was dinging over and over again.

"Is everything ok?"

He pulled out his phone, a worried brow on his face, which quickly changed to humor.

"All is good. Let's just say the boys are both eagerly awaiting the end of this dinner and want to kill me."

I sucked on my bottom lip. "Me too. The after dinner piece... not wanting to kill you."

Awkward.

I sighed at myself before running my hand up his leg and over his crotch.

"You really are trouble."

"Yea. Not the first time I heard that." The last time was... you guessed it. High school. Chemistry class. Seeexxy.

Why was I so in my head right now? I needed to get out of it and just enjoy tonight.

We pulled up to the convention center, where the gala was, twenty minutes later. Most of the car ride had been quiet, with Callum running his fingers along the inside of my palm while he looked absentmindedly out of the window. I'd pay all the money in the world to know what was going on inside of his head. Part of me hoped he was trying to figure out how he could live the rest of his life without me in it. That tonight and possibly some other night wouldn't be the end of us. Of this.

This was wrong. I shouldn't have asked him to come. Why did he say yes? He said they don't do dates. Everyone was going to think we were a couple, and he was my boyfriend. Did I really want to go through the entire night correcting them? Did I want to even correct them? What would I say? No, this hot ass man isn't my boyfriend. We're just friends with benefits for the rest of the week?

I felt his hand slip around my back and felt a warmth and tingle shoot up my spine. "What's wrong Everlee?"

Shit. Even the way my name rolled off his tongue. "Nothing." I lied.

He grabbed my hand and pulled me off to the side, away from the red carpet, which had been rolled out the entire length from the roundabout to the front door.

"Everlee."

"It's nothing, really. I don't want to talk about it."

The back of his hand brushed along my cheek. "I'll let it go for now."

I tried to smile, but knew I didn't succeed. I was going to ruin this night before it even started. Get your shit together, Everlee. That's what Lizzy would say. She'd be jumping up and down in front of me, hyping me up. She'd tell me to get that donkey dick or some other crazy name she'd blurt out and say to just have fun.

I grabbed his hand and pulled him back onto the red carpet as we continued our walk. There were a few couples in front of us, so we didn't have to wait outside long. I noticed a few of the dresses from the shop I got mine at and loved mine even more. Theirs looked nice on them, but I truly loved this one.

We got up to the huge heart-shaped balloon arch at the front and had to take a picture. I was going to decline, but Callum pulled me over insisting.

When we walked in, we stood for a second at the doorway, admiring all the exquisite decorations. They really went all out for this.

"What did you say this was for again?"

I laughed. "I guess I didn't say. This is one of our largest customers. They are hosting this gala to raise funds for one of their charities. Our company bought several tables as a show of support. They did it on Valentine's Day, because it was a special day for the charity owner."

We walked over to a desk where the charity had set up a station for any other donations.

"Good evening. Don't you make a handsome couple." The older lady beamed. She was wearing a draping black sequin dress with a pearl necklace and matching earrings.

"Thank you." Callum chimed, reaching his arm around me. "I think so too."

"Thank you so much for coming tonight and supporting us, it really means the world to us and these children."

Callum smiled. "Can we still make donations?"

"Yes, of course." The lady perked up.

Callum reached into his pocket and pulled out his checkbook. I watched him, then had to look again. Ten thousand dollars. Holy shit. Who was he?

He handed the check to the woman, who nearly choked, and I'm pretty sure a tear formed in the corner of her eye. "Thank you so much, Mr. McCall."

McCall. Him and Jax were brothers? Would make sense and I guess I could see it. Tall, dark, and handsome. Alpha, beta. I'd have to guess Jax was a little younger, but not much.

"Can I give you a hug?" The woman was asking, already walking around the table.

"Of course." He opened his arms and the older woman walked right in and looked so tiny compared to him.

She patted his chest. "I don't want to get make-up on your suit." She grabbed his hands and then looked at me. "If I was younger, I'd give you a run for your money."

"Any man would be lucky to have a good-looking woman like you." Callum cooed.

The woman blushed and walked behind the table and scribbled something down. "Here's a receipt for your records. What name would you like to be added to the scroll of donations at the end of the event?"

"Anonymous is fine."

She reached forward and grabbed my hand. "You're a lucky woman."

"Don't I know it." I grabbed Callum's hand, and we headed to the bar.

"Do you want an old-fashioned?" He brought my hand to his lips, placing a gentle kiss on my knuckles.

"Will it be as good as Emmett's?"

"I doubt it. He's truly perfected it."

"I'll try it and switch if needed."

While Callum ordered our drinks, I looked around at the people filtering into the building and still didn't recognize anyone.

He handed me the drink, then placed his fingers on my lower back, his pinky dipping just below the edge of my dress, grazing the top of my ass. He leaned over. "I can't wait until my cock is buried–"

"Everlee?"

We turned, and I saw Mr. Randall walking over with Annalise, my assistant, a step behind him. She saw Callum and her eyes grew wide as she leaned back, clutching her chest, mouthing damn. I chuckled briefly, then turned my attention to Mr. Randall. "Hello, sir."

I felt Callum's fingers dig gently into my back. Was he jealous? Obviously, he knew it was a different kind of sir.

"So glad you could make it and bring a date." He motioned towards Callum. "I really thought you were going to call out sick." He chuckled. I chuckled. We all chuckled. But if he only knew the truth. That is why I was chuckling.

"Callum, this is Mr. Randall, CEO of McClintock Enterprise."

"Very nice to meet you. I'm glad I made the invite list." He said, removing his hand from my back to shake Mr. Randall's. I felt the cool air hit my skin where his hand had been, and I missed our connection. Seconds later, it was back, and I breathed a sigh of... not relief, but of comfort?

"We'll see you in a little. Going to walk around and find more people, then head towards our table. The chef is going to walk around soon to introduce herself before everything starts. I heard she's going to do a cooking demonstration on the stage of what we're eating tonight."

"That sounds exciting."

Callum nodded, but didn't speak.

Mr. Randall and Annalise walked away when Callum looked at me. "Who's the chef tonight?"

I shrugged. "Someone from France. I'm not sure. I wasn't paying attention to anything related to this, because truth be told," I leaned in close. "I *was* planning on calling out sick, but you sort of put a wrench in those plans."

"Glad I could oblige," he smirked.

Hashtag WendyDick

WE FOUND OUR NAMES on the seating chart at the entrance of the grand ballroom and weaved through the maze of tables to find our seat tags. The room was stunning. The ceiling had large pieces of pink and white fabric drooped between golden rods nestled in between enormous chandeliers. The tables were large round circles which sat ten people, covered in white tablecloths with a pink or red accent stripes down the middle. In the center were large glass cylinders filled with white, red, and pink pebbled hearts coupled with golden arrows sticking up the middle. And the place settings were brushed gold chargers underneath white porcelain plates with a golden rim. They had really done up the valentine's theme, but it was elegant, not gaudy.

We found our seats and sat there quietly, watching people file in. Something was weighing on Callum, but I didn't know what. Nothing had really changed much since we arrived, so I couldn't figure out what it was.

"You know." I started, then stopped, grabbing his attention. "That was really nice what you did earlier. The donation. It's not why I invited you."

He smiled. "I know why you invited me."

"Because I seem to have a problem attracting decent men that want to stick around?" His head tilted to the side disapprovingly. I was trying to make a self-deprecating joke, but I could see how it could have been perceived as a jab at him, so I added. "And your cock, of course."

"With a filthy mouth like yours," his thumb padded over my chin, "I don't see how you don't have guys lining up."

"Callum?" a woman's voice with a soft accent chimed behind us.

Callum's eyes fixed on mine knowingly, and it took him a second to turn around.

"Callum. It is you." Her gaze quickly flitted to me, then back to him.

"Sophie." He said, standing up and moving to give her a hug. "Everlee mentioned a highly sought after French chef was being brought in and I wondered if it is you."

She held her hands to the side, smiling. "I guess I shouldn't be surprised you'd be at an event supporting children. I know how much these organizations mean to you."

They did? I felt... jealous. Why didn't he tell me how much the charity meant to him? I guess I should have known since he just gave them ten grand, but still...

He smiled, "Yes they do." He turned to look at me. "Sophie, this is Everlee."

"Your date, I presume?"

The way she said date didn't sit right with me. It felt like there was a hint of distaste in the word, or maybe that was me reading into it because I had a feeling she was one of his past women.

"You look stunning." She offered, grabbing my hands and pulling me in to give me a kiss on each side of my cheek. She studied me for a second, then turned back to Callum. "How's Emmett? I miss him. All of you, really." Even though she wasn't directly looking at me, I could tell she was watching my reaction out of her peripheral.

"Emmett's doing good. He recently just opened up his own restaurant here in town. Bo La Vie."

She chuckled, clasping her hands together. "Good life. Yes. I suppose you all live the good life, don't you?" Her words wandered off.

"You should come by. The guys would love to see you."

"I'm only in town for a few days."

"Perfect! You can come by our club one of those nights."

"A club with you and the boys?" She smiled. "Could be trouble."

"So that's a yes?"

"Oui. Now I have to get backstage and get ready to wow you all with my expert culinary skills. Enjoy your dinner!" She leaned over and gave him a kiss on the cheek. "Ta- Ta. And nice to meet you Everlee!"

Callum watched her walk away, and then slowly turned to me. I was fighting a mixture of emotions right now. Jealousy. Anger. Envy. Sadness. So many things. She was one of their... their women. She was a world renowned chef, and I was just... me.

Callum's hand drifted to the side of my face. "Everlee." His words were soft, like he was reading every single emotion that was flitting through my mind.

"She was one of your..."

"Yes. But it was a long time ago. She has since moved on and has a wonderful husband and three beautiful children. We get a Christmas card every year from them."

"It's fine." I said in that typical girl voice that says I'm totally not fine. But I was trying to be. I knew I didn't have a right to be anything but happy he was here with me. I was going to go to his place tonight to have the best sex of probably everyone in this ballroom and easily the best sex of my life.

"Your pussy is the only pussy I want my tongue in, my fingers in and my cock in. No one else's."

"Until when? This week and then I'm gone? Time to move on to the next woman?" I held my hand up. "I'm sorry. I shouldn't be saying this. I knew what I was getting into when I signed the contract."

He grabbed my hand and brought it to his lips. "I don't know what our future holds. But I don't want the could be, to get in the way of the now. If you've changed your mind and don't want to come over tonight, I'll understand. No hard feelings."

"No. I want to come over."

"Let's have fun here, and then we'll see what happens. Ok?"

I nodded. "If you'll excuse me, I'm going to run to the lady's room."

"I can walk you."

"No. I'm ok." I knew I was being immature right now, and I was really trying not to let my emotions get the best of me, but it was tough. Since I'd left Dick, my self-confidence had been completely shot, and it wasn't until these guys that I started to get that back, but seeing her and... her status... I couldn't help but wonder what they saw in me...

He sat back down. I could feel his gaze on my back as I walked away.

Get your head in the game, Everlee. This is why I hated the holiday. It was some ploy to make people express how much they mean to one another. Why not do it all the time? Why wait for one single day in a year?

I walked into the bathroom and stood in front of the mirror with my hands on the sink, staring at myself. I hated I didn't bring my phone with me. I could really use a Lizzy pep talk right about now. Have her tell me to ignore the insanely talented chef that made all of this amazing food and focus on the fact he's here with me. On a date. Even Sophie took notice of that, something perhaps she never had? Lizzy would say that Sophie was jealous of me because she knows I'm getting all those cocks tonight and she's not. Only Lizzy wouldn't say that because she can't know about the quadcocks just the unicock.

I washed my hands and patted them dry with the warm towel that was rolled up on the sink.

Focus on the quadcock and the fine ass man sitting beside you tonight.

I opened the door with a renewed feeling and walked right into dickface, waiting outside the stalls.

"Everlee?"

"D... Richard?" I should have called him Dick, but I was trying to be mature - at least to his face.

"Wow. You look amazing." His eyes were bugging out of his head, which gave me a modicum of satisfaction. If only he had looked at me this way when we were together.

"What are you doing here?" We both said in unison.

"I'm here for work."

His brow furrowed. "Wendy too."

Wendy. Wendy and Dick. Hashtag WendyDick.

"I saw your company listed as a sponsor, but didn't think you'd be here."

"What?" I asked accusatorially.

"Well, you hate this holiday."

"I wonder why?" I held my hand up. "Nevermind. I will not get into this with you. Have a pleasant night."

"Richard? Who is this?"

Fuckballs on a wall. Could this night get any more awkward?

I turned around and saw a petite woman walking out of the bathroom, wearing a bubblegum pink a-line dress I've seen two others wearing so far and laughed inside. I didn't hate her because she was with my ex. I hated both of them because she knew about me and didn't give two shits when she fucked him... for months.

"Oh. Everlee."

"Hi. Let me guess. La Belle?" I asked, pointing at her dress.

She looked down and frowned. "Yes."

"Must be a popular style." Zing. From what little I knew about her- yes, I post breakup snooped. I was lonely, pissed, and bored. She prided herself on fashion and the fact she was wearing the same dress as at least two other people meant she was beyond angry. She was probably in the bathroom crying.

Well, that flipped her bitch switch on because her eyes narrowed and were shooting arrows at me. Little cupid's arrow. Pew! Pew! Pew! "I didn't think you were dating anyone. Did you come alone?"

"One. The fact you're snooping to see if I'm dating anyone is weird and, frankly, not healthy. And two-"

"And two. She came with me. Rather, I came with her." I looked behind me to see Callum approaching the group, slipping his arm around me. He lightly rubbed my back. The final count down song played in my head as he approached and I was fist pumping in my mind.

"I... uh... uh... ok."

"Richard." Dick said, sticking his hand out.

"Callum." He grabbed his hand and shook.

"So you two?" Wendy asked, pointing between the two of us.

"Yes, Wendy. Would you like to fuck him too?"

"Baby, you can't just pimp me out to people. Plus, I only have eyes for you." He kissed the top of my head.

"Welp. Guess he's not interested, but this one still is for now." I pointed at Dickface. "Unless that's why you've been stalking me, because you thought he and I hooked back up. Don't worry, we haven't, nor will we ever. Once a cheat, always a cheat. Good luck with that. Hope it works out for you." I turned and walked away, with Callum right by my side.

Holy forking shirtballs, that felt good. My heart was racing, and I felt like jumping up and down like a boxer in the ring. Ahh! Whew! I definitely felt like Ali right now, but like if he was words. Wham bam thank you ma'am!

Callum grabbed my hand and pulled me into the stairwell.

"What are you doing?" I squealed.

He pushed me back against the wall and took my mouth in his. His kiss was needy, hungry. I don't know if he was trying to prove something to me, but I was here for it. His hand slipped down the back of my dress, dipped inside, then he paused, looking at me.

"Fuck Everlee. No panties again?"

"It didn't fit with the dress."

"Do your clothes ever work with panties?" He took my mouth in his again and continued moving his hand over my ass and found my clit with the tip of his finger. "You're so fucking wet."

I arched my back, rotating my hips so he had easier access, causing a moan to escape my lips. He slid his hand out, sucking me off his fingers, and then kissed me once more. "Dinner can't come soon enough. Because I can't wait to get my dessert."

I ran my thumb over the bottom of his lip, wiping away the hint of my lipstick. It was supposed to be smudge proof, but perhaps they didn't do testing for playing aggressive tonsil hockey.

Dinner came and went and it was better than fantastic. There was some sort of lemon butter dill salmon and wagyu beef filet with scalloped potatoes, asparagus, mushrooms, and salad. It was really way too much, but when it's that good...

When desserts came out, Callum leaned over and whispered not to fill up, because we'd be having dessert at home, which sent a tingle up my spine.

After dinner, they brought out a band and people filed onto the dance floor. We were going to leave, but Mr. Randall insisted everyone get on the dance floor for a group picture. We stayed for a few dances, because WendyDick was out there too. It was Callum's idea to stay. At first I didn't know why, but then I found them.

Callum grabbed my right hand with his and placed his other hand on my lower back, pulling me to him.

"I love this dress on you, but I think I'm going to like it more when it's off."

His thigh found its place between my legs, which rubbed on my sensitive spot.

"Callum." I panted.

He lightly brushed his knuckles along my cheekbone. "I don't know how I'm going to quit you." His lips took mine softly, his tongue slipping in and gently dancing with mine. I felt a flush move around my body, and it was like everything had faded out. The sounds, the music, the people, it was only just us two.

He stopped kissing me and the world came crashing back around me. My head was in a daze and when I looked around, I saw several people looking at us, one of them being WendyDick. Yea, they were a unit now. Dick's eyes were narrowed and angry and Wendy's were in awe. Bitch was jealous, and I was ecstatic.

"Want to get out of here?" He murmured, his lips gently brushing against my ear.

"Yes."

He grabbed my hand and whisked me off the dance floor like you see in those ads for perfumes.

It was time. My stomach was filled with knots and butter-flies at the same time my heart had a fine crack etched into it, ready to break.

Whipped Cream, not just for food

THE CAR RIDE WAS quiet as the anticipation and nerves were building. Brady pulled up to their house, and Callum stepped out first and moved around to open my door.

He stood outside with his hand outstretched. "My lady."

I grabbed it and with each step, my stomach twisted more.

"Are you ok?"

"Yea, just a little nervous. Mostly excited."

"If it's ever too much, then just tell us."

He opened the door and there were rose petals along the floor at the entrance with a bottle of champagne and two glasses on a tray.

"Oh, geez." Callum rolled his eyes.

"What?" I chuckled, nervously.

"I may have texted and told them about Sophie."

"Oh."

"So they may have gone a little overboard on decorations."

I looked down the hall and saw streamers hanging down, separating us from the kitchen.

"So they don't always do this?"

"Not at all. You seem to have changed everything up."

So he's saying there's a chance.

I was going to take my shoes off, but Callum stopped me. "Let's let the boys get a glimpse of you in your outfit before we take anything off."

I nodded and waited as he poured us each a glass of champagne. I took a sip and let the bubbles slide down my throat.

We walked into the kitchen and the boys were standing completely nude with whipped cream sprayed around their cocks. I felt a heat rush through my body, pushing all my nerves out.

These men were all mine tonight.

Suck it Wendy!

"Fuck, you look divine!" Knox mumbled.

"Hot... so, so hot!" Emmett continued.

"Beautiful." Jax said. Always simple, but effective.

Knox walked over, circling me like a shark circles its prey. His hand ran down my spine slowly as he trailed kisses from my shoulder up to my neck. "I've been waiting all night to taste you." My eyes found Callum standing beside the counter watching us, his gaze hooded and his bulge growing.

Knox's hand skimmed up to my shoulder and gently pushed the strap off to the side. My eyes moved to Jax and then to Emmett. They were so hot, standing there with nothing on but some whipped cream.

"Emmett. Join Knox." Callum commanded.

Emmett slowly walked over. "Hey trouble." His lips pressed against mine as his tongue pulsed in. His kiss differed from Callum's, but was still sexy and provocative. He pulled off my lips and began working his way down my neck to my collarbone as he gently eased the other shoulder strap off. The only thing holding up the dress at this point was the curve of my breasts.

"This has to go." Emmett said quietly, giving the dress an extra tug, so it slid down my body, falling into a puddle of sequin red fabric at my feet. I was standing in front of them, completely nude. Well, except for my shoes. Those were still on.

"Fuck, you look so good." Jax ran his teeth over his bottom lip as he stood watching me. My stomach was twisting with anticipation.

"Jax." Callum called. "Go taste her."

Jax stalked over, his dark eyes focused on mine, and he dropped to his knees.

I felt like I was going to come and he hadn't even touched me yet.

His tongue gently ran up between my wet folds slowly, from back to front, landing on my clit.

"So sweet." He mumbled against my pussy.

Knox and Emmett were still kissing my neck and shoulders when Callum gave another order. "Take her breasts."

They each took a breast in their mouth, their tongues swirling around my nipple before taking it between their teeth gently. My hands were having a hard time finding their place between Knox and Emmett's heads or Jax's.

My gaze shifted back to Callum, who was still by the counter watching us. A moan escaped my lips, but my eyes never left Callum's as Jax continued his gentle assault on my pussy.

"So perfect." Emmett moaned.

Callum walked over to stand behind me, his hard cock pressed against my backside. He snaked his hand around my throat and then turned my chin to look at him. My lips parted as Jax was moving me closer and closer to climax, but Callum took it as an invitation. His tongue swiped across my bottom lip before taking my entire mouth in his. His kiss was passionate. Hungry.

My hand reached around the back of his neck, holding him to me. I was in heaven. All their mouths were on me, licking, sucking, and fucking. My hips were thrusting as Jax's tongue pressed in, pulsing in and out, while Knox's finger slid down and began working my clit. "Oh... oh my."

I moaned. My legs were getting weak as I was climbing orgasm mountain. I saw the summit, but then Jax pulled away, as well as the others.

I was left panting and wanting. Bunch of assholes.

"Let me taste." Emmett said to Jax. They both looked at me as their lips touched.

Damn. I did not see that coming, but it was so hot. Emmett pulled back a second later. "Yes. She does taste divine."

"Let's get you to the table." Jax offered.

With everything going on, I hadn't even noticed the table had a variety of fruits, whipped cream, and chocolates on it.

"What's this?" I asked, chuckling.

"Once you climb up there, it will be our dessert." Emmett said.

Jax guided me over with his hips and cock pressed into my backside. His teeth grazed along the edge of my throat. "I can't wait to sink my cock into your tight little pussy." He said before nibbling at my neck.

"Samesies." I whispered back in a low voice and regretted it almost immediately.

Stupid. Fucking stupid. Samesies. What the hell? I needed to work on my bedroom talk because that... that was an epic fail.

His hands gripped my hips, and he lifted me up like I was nothing but a feather and placed me on the table. He bit my ass just before I sat down. There was a red satin pillow at one end, so I laid my head down while Callum slowly unbuckled my shoes, letting his finger lightly rub and graze along all the sensitive parts of my foot, causing my whole body to tingle.

Knox and Emmett walked to the back of the table and each grabbed a can of whipped cream and began spraying it on my body. Emmett sprayed over my breast and Knox around my hip bone, to the apex of my legs. After Callum sat my shoes out of the way, he came back and began rubbing my feet.

I didn't know what I had in mind about tonight, but this was definitely not it. The amount of attention and care... I felt like a goddess or perhaps like their queen.

Jax grabbed a can of whipped cream and mirrored what Emmett was doing, circling it around my other breast. Once they were done, they began decorating my body with various kinds of chocolate and strawberries. I peeked down at one point and between the white whipped cream and chocolate, I felt like the Valentine's Day version of a snowman.

"This may be our best creation." Emmett bragged.

"She looks delicious." Jax said.

"I can't wait to taste her." Knox said, swiping his tongue at a piece of whipped cream on my stomach.

I heard a ding and Emmett excitedly scurried into the kitchen. A moment later, he was back with two bowls. "Hot chocolate."

He stuck his finger in the bowl and smiled, licking it clean.

He gave a bowl to Knox, who gently poured it down the center of my makeshift bra and then swirled it around each breast, the heat contrasting with the cool whipped cream. Emmett took his and began pouring it on my stomach and swirling it around the mound of white over my pussy, then down each leg.

I was a mess.

I had whipped cream, chocolate sauce, strawberries, and chocolate morsels all over me.

"Who wants dessert, guys?" Callum asked.

They all raised their hands and moved towards me like animals diving onto their prey. Knox sprayed the remaining whipped cream on my nose and my lips. A second later, his tongue was lapping up the sweet cream and oh, his kiss. He was fast and wet, his tongue skillfully moving with ease.

I hadn't noticed someone had crawled onto the table and landed between my legs, but a second later I felt their tongue licking through all the creamy sweetness, causing a moan to reverberate through my body and my back to arch off the table.

"So perfect." Emmett mumbled. Before licking the chocolate up my body to my breast.

With all this attention on me, I felt like I should give something back. I reached my hand to grab Jax around his hard cock and heard him let out a sigh. I ran my hand down it, the whipped cream making it slick, and pumped slowly. I turned my melted gaze to him. "I want to taste."

His eyes fluttered with excitement.

I scooted up the table so my head was hanging off the edge. The tip of his cock pressed to my lips, so I swirled my tongue around, lapping up all the whipped cream before I sucked him into my mouth.

"Shit Everlee." Jax hummed in a deep and gravelly sound of appreciation. "You suck cock so good."

"Doesn't she though, brother?" Callum asked, lifting his head from my pussy.

He thrust into my mouth again and again, getting faster and faster. I felt hands rubbing all over my body, warm and sticky from the chocolate.

"I say we move this party into the bedroom." Emmett suggested, eating the last strawberry off me.

They all stopped thrusting, licking, and sucking and looked at me. Their eyes were so intense with hunger, all I could do was nod.

Emmett scooped me up in his arms, garnering a squeal from me. He ran up the stairs and down the hall and it took me a moment, but I realized where we were going.

The voyeur room. Only this time we'd all be in there.

Emmett threw me onto the bed and crawled over top of me. "My turn for a taste, trouble." He slid his body down mine, lifted my legs over his shoulders with authority, and buried his face. He was hungry like a man who hadn't seen food in days and I was a plate of all his favorites.

"Oh." My body did a wave on the bed. "Shit Emmett."

"He has a mouth of the Gods." Knox mentioned.

"I'm about..." my entire body tingled as my orgasm hit me fast and hard. "Too late."

Jax brushed his hand across my cheek as my insides were still clenched. "We're all clean and get tested frequently. Do you want condoms or no condoms?" He asked breathlessly.

"I want you all to fill me with your cum." I panted between waves of bliss.

He smiled a devilish, wicked smile. "We're going to fill every hole of yours with our cum. You are ours. Now open that dirty little mouth and suck my cock."

He barely waited for it to be fully open before he thrust it in. Remnants of the sweet cream lingered on his cock, making me want to devour it all the more. "That's right Everlee."

I saw Callum climb on the bed through my peripheral and just watch me suck his brother's cock as he slowly stroked his own, his teeth scraping over his bottom lip.

"I think it's time we give our girl what she wants." Callum said, and everyone froze.

Knox stepped forward and lowered himself on top of me. "Are you ready, Ali?"

I nod.

"Words baby." Callum reminded, using his fingers to glide my chin towards him.

"Yes. I'm ready."

Knox lined up the head of his cock, teasing me. I looked up at him as his head lowered to mine, taking me into a kiss. "I'm going to love fucking you."

"Samesies." I hear whispered and catch Jax out of the corner of my eye with a grin spread across his face.

I cast a nasty glare at him, causing him to chuckle the same time Knox presses in. I whimper out as pleasure spreads across me.

"You feel so fucking good." Knox growls, pressing into me again.

"More." I cry out with a guttural moan.

In a quick swoop, Knox rolls us over so I'm sitting on top of him. I gaze around the room and all the men are looking at me, their eyes hungry while they stroke themselves. I feel so wanted, so alive. My body is already buzzing, preparing for another orgasm, as I continue to ride him harder.

"I need more." I call out again.

Knox leans back so I'm laying on top of him. I feel a pair of hands on my hips as something wet slides over my forbidden area. I clench as the sensation robs me of my breath.

"Are you ready?" Emmett asks, pressing his fingers into me, prepping me.

"Yes." I rest my head on Knox, who stops moving for a minute so I can take Emmett. He slips his cock in past the tight ring of muscle. It's been a while since anyone's been there, but the feeling comes back. He pulls out slowly and pushes in again, holding himself there, while I stretch and adjust to his size.

"Your ass takes cock so well. It's like it was molded for my dick." Emmett says as he pushes in again, hands rubbing along my back.

This time, Knox begins to move below, both in rhythm. I feel so incredibly full that it's hard to describe. It's one of the most intense feelings I've ever experienced. It was like my body was singing.

"I can feel your cock inside of her," Knox moaned, pressing in again, picking up speed.

"More." I rock back, pressing into Emmett, as his hands glide down my back and around my side to find my clit. "Oh, shit."

I hear Jax say something over my shoulder and see Emmett nod. Everyone slows for a second just as I'm about to have another orgasm. I feel Emmett's cock twitch in my ass as he takes Jax in his. Oh my God. I was not prepared for this. I stayed frozen, watching Jax plunge into Emmett with his cock. It was one of the hottest things I'd ever seen. All muscles, tattoos and pure raw sex.

"You like that, Ali?" Knox asked from below. "I can feel you dripping down my cock."

Emmett thrusts in again and now it's like I'm being fucked by the three of them. His thrusts feel different, deeper. Knox lines up with the thrusts from Emmett and we continue. My orgasm was close before we paused, but it's not far away, sitting right on the edge.

Callum stepped up in front of me, his cock in hand. "Do you want some?"

"Yes, please." I blurt out.

"Yes, what?" His blue eyes narrow.

"Yes, Sir."

"That's a good girl." He rubs his fingers over my swollen lips, then grabs the back of my head and guides me to his cock. He presses it in and my insides quiver with excitement.

How could something that should be so wrong feel so right? I was theirs and they were mine. I felt my orgasm building. It was a like a deep wave within my body and I could tell when it crashed, it was going to be like a fucking tsunami taking everything with it.

I pressed back harder into Emmett and Knox while Callum fucked my mouth. The sound of wet smacking filled the room as everyone moved in perfect rhythm, opposing sides, but meeting inside me. It was beautiful. Poetic. I could understand why they limited this, because it was fucking magical and I never wanted it to end.

Emmett continued to work my clit until I felt it. The wave of the tsunami cresting and then crashing.

"Fuck, Everlee." Knox said, just before he came. A second later, it was like a chain reaction. Emmett whimpered, followed by Jax.

My eyes looked up to Callum, head of this sex train and house. I feasted on the beauty of his body marked with all his tattoos, scars, and muscles that were flexing with each thrust. I grabbed the base of his cock, confident the boys would hold me up if I fell, and pulled him deeper. I squeezed each time I brought him in. My eyes were watering as he continued to thrust, his fingers getting wrapped up in my hair, holding it in place as he fucked it hard.

"Get ready baby." He grunted.

The taste exploded in my mouth and I swallowed him down as fast as I could. I moved my hand from his shaft to his balls, rubbing and squeezing them to get every last drop out.

"Fuck baby." Callum heaved, before pulling out and gazing down at me with fire in his eyes.

I collapsed on top of Knox, while Emmett gently pulled out and then Knox. Jax and Emmett moved to the set of dressers on one side of the room and grabbed wipes or something, because it looked like they were cleaning themselves up.

"I'll be back." Jax said, still stroking his cock as he walked into the adjoining room.

I knew what was there, and I was excited. The ginormous bathtub. I vaguely remember it from the night Callum and I were in this room. He moved me in there to clean me and take care of me. They all did.

A few minutes later, Jax walked back in. I lifted my head off Knox's chest, letting his heartbeat lull me into a blissful comfort. "It's ready."

"Come on trouble." Emmett said, scooping me off Knox's chest.

Knox cried out, "Hey, you're taking my blanket."

I reached out to him as Emmett carried me further away. "Don't worry. He'll come."

"He already did." I mumbled, taking Emmett's nipple ring in my mouth and twirling my tongue around it.

He looked down at me, a smirk on his lips. "Yes, he did." He kissed the top of my forehead.

We were walking into the adjoining bathroom a moment later and, being more awake this time, I realized it was more like an indoor spa. It was massive and what I thought was the bathtub before looked to be the size of a hot tub. It was a huge porcelain square tub in the middle of the floor. It didn't seem to have the bubbles like traditional hot tubs, but that could be because they weren't on. On the far wall behind the tub was a row of rainfall shower heads spread over ten or more feet with jets on the walls. On the right of the room was a smaller room, encased in wood, perhaps a sauna?

Emmett dropped me off at the bathtub... er, hot tub? I still wasn't sure what to call it. I climbed in, and a moment later, the boys were joining me. Jax flicked something on the switch and music played throughout the room. The lights dimmed and another set of lights turned on in the hot tub. They were changing from purple to pink, green to blue. He must have poured some sort of scent packet into the water because lavender and lemongrass stirred through the air.

I sat back against the wall with Emmett on one side and Jax on the other. Callum and Knox, both across from me. The water felt amazing and then a second later, I felt the jets turn on, blowing hot water down my back with one on the seat, blowing through my legs. It wasn't as forceful as the others, but positioned in a way that made me not want to clean up. If my time with them was limited, I was going to make it count.

Callum and Knox grabbed a foot and began rubbing. I moaned, tilting my head back on the side of the tub.

"Oh baby, don't do that or we won't make it out of here." Jax warned.

I turned to look at him, my head still tilted back at the same time Callum hit a spot on my foot, eliciting another moan.

Jax's hooded gaze raked across my face, to my neck, to my breast that were playing peekaboo with the colorful waves of water. I guided my hand to his cock and felt it getting hard again. He looked at the rest of the boys, then looked back at me.

"Do you want my cock?"

I bit my bottom lip and nodded.

He slipped his arm around me and pulled me over to sit on his lap, facing him.

"No." I said. "I want to watch them, watch you fuck me."

"Jesus." His lips crashed to mine for just a second before he turned me around and seated me on his cock. I slid down, my hands rubbing over my breasts. My eyes were locked on Callum as Jax guided me up and down. I kept one hand on my breast and slid the other under the water and worked my clit.

A puff of breath escaped as I rocked my hips back and forth on Jax. I saw Callum's hand slip from the edge of the tub under the water and I shook my head. He stared at me in shock. "You're next." I looked at Emmett. "And then you. I want you all in me."

"I think I'm in love." Knox shouted, garnering a chuckle from everyone. My laugh was stifled as Jax's hand moved over mine and he began to rub my clit and his mouth brushed over my neck, causing my already pebbled nipples to harden even more, if possible.

Jax pumped harder and faster, the water slopping on all sides. Fortunately, the entire room seemed to be designed as a wet room with tiled floors and drains, so no one was concerned about water getting out.

"Fuck me Jax. Harder."

I couldn't get enough of him. I couldn't get enough of the boys watching me. It was so hot and erotic.

"My turn," Emmett shouted.

Jax pumped a few more times before he pulled me off him. I waded to Emmett where I turned around and sank onto him. He felt different from Jax inside of me; he moved slower, gyrating his hips more.

I stared at Jax as Emmett pumped into me, my fingers pinching my nipples with each thrust. Emmett's hand ran down my spine all the way to the top of my ass, where he pressed at my hole.

I felt my eyes go wide with heady anticipation. Emmett leaned forward and bit my neck, sucking my fevered skin into his mouth, his tongue swiping over his marks. "Good girl." He murmured before slipping his thumb in. I felt my core tightened and my clit throb as a shot of pleasure coursed through my body. "You like your ass being played with, don't you, trouble?"

I nodded, biting my finger.

"Good. Because I'm an ass guy too." He thrust me up slowly as his thumb swirled around in my hole.

"Oh God."

"No, trouble. I'm just Emmett." He pumped faster and faster. I felt my insides clenching and squeezing. I don't think I've ever had this many orgasms so close together. Each time they were more intense, but took longer to achieve.

I watched Jax. His eyes were focused on me, teeth set on his bottom lip as his arm pumped under the water ferociously. He was so hot. The tattoos creeping up his neck flexed with every thrust and I noticed one on his pec, just above his heart I hadn't seen before. It looked to be some sort of frog, but just the bones of the frog. I'd seen it in pictures, but couldn't remember where.

Emmett popped me off, moving with precision as he rolled me over and lifted my legs over his shoulders and over the edge of the tub so I was floating on my back.

"You cheat." Callum teased. "Now she's definitely going to come."

Emmett cast a small wink and then brought my pussy to his face, and his tongue darted in. My back arched, sending my head under water. Super graceful. One point for the water. Zero points for me.

Jax was moving a second later, pressing his hand under my back while his mouth clamped around my breast.

"Dibs!" Knox shouted, moving to the other breast.

A low guttural moan escaped, like it was pulled from the depths of my soul. I was riding Emmett's face like it was the fucking merry-go-round of sex town, my legs clamped to his head and calves pressed onto the side of the tub. "Fuck.

Me. Oh. My. Ah. Shit." The orgasm was so intense, my toes literally curled as the muscles in my body constricted like the orgasm was sucking everything out of me. I could feel my muscles pulsing repeatedly and then I just sprawled out, happy to have the boys holding my back.

"You're like a little sex fiend."

"I've not had sex in over six months and you all are putting me on a limit. So I plan on cramming as much of that six months into one night as possible."

"Why anyone would be stupid enough to lose you is beyond me." Callum said, stroking a piece of wet hair behind my ear. He grabbed my arm, and I floated over to him, as he pulled me onto his lap and cradled me. "Now for the pampering that was supposed to happen."

Knox reached over the edge and grabbed a bucket or something and dipped it in the water. Callum placed his arm under my neck so my head tilted back and the water poured over my scalp. It was relaxing. A moment later, they were working shampoo into my hair, lathering it around. I felt my eyelids getting heavy as relaxation settled into every fiber of my body.

"Are you falling asleep on us again?" Jax chuckled.

"It just feel so good." I mumbled out.

Emmett and Jax both had washcloths lathered in soap and were wiping them up and down my legs, through my legs and around my feet, while their other hand gently massaged and squeezed.

I was in heaven.

I had somehow died and was in heaven.

I was in the bathtub with four devilishly hot men who sexually satisfied me repeatedly, who are now washing and massaging me.

I must have been in that in between space of sleep and awake, because a second later, I felt myself being carried, but I was too lazy to open my eyes.

"I can't let her go, Jax." Callum whispered.

"You know the rules. It's why we put them in place. So no one gets hurt." He responded, his voice achy.

"What if we all vote?" Knox asked, before his words fell to a whisper.

"Now is not the time to discuss this." Jax said, his voice more stern, but still with a crack laced throughout.

"He's right. We have the club these next couple of days, so it will be hard to see her." I felt his gaze on me, so I pretended as best I could to maintain my steady, slow breathing and not let my eyelids flicker. I didn't want them to know I heard this because I don't think I was supposed to. "She's just perfect."

"You're infatuated."

"I don't know. You know I never get attached, but she's... the moment I saw her, I could tell."

Jax must have given a look, because there was silence for a bit.

"We'll see you tomorrow morning." Callum said before walking away.

Unexpected Visitors

I FELT LONELY.

I shut down my computer and walked home. It was Friday. The weekend. I should be happy. Excited. But I wasn't. I missed them. How stupid was I? It was only one night, but that one night was magical. I was still a little sore, but it only served as a reminder of what I wanted.

Them.

Lizzy called Thursday afternoon to get the download on the gala and the date with Callum. I told her as much as I could. Her favorite part was me telling off WendyDick and Callum swooping in and making Wendy's panties wet. Probably Dick's too if he was being honest with himself, because who wouldn't get a hard on for Callum. He was perfect. Tall, dark, handsome. I felt my core tighten just thinking about him.

Lizzy, unfortunately, didn't get engaged Wednesday. She said she was ok, and only kidding when she was talking about it, but I knew the truth. She wanted it, even if she wouldn't let herself admit it. But in a way, I'm glad she didn't, because there's no way she would have had a long engagement. Being married has been the top of her priority list and since they've only been together for a couple months, I didn't want her getting into a situation she'd potentially regret. I really liked Tony. I just wanted them to be together a little longer.

My phone dinged. Part of me hoped it was one of the guys, but it was Lizzy.

Lizzy: *Bitch. Get your getup on and let's go out. I'm thinking... VIXEN!*

Everlee: *Ha. No.*

Lizzy: *What? Don't you want to see him?*

Everlee: *Yes. But I don't want to be the needy girl showing up at his work. Awkwardly sitting in a corner watching him.*
Everlee: *Pretty sure that wouldn't go over well. Stage five clinger.*

I had a feeling this should probably be a phone call, but I was too lazy to make the transition. Which was stupid since it was only the push of a button.

Lizzy: *Psshh. I'm thinking you go there and dance your heart out.*
Lizzy: *Make him jealous.*
Lizzy: *Show him he needs to LOCK. THIS. SHIT. DOWN.*

Everlee: *Have I ever told you that you're too much?*

Lizzy: *All the time. But you love me.*

Everlee: *Yes, I do.*

Lizzy: *So?*

Everlee: *I don't know.*

Lizzy: *See you there at ten.*

Everlee: *Ten?*

Lizzy: Yes, you old hag.
Lizzy: Dust of your granny panties and let's go!

Everlee: Fine.

I looked at the clock. I had just over four hours to kill.
There was a knock on my door.

Had Lizzy really come all the way over here to make sure I was going out, and the call was just to warm me up in case I said no? I laughed, opening the door. "You couldn't wait-"
Dick.

"What are you doing here?" My face fell.

"I want to talk to you."

"I'm pretty sure there's nothing that needs to be said between us."

He looked over my shoulder, like he was looking for someone. For Callum.

"What do you want?" I sighed.

"I broke up with Wendy."

"Do you expect me to care?"

"I broke up with her for you." His voice got louder.

"Sucks for you, because this is never happening again." I pointed between us.

"Come on Ev. We were good together."

I nodded, my lips flattening into a hard line, lowering my voice to a thoughtful tone. "We were so good, weren't we?"

He nodded.

"So good that you were sleeping with at least three other girls while we were together. It wasn't that I wasn't putting out. Because damn."

"It wasn't you. It was me. It is me. I have a problem."

"No shit, Sherlock."

"Stop. Will you let me in so we can talk?"

"No way in hell."

"You looked so good on Valentine's. God. I couldn't get you out of my head."

"I know I looked good. My date thought so too."

"Your date? So you aren't serious?"

Shit.

"It's none of your concern what we are or aren't. You need to leave."

"Come on Everlee. I will do whatever I have to, to make it up to you."

"Fine."

"Fine. Name it!" He answered excitedly.

"Go without sex for a year. No sex, no oral, no jacking off."

"That's impossible."

"No shit. So is this."

He shook his head. "But I dumped her for you."

"Well, at least you seem to be breaking up with girls before you try to bang another one. That's progress and I'm proud of you. But when I say there is literally no chance in hell of us getting back together. I mean it. Zero. Zilch. None. Nada. Zip. N-"

He held his hand up to stop me from speaking. "Fine. But I'm not giving up on us."

"Sucks for you."

"I'll win you back."

I pressed my forehead on the frame of the door, debating if I should say anything else before slamming it in his face. It was clear he didn't know how to take no for an answer.

"I think she said no, buddy." I heard a voice boom from down the hall.

I looked up and saw Jax sauntering down the hall in dark jeans and a navy blue pullover, looking like he just stepped out of a Calvin Klein ad.

"Who are you?" Dick asked, quivering a bit in his shoes at the Goliath of a man stalking towards him. The tattoos on his chest poking out just a bit.

"None of your concern."

"Ev. I'm not going to leave you here with this stranger."

"Seriously, what the fuck?" I couldn't even control my outrage. Who did he think he was? I hated this about him, always assuming he knew me and what I wanted and what I liked. He had me fooled for a long time that I wasn't good enough or pretty enough, or just simply... enough for any man to want me. I didn't realize at the time, but he'd manipulated my life in such a way that I'd lost most of my friends, making my whole life centered around him. Fortunately, for me, Lizzy is a stubborn cuss who doesn't give up easily. She gave me space, but was never gone. She always saw what a douche bag he was, and it took me until after he was out of my life for me to see the hole I'd gotten myself into.

"I know most all of your friends."

"For the old me, but you know what I learned when you cheated on me. I learned that all of *our* friends were really just *your* friends. I had to rebuild my life. But you know what? I'm good with that. I learned I don't need you or any of *your* friends. I'm happy now. I feel complete and, more importantly I feel enough."

Jax pushed past Dick.

"I knew I should have never come here. Wendy was good, much better than you."

Jax looked at me and then at Dick. "You will not stand here and try to guilt trip her into feeling sorry for your weak ass. She doesn't need you and the fact you can see that too is tearing you up inside to the point where you feel you need to belittle and degrade her. If you don't walk your tiny timbuck, scrawny ass back down the hall, I'm going to help you and I can guarantee you don't want me doing that."

"You don't scare me."

"I'm not trying to scare you, princess. I'm merely just giving you a heads up, so when I lay my hands on you, you can't say I didn't warn you." He took a step forward.

Dick looked between us uneasily, and all I could do was raise my chin slightly and look down my nose at him.

"You're so going to regret this." He mumbled before storming away.

"Doubt it, dickweed." Jax said, slamming the door.

I did the super cliche thing and ran into his arms. He wrapped me in a bear hug and held me there for what felt like forever. "You smell good." I said, pushing off him a moment later.

"I take it that was the ex Callum met?"

"The one and only."

"Seems like a charmer."

"He could be. I fell for it at one point."

Jax ran the back of his hand down my cheek affectionately, staring into my eyes, causing a tingle to stir in my core. I should not feel this way about him. With any of them. I should look at this for what it was. Sex.

"What are you doing here?" I asked, walking into the kitchen to grab a glass of water.

He looked around my living room and kitchen area. "Just wanted to check on you."

I walked towards him. "Wanted to check on me?" I didn't believe him.

"Good thing I did since the charmer was here."

I pressed my hand into his chest. "I'll have you know I don't need you or any other man fighting my battles for me. I'm a capable woman."

He looked down at my hand that hadn't moved and I nearly stumbled backwards. "I've seen how capable you are."

"Don't you forget it." I walked into the bedroom to flip the light off, but when I turned around, I walked smack into Jax's chest.

"What was that?"

"What was what?" Shit. There was no way he saw my wall of boyfriends.

"On your shelf."

"Nothing." I threw my hand on the door frame of the bedroom.

He chuckled. "That was not nothing."

Fuck. Shit. Mother ass. "Pretty sure it was nothing."

He pushed past me with ease and flipped the light back on. "Oh, baby." He said in a low and sultry voice.

"What? A girl has needs that need to be met."

"Yes, she does and if that's what you've been using... I mean, the green one is the only one that looks anywhere close to satisfying you, the others just look like they'd piss you off."

He walked into the room. My room. My bedroom. And was looking at all my boyfriends like he was trying to solve the world's toughest problem and here I was, following him around like a lost puppy. Not a lost puppy. Like a freaking horn dog.

"Do you need any *needs* met right now?" He asked, turning to look at me.

"Gah- what?"

"Do you have any *needs* that need to be met?" His hand brushed the hair behind my ears and I felt the energy in the room change.

"Are you offering?" What kind of question was that? I asked, beating myself up internally. "Is that... allowed?"

He chuckled, "Do you ask that of Callum?"

I puckered my lips at him. "Fair point."

"So I'll ask again... do you have needs?" His tone was low and gravelly, as his face inched closer to mine. I could feel his warm breath dancing across my face as I moved to close the gap between our kiss, scraping my teeth over my lip.

I nodded.

"You need to stop doing that." He inched closer, his lips only a breath away.

"Doing what?"

"Biting your lip."

"Like this?" I teased, sucking my lip in and letting my teeth slowly scrape over it.

His hand clamped around my neck and he drove me back into the wall, my back pressed against it, and he stared at me.

"If you're trying to scare me, it's not working. It's only turning me on more."

He let out a low, dark chuckle. The sound sent a wave of pleasure straight to my core. "I know." He took my mouth in his, forcing his tongue in.

I whimpered out a moan as my knees gave the slightest buckle. He kissed so good. It was like... like I was riding a unicorn through the clouds. I know that doesn't make sense, especially since he was nothing like a unicorn and the passion, the lust, behind the kiss was nothing like gently floating on a cloud, but damn, it was heaven.

My hands fumbled with the buttons on his pants. It had been so long since I'd had to undress a man in the heat of passion, I felt like a complete novice. I felt him smile under our kiss and his hands made quick work of the buttons and I sank to the floor, sliding his pants down with me. I grabbed his cock in my hand, wrapping my fingers tightly around the base and pumped it a few times into its full erection. I looked up at him, his eyes watching me as I pressed my lips to the tip of his cock, waiting for him to stop me. To tell me this wasn't a good idea.

I counted to three in my head, because that's all I was giving him. I sucked him in hard and fast, without finesse. He drew in a deep breath as his muscles tensed and he pressed against the wall to hold himself up. Hearing his moans was like adding fuel to the fire. I ran my tongue down his cock and back up again, coating it in my saliva. I rolled my tongue around his head, licking the precum off, before sucking it back in again. He blew out a breath that shook in his chest. I pumped my hand up his cock as I pulled off and then thrust it back in again, feeling him hit the back of my throat.

His hands tangled in my hair, holding me there as his hips moved. "I don't know if you can handle me trouble."

I looked up at him with my cheeks hollowed out around his dick.

"But goddamn, you suck cock so good." He thrust in fast, his cock hitting the back of my throat, causing my breath to catch and my eyes to water. He was rough, rougher than anyone I'd ever been with, but I liked it. The raw power of it all. I got a glimpse on Valentine's, but I could tell he was restraining himself.

I felt my gag reflex fighting me, but I closed my eyes. One to hold back the tears and two to relax my mind and my jaw. I wanted to take him all in, show him I was good enough. I sucked harder, almost begging for each thrust. My hand rested at the base of his cock, no longer able to keep up with the momentum of his thrusts.

I felt my saliva leaking down my chin as he pumped faster and faster, lost in the haze of it all. I wanted all of him. I wanted to taste him. I squeezed the base of his cock, rotating my hand in small twists.

I felt him raise on his tip toes once and his hands fell from my hair. "Fuck, Everlee." His hands pressed to the wall as he relinquished control in those last seconds. I knew he was getting close. I pumped two more times and felt the warm shot explode in my mouth, hitting the back of my throat. I swallowed down as fast as I could while continuing to pump, getting every drop out.

He lifted me from the ground and wiped his thumb across my chin and kissed my swollen lips, his tongue swirling in my mouth. He pulled out and looked at me. "My turn." A wicked grin flashed across his face. He ripped open my shirt, the seventeen buttons flying in every direction. I mourned the loss of one of my favorite shirts only for a second. It was new, and it made my boobs look great, but damn. Seventeen buttons? Hashtag poor planning.

He slid the bra off my shoulders, unhooking it in under a second, and took my breast in his mouth. I was eager to feel his tongue ravage it. It was a risky move given his aggression because I could lose a nipple, but I'm pretty sure it'd be worth it.

He grabbed me off the wall and tossed me on the bed like a rag doll. I moved to scoot to the center, but he grabbed my legs and pulled me back to the edge. "Where do you think you're going?"

I knew it wasn't a question that needed an answer. I was in his control and my goodness.

He unbuttoned and yanked my pants off, tossing them behind him. I heard the rattle of bottles shaking and presumed they landed somewhere on my dresser. He delicately pulled my underwear down, a stark contrast to his other movements as his eyes raked over my body. It wasn't often I was completely naked in the daylight in front of a man. Well, it wasn't before a couple of days ago, but even now, I didn't feel shy.

I felt... alive. Confident. It was intoxicating.

"I want you to finger fuck yourself. Show me how you do it when you're by yourself."

I studied him for a second and then slowly slid my hand down to my throbbing clit. Shit. I was soaking wet. I rubbed a few circles over my nub before slipping two fingers in. My back arched off the bed as my hips rotated up.

His eyes were watching me intently. "Keep going. Faster. I want to watch you come."

I bit my bottom lip and pressed my fingers in faster, while my other hand grabbed my breast, pinching my pebbled nipple between my fingers.

"Keep going," he commanded as he walked away from the bed to my boyfriends.

He grabbed two, a thinner bright pink one with a string on one end and the green monster cock. The pink one was a gift with purchase that I'd yet to use, though the thought had crossed my mind more recently.

"Which one should I use?" He held them up.

I shook my head, unable to decide, unable to focus. The wave was building. I have never masturbated in front of someone before and I thought I would feel different about it, but I didn't. I spread my legs wider for him, as I pumped my fingers in faster, my palm pressing on the outside of my clit while my fingers curled on the inside.

"Good girl. I can see it."

I closed my eyes, the sensations riding me. The need. I moved my hand faster and faster to the point my wrist was hurting, my arm was hurting. I held my breath, urging the orgasm along and BAM! It hit so hard, my core clenched and raised me off the bed while I continued to fuck myself. It had been so long since I'd not used any toys, I forgot what it felt like.

Jax jumped on the bed, grabbed my hand, and stuck both fingers in his mouth, sucking them off. He took my breast in his mouth, swirling his tongue across it, then moved to my neck, where his teeth scraped down and he sucked on my fevered skin. A moan slipped from my lips. His hand crept down my stomach and rubbed over my clit, causing my body to twitch, because it was still so sensitive.

"Let's try this one first." He looked down briefly, and I heard the buzz start up. I could tell by the hum it was the smaller one. He looked back at me, his face just inches from mine, as he slowly slid it in. A shudder of breath escaped, followed by another moan. He pumped pinky the vibrator in several times slowly, and then pulled it out and ran it over my tight hole.

My eyes darted to his as I realized what he was doing and what his intentions were. He lowered his mouth back down to my neck, sucking on my skin again. I rolled my head over, because the gentle sting, coupled with the swipes of his tongue, was amazing. After pumping pinky in a few more times, he pressed it at my hole. He took my mouth in his as he pushed pinky in slowly. He pulled it out and then pressed in again, the vibration making my hips thrust.

I grabbed him by the jaw. "Give me your cock now."

"Yes, ma'am."

He jumped on top of me and ran the head of his cock down between my wet folds before slamming it into me. My head dug into the bed as he slammed into me again.

Between the vibration in my ass and the complete fullness of him, I felt my body spooling up for another orgasm.

"You told me to fuck you harder when we were in the bathtub."

I nodded.

"I plan to fuck you so hard, you forget your name." His lips took mine unforgivingly as he tilted his hips and slammed into me again. He grabbed each leg and swung it around in front of him, throwing them over his shoulders, so the bottoms of my feet were pointed to the ceiling and my calves cupped his ears. He wrapped both his arms around my legs and raised on his knees and began thrusting in hard and fast. I could feel a pain inside as new depths were reached while pinky continued to vibrate in my ass. After several thrusts, he pulled out and flipped me over so my stomach was on the bed.

"You want more now?" he murmured in my ear.

"Yes. Jax. Give me more."

"As you wish."

He pulled me onto all fours, then pushed my back down, so my ass was up in the air and my chest was on the bed. He thrust inside of me and the moans were coming fast now as he was pumping the breath out of me. His hand moved around my hips and landed on my clit. "Holy shit Jax." I groaned out.

His finger circled, as the wet slaps of his cock sliding into me echoed across the room. The headboard was slamming into the wall, but I didn't care. I had to listen to Phillis and Larry bang their headboard on the first of every month, and now it was my turn.

His grunts mingled with my moans and the buzz of the vibrator. I was so close that it almost hurt and then it hit me so hard, my chest bucked off the bed only to be quickly pressed back down. I yelled so loud, as the orgasm washed over me, curling my toes, causing every muscle in my body to tense. He yanked the vibrator out and slung it somewhere and his hands gripped tightly into my hips, taking what was his.

I felt it when he burst inside of me, his cock twitching as he rode his own orgasm before collapsing on my back. The echo of the vibrator was the only sound aside from our labored breaths. He pulled out, and I rolled over, looking up at him while he fell to his side, his arm draped around me.

"Had enough?"

"If I said no, would you believe me?" I smirked.

"Insatiable." He kissed my nose.

I'd had enough for now. As it were, I would not be able to walk tonight.

He fell to his back and pulled me up to his chest. I laid my head on it for a second, listening to his heartbeat, and then propped my chin on his pecs, tracing my finger along his tattoos.

"What does this one mean?" I asked, running my finger on the frog looking one I noticed a few nights ago.

Without looking, he answered, "I was in the SEALs and my buddies and I got them."

I propped up on his chest. "You were a SEAL?"

He nodded, and I got the impression he didn't want to talk about it, so I let it drop. It explained several of the scars he had scattered around his chest and abs, and the one I saw on his leg. They were battle scars, mostly wide, so I'm guessing a knife, but there was a circular one near his clavicle that looked to be a gunshot scar.

I laid my head back on his chest for an immeasurable amount of time. "So, why did you come by? Or was it to make up for the last time?" I teased.

He pushed me off him and jumped off the bed, a smirk tugging on his lips. "Well, it wasn't to fuck you. That just sort of happened."

"It did, did it?"

He nodded, slipping his pants back on.

He reached into his pocket and pulled out a small purple silicone looking thing.

"What's that?" I had an idea, but I wanted him to confirm before I jumped to conclusions.

"I think you know what this is."

"What am I supposed to do with that?"

"I think you know what you're supposed to do with it." He smiled and tossed it on the bed before he reached down to shut the other vibrator off.

"The boys want to see you tonight at the club."

"And I'm expected to drop all my plans and come?"

"If you come is up to you, but we expect you to show up." He winked.

"I see what you did there."

"Just be sure to turn it on before you arrive. We'll tell the bouncer to be expecting you."

"And Lizzy too."

"And Lizzy." He knocked his knuckles on the door. "Try not to miss me too much."

"I've already forgotten you were here."

"I doubt that, love."

He was gone, and I was left wet and fucked on my bed.

PPE... not personal protection equipment...

"THIS LINE IS INSANE." Lizzy said as we were walking up to Vixen.

"Good thing I know somebody." I opted for a black sequin strapless dress tonight and low heels. I wouldn't have worn panties, but having this purple pussy eater thing in, made me nervous. I didn't need to be dancing and birth it on the dance floor. That would be super awkward.

We walked up to the bouncer and before I could tell him who we were, he opened the rope for us. "They'll see you upstairs."

"Upstairs?" Lizzy shimmied her shoulders. "Look who's all fancy now."

"Stop." I batted.

I remember there being a staircase on the left when we walked in that swooped up to the top level. I didn't know of any other, so we walked along the hall towards the main dance floor until we found it.

Another bouncer was standing there and waved us through.

As we were climbing the stairs, I called over my shoulder, "Are you sure Tony won't have a problem with you being here?"

"No. He's at a work dinner or something. He said he may swing by later tonight, depending on what time he gets done and where we're at."

It was already ten o'clock, and I knew Lizzy said he was working on closing a big deal, which often meant lots of late nights and expensive dinners. I couldn't imagine him wanting to come out to a club after all that.

The upstairs was a little quieter. There was a bar in the center and oversized booths scattered around the floor, with a small dance space in the middle. It curved around the downstairs so that whoever was up here could watch what was going on from almost every angle.

"There she is." I heard a voice boom.

Callum.

I found him on the opposite side of the room, walking towards us with his arms outstretched. Class and sophistication. Sex and Power. That was Callum McCall, and he was intoxicating.

"Hello ladies," he cooed, sliding one hand into his pocket.

"Hey."

"I wanted to formally introduce you to someone." Callum offered, pulling his hand out of his pocket.

I saw her walking over out of the corner of my eye. She was sophistication bottled up in a petite little frame with a pixie haircut. Her dress was a black spaghetti strap v-neck.

Lizzy grabbed my arm, recognizing her immediately.

"Everlee. Lizzy. I want you to meet my good friend, Sophie."

Lizzy was the first to step forward because she wasn't tainted by the fact Sophie was Callum and the guy's ex-lover. She threw her hand out to shake Sophie's. "Oh my. I. What?" Lizzy glanced at me, then back to Sophie. "I'm sorry. Just fan-girling over here. I bought your cookbook like two years ago and," she kissed the tips of her fingers before continuing excitedly. "And then I started watching your cooking show and your other at home show, then I saw you were in town." She patted the air down. "Needless to say. Huge fan."

Sophie chuckled softly, "Well, thank you. I love meeting fans."

Lizzy thumbed both her fingers at herself. "Right here!"

I laughed because I hadn't seen Lizzy this excited to meet someone since we got backstage passes at a Michael Bublé concert.

Sophie turned towards me. "Everlee. So happy I get to formally meet you." She quickly glanced at Lizzy, "Callum has told me so much about you."

I looked at Callum, wondering what in the world he could have said or if she was just being nice. He pumped his eyebrows, but I was still uncertain.

"I've reserved the upper floor for us tonight," Callum said. "As well as the bar. Drink whatever you'd like." He directed us over to one of the large semicircle booths against the wall, out of sight from the floor below.

Sophie held out her hand. "Lizzy, would you like to come to the bar with me to pick out a shot for the group?"

"Not me," Callum said, waving his hand.

Sophie glanced at me, encouraging me to work on Callum. "Just one?" I pouted, sticking my bottom lip out, before mouthing sir.

He glared at me. "Fine. One. But that's it." He gave me a hard glare that told me not to push it.

I grabbed his leg and squeezed, feeling his thigh muscles flex inside his pants. Butterflies danced in my stomach and I had to look away to get ahold of myself. It felt like there was a little sex fiend nympho inside of me who'd been let out of her cage. I don't know if it was because I had been six months celibate, or these guys, but damn. It's like she was a scavenger looking for that dick, all bent knees, hands at the ready, flitting from one place to the other.

I watched Lizzy and Sophie at the bar. Lizzy was going on about something, and Sophie had a soft smile on her face, listening to it all. I appreciated she didn't use her past with Callum to sway him, but instead left it to me. Like she was telling me she wasn't a threat.

I felt his cheek brush against my hair, before I felt his warm breath on my ear. "I hear you had a good time with Jax this afternoon." There was a playfulness in his voice.

I looked back at him, our face inches apart. "What are you talking about?"

He chortled, "Your poker face is getting better, but you have to understand. For us, we share everything. We can't afford to have secrets." His hand ran up my spine, causing a wave of goosebumps to spread across my skin. "Did you do as Jax asked?"

I looked at him and nodded cautiously. "Good girl." His head darted back to the girls, who were carrying drinks. Sophie handed me my shot while Lizzy gave Callum his.

"To a good time tonight and a joyous trip to visit old friends," Sophie peeped.

"Here, here," Callum said before we all tilted the shot back.

Lemon Drop shot, a Lizzy go-to.

"Oh, this is quite delightful," Sophie said with her soft French accent.

"Oui," Lizzy laughed.

"Here are your other drinks," The bartender said, arriving with a tray of three martini glasses.

"Pineapple Cosmo," Lizzy offered when I looked at her.

I took a sip at the same time I felt a slight tingle from below and nearly choked, swallowing the drink down.

I dabbed my mouth with the cocktail napkin and cut my eyes to Callum, who was leaning back against the chair, looking as cool as a cucumber. One hand in his pocket, one hand on the back of the chair, not like a man who had control over me right now with the press of a button.

The purple pussy eater began to vibrate more against my clit and my g-spot. I leaned forward in the chair, clamping my legs together, but tried to play it off that I was putting my drink on the table. The vibration slowed to a point where I thought it was cutting off, but it just stayed there, low and steady.

Lizzy and Sophie started talking about something, so Callum leans forward, his lips brushing against my ear as his hand clamped on my thigh. "So tell me again. Did you have a good time with Jax this afternoon?" he whispered.

I nodded and the vibration picked up speed. I felt my core tightening and my nipples pebbling. I clamped my fingers around the edge of the chair.

"Use your words Everlee."

"Yes..." I had to pause for a second as the wave was building.

"Yes, what Everlee?" He pushed.

"Sir," I pant out quickly and the vibration dies.

I let out the breath I'd been holding, because it was the only thing keeping me from rocking in my seat and having a full-blown orgasm right here in front of everyone.

"Good girl." He kissed my cheek, then stood up. "You ladies have fun. I need to go check on some things, but I'll send Jax over here to keep you all company."

I huffed as he walked away, because this thing was still inside of me like a ticking time bomb waiting to make me explode.

Why in the hell did I put this thing in? Give him this much power?

Jax walked over a moment later, looking as casual and sexy as ever. I tried not to react around him, because Lizzy still didn't know which was really annoying. If they would have allowed me to tell her or at least have her sign some NDA too, then I could talk to someone about all this crazy shit. Although, perhaps I could talk to Sophie about it.

Would that be weird?

Sophie stood up, kissing either side of Jax's cheek. "How are you, darling?" she asked, grabbing both his hands.

"Doing well." He nodded towards Lizzy and moved to give me a hug, his large hand pressing into my lower back. "Glad you came."

"Not yet," I teased, causing him to chuckle.

"Not yet," he repeated before pulling away and taking a seat between Sophie and I.

I caught Lizzy looking curiously at us, but she said nothing.

I listened to the conversation Sophie and Jax were having about her new restaurant in France when I was surprised by the vibration between my legs again. I blew out a small puff of air, as my orgasm was edging closer. I quickly scanned the floor and saw Callum talking to Knox about something, but he was using both his hands.

The vibration stopped.

Shit.

I slowly turned to Jax, whose hand was in his pocket, coolly carrying on a conversation with Sophie.

He asked another question, but I wasn't paying attention because the vibration picked back up. He was toying with me.

"Are you ok Ev?" Lizzy asked.

I nodded. "All." It vibrated faster, causing the word good to be elongated, before the toy shut off again.

Was there a range for this thing? How far could I get away from it to have it not work? Did I want to do that?

Jax kept the vibrator off for a while after that, letting my body relax and ease into a false sense of security, but I should know it wouldn't last forever. The not knowing was exciting though.

After sometime, Sophie suggested we go downstairs and dance, to which Lizzy and I agreed. The music was pumping and with only the three of us up here- excluding the boys, of course- it wasn't really a dance scene.

Jax said he needed to take care of some things anyway, but he or Knox would check on us. Emmett was at Bo's tonight and hated he couldn't be here with the three of us, but apparently Sophie spent the day there, working in his kitchen.

We started heading down the stairs, and Lizzy grabbed my arm gently. "What's with you and Jax?"

"What do you mean?"

"The way he looks at you."

"How?"

"Don't pretend you don't see it."

"I don't know what you're talking about."

"Like he just ate you for lunch."

Dinner, I wanted to correct. "That's just him."

"Well, don't let Callum see."

Callum would love to see and love to watch him fuck me. A flash back to Valentine's Day in the bathtub caused my stomach to tighten.

The heavy bass from the speakers started thumping through our bodies.

"This is great, no?" Sophie shouted back to both of us, grabbing our hands and guiding us onto the dance floor.

"So fun." She was impossible not to like. I literally tried not to like her, but she's this little ball you want to wrap your arms around.

I glanced up and saw Jax, Knox and Callum standing shoulder to shoulder watching us. I rubbed my hands up my dress and over my breast, then through my hair, never breaking eye contact.

Big mistake.

I was dancing with the devil, and I didn't even have a pitchfork.

The vibration started again, slower this time. Lizzy grabbed my hand and started swaying her hips from side to side, working her way down, wanting me to follow. I tried, but sticking my ass out and swaying from side to side nearly sent me into convulsions.

The boys must have seen, because the vibration stopped. They were toying with me. Bringing me to the edge and then cutting it off. My panties were a sopping mess now, but at least I was standing and not sitting.

"You're acting really weird tonight."

"Sorry. I felt my hip pop," I lied. Seemed like it could be legit.

"Do we need to get your cane, grandma?"

"Shut up." I pushed her back and swayed all the way to the floor and back up.

"There she is."

The three of us danced in our little bubble for a while. When I looked at the clock, it was just after midnight.

"I'll be back," Lizzy called over the music. She signed the word for bathroom.

As soon as she was gone, Sophie was by my side, holding my hands. "How are you doing with all this?"

"All what?"

"The four of them?"

I hesitated for a moment, because it felt weird. If I shared, then would she share? And did I want to hear that? But the other part of me was dying to talk to someone about it, so I went for it and hoped I didn't regret it.

"It's tough."

She nodded. "You may think you want it long term, but it's hard."

"How so?" We were still half swaying to the music, but you could tell we were more interested in having a conversation than dancing.

"Callum says you've only had one group event?"

"Yea." I frown and she laughed.

"It's addicting, but then feelings become real. Attachments form. You will make yourself believe it can be a thing, all of you, but then you have to step outside your bubble and the real world hits you. The world doesn't see love the same way the guys do. They are all, for the most part, one man, one woman. It's archaic. Sure, same-sex couples are being accepted more and more, but could you imagine showing up for Thanksgiving dinner with four men or going on a date? The world will put pressures on you." I could tell she was speaking from her own experience. Is that what happened to her? They thought they could be something more... I knew Europe was more free love and what not... did they get bit?

"Polyamory is a thing, though."

"Right, but they usually get away from city life, from the public, to avoid the daggers and swords being thrown."

I sighed. I agreed with what she was saying, but I didn't want to believe it. I wanted to believe we could make it work. They were all different and I could already feel myself getting attached. It hadn't been long at all, but it's easy to get swooped up in their life. Their world.

"I'm not trying to be a Debra Downie. I was you."

I chuckled at her mispronunciation of Debbie Downer.

"I always get it wrong. That's what you were laughing about?"

I nodded. "Debbie Downer."

"Yes, that. But as I was saying, I was you until I wasn't. I had to make the choice to leave them. It was hard, but we were wrapped up in a cocoon for so long we fooled ourselves into thinking it was all going to be ok."

"The contract I signed limited our engagements to a few, but no more."

She smiled. "From what I've heard, you've already had a few and some, but one group..."

My lips tugged to the side. "Maybe I can just have sex with them one at a time and never have a group play, and then we can go on?" I was mostly teasing.

She gave me a hug. "I don't think they will let that happen. They have to protect themselves too. They aren't robots." She gave me a hug, ending the conversation just as Lizzy walked back.

"What did I miss?" she asked, jumping right back in.

"Oh, nothing much, darling. Want to go back upstairs and rest our feet?"

"Sure."

We walked upstairs where the three men were waiting for us, looking as handsome as ever.

"We saw you dancing and were just about to come down and join you," Callum teased.

"You lie." Sophie booped him on the end of the nose.

"You're right. They weren't, but I was," Knox said.

"We came back up to rest our feet," Sophie said, walking over to our booth.

"Everlee and I will get you all some drinks." Callum placed his hand on my back as he ushered me towards the bar, but stopped short. "What were you and Sophie talking about?"

I studied his face for a moment. I had thought perhaps he instructed her to lay the groundwork, but now I wasn't so certain. "Nothing much."

"Everlee," his voice lowered.

"She was talking about you all and how I need to be prepared to let you go when this is done. Whenever it's done."

He looked down his nose at me.

"That's all. I mean, she said the world isn't ready for a relationship like ours- Sorry. Not to imply we are in a relationship. I know we're just having fun. But that's also what she said. That this needs to end before feelings get attached."

His lips hardened into a flat line. "Yes, that is all very true."

I felt there was a but coming, but he didn't continue. Was I hopeful for a but? But, we don't want to give you up. But, we can find a way to make it work. But, you've shown us we can have it all.

We walked up to the bar, and I was too enthralled with all the ways that conversation could have gone that I didn't even pay attention to what he ordered. They may not be robots, but I felt like one right now. I wanted to be a robot, because whether or not I wanted to admit it, I was getting attached. How could I not?

I knocked back a shot and sat the glass on the table and walked over to the bar and ordered another.

"What's wrong, jellybean?" Lizzy asked, meeting me.

"Nothing toucan Sam." My brow furrowed. She definitely knew something was wrong now. Anytime I added two things together that made little sense, it was like a dead giveaway.

She grabbed my arm. "Everlee. You tell me right now. Do I need to lay someone out?" She reached up to take her earrings out.

I laughed, grabbing her arm. "Keep your earrings in. All is good. I just... I like them."

"Them?"

I shook my head, scrambling. "I like Callum and all his friends. They are just... they just seem great. So much better than dickface. You can tell a lot about a person, by the friends they keep."

"Is that why you keep me around?" She nudged my arm.

"The only reason. I'd have gotten rid of you a long time ago, but then people would think I was super boring."

She threw her head back, laughing. "Yes. Yes, they would have." She Z snapped the air and waved me back over to the group.

Callum patted the seat between him and Knox. I leaned over and gave Knox a hug, and he managed to plant a quick kiss on my ear. "You look so hot tonight."

I put my hand on Callum's leg to hold up appearances we were in an exclusive relationship and I felt guilty I couldn't be like this with all of them. But they seemed to understand their roles in front of people who didn't know. I imagine if Lizzy wasn't here, it wouldn't be a problem, but I wouldn't choose them over her. No matter how good the sex was.

When you're playing Hide and Seek as adults, it's bound to end in a good time

----

"You seemed quite, during the last hour," Callum noted in the car ride back to his house. Lizzy called Tony, and we had just dropped Sophie at her hotel.

"Sorry."

"What's going on?"

"Nothing. I mean something. But I don't want to talk about it right now."

"Do you want to do something else instead?" He closed the gap between us as his hand moved up my thigh.

I wanted to say no, but I couldn't. I just wanted to fuck and forget. "I'd love to do something else."

"Music, Brady. Make it something loud."

Were we really about to have sex in the back seat of a moving car, with the driver an arm's reach away? There was no way.

"I've been thinking about your pussy all night."

"I've been thinking about it too since you men thought it would be funny to edge me all night with the remote-controlled vibrator you gave me. You better be glad I was dancing on the floor that one time, because I would have definitely puddled all in your seat. My panties are a complete waste now."

"Then let's get rid of them."

"Already did."

He sucked in a breath before his hand slipped under my dress and swiped over my wet folds.

"Fuck me, Everlee." He sucked his fingers and then reached into his pocket and flipped the switch for the vibrator.

I shot a nasty glance at him and tried to close my legs, but he held them open. "No, baby."

My fingers dug into the cushion of the seat as he came in for a kiss, taking my mouth in his. His tongue swirled around as my body began to grind. I was about to crest the top of orgasm mountain and then he cut it off.

I sighed into his mouth, welcoming the brief reprieve, but it was almost turning into torture. My body was so spooled up right now I felt like the next smallest bump or vibration would set me off on a cataclysmic orgasm that would probably show on the Richter scale.

We got home. No. We got to his house, and he scooped me up and carried me in. I was fairly confident, once again, my pussy was hanging out, but we were in his private drive and Brady stayed in the car so there was no one to see.

When we got in, the others were waiting in the living room. Emmett's hair was wet, like he'd just gotten out of the shower and he was only wearing a pair of black joggers that hung low on his hips.

"I think she's ready, boys."

Fuck me. I went limp in Callum's arms.

I was ready for Callum, but all of them?

Headline tomorrow reads. Mysterious Seismic Activity reported last night. Cause still unknown.

"Do you want to play a little game?" Callum asked.

I nodded, not sure why. Because the last time they asked me to do something, I ended up with the purple pussy eater inside of me.

"Did you ever play sardines growing up?" he inquired.

"The reverse hide and seek?"

"Exactly."

I nodded. Excitement filling me.

"Only we play naked."

My eyes grew wider.

"You hide first." He winked.

"How much time do I get?"

"How much do you need?"

"Ten minutes."

"Ten?"

"This is a big house and I want to make it good."

"Fine. Round one is ten minutes."

Round one? Thankfully, tomorrow was the weekend and I could sleep as long as I wanted.

I started walking through the kitchen.

"Don't forget. No clothes!" Knox shouted.

"And no orgasms unless there are two or more people hiding with you."

Oh shit.

I took off, but not before turning around to watch the guys stripping out of their clothes.

I felt the vibrator kick on. I'd forgotten about it and it caused me to squeal, which garnered several laughs from the living room.

After a second, it turned off.

I had no idea where I was going. The fun thing about playing sardines when I was a kid was to find the smallest space you could. Every time someone found you, they had to fit in there with you or they were out. Trying to see how many ten year olds could fit into a cabinet was something to behold. I was doing the same thing now, only instead of hands and knees, it was going to be ass and cocks.

I walked around the second floor, not sure how much time I had left. I didn't know what was up here, but they said nothing was off limits and I'd have to assume if there was a room off limits, they would have locked the door. I picked a door at random and dropped my dress in front of it, then hurried to the voyeur room, where I dropped my heels.

I opened a door at the end of the hall to find another set of stairs going up. I walked in, the low level lighting illuminating the stairway, and gently closed the door and ascended the stairs, where I found another door. I stepped out and was shocked. I was on their roof. But it wasn't just any roof, but a rooftop bar with all the lighting, games, a pool, and a hot tub. I was definitely going to hide here, but where?

I walked around the floor and was in awe of the amazing views they had of the cityscape in the distance, but loved this space was still private.

I shook my head to clear it. I needed to find a place to hide. I moved quickly and settled on the turf, behind a row of chairs that overlooked the cityscape. I could at least admire it while I waited.

A cool wind blew, causing me to shiver. Why did I think it was a good idea to come outside on the roof of their house and hide in the nude in the winter? I didn't feel the air at first because of the excitement and anticipation, but now I had been outside for a moment, the weather was starting to bite.

The steam rising from the hot tub and the gurgling of the jets were a siren's song.

"Yea. Fuck this. A hot tub is an equally good place to hide."

I stood up and pulled the purple pussy eater out and dropped it on the ground before I climbed down into the inset hot tub. The hot water stung my skin, but only for a minute. I let out a sigh as I sank all the way down and let the jets and bubbles drown out any thoughts.

"Found you."

I heard the rough and deep voice of Jax. Of course, the ex-SEAL would find me first.

I opened my eyes as he was slipping into the water. He was so smooth and graceful the water hardly moved. I couldn't help but wonder what he was like in the field. What he looked like in all that tactical gear and face paint, moving through woods and water.

He floated over to sit beside me, and I put my hand on his thigh. "I was over there." I pointed to the chairs, "but you all took too long and I was freezing my ass off."

"I'd hate if that happened. Such a fine ass it is," he said, lifting me onto his lap, grabbing my ass in the process.

"How did you find me?"

He shrugged. "I looked for a bit, but when the others kept clearing rooms, I decided to use the cameras."

"You cheat." His pec flinched when I palmed his chest.

"I wanted to find you first."

"Why is that?" I flirted.

"More time to play with you. I know you're ready to explode after how much we tortured you tonight."

"I'm glad you can appreciate the hell you all put me through."

"You liked it or you would have taken it out."

Our gaze lingered longer than it should have. "I guess you're right."

He smiled. "Now be a darling and ride my cock while we wait for the others."

"I thought you said no orgasms with less than three people."

"There won't be."

"So you're going to continue to edge me?"

"Hopefully not, because I want to fuck that pretty little ass of yours."

I popped up from his lap and centered myself above the tip of his hard cock.

"So you want me to just ride you?"

He nodded, raising his hips up a little.

"No, no, no." I batted my finger in front of his face.

He threw his head back laughing, the muscles in his neck and the Adam's apple in his throat bobbing.

"Payback is a bitch."

"Careful sweetie. One of us is trained in torture."

I leaned forward and kissed him hard. His hands wrapped around my back, pressing me to him. I sank down on him slowly and we swallowed each other's moans.

"Fuck, you feel so good," he whispered against my lips.

I slowly raised up and then lowered back down. "Samesies." I smiled against his lips.

"I don't know if I can keep to the rules." He pulled my hair down so the back of my head hit the water, as he took a breast in his mouth. I loved how rough he was with me. I don't know if just anyone could do that, but I trusted him and it turned me on.

The vibration from my silicone friend was buzzing across the floor. "Ooh cheater, cheater. Should we let your moans be the guide for the guys? I mean, technically, if they find you before you orgasm, we aren't breaking the rules."

"What if your neighbors hear?"

"Fuck the neighbors."

He took my breast in his mouth, running his teeth over my pebbled nipple, sending an erotic sensation down to my clit. I moaned out.

"I don't think that was loud enough." He let go of my hair, lifted my ass, then slammed me back down again. I moaned out louder. "Closer."

He pressed his finger on my clit and I felt my walls clench around his cock. A low guttural moan escaped, and he looked at me. "Oh, you are close, aren't you? Maybe we should stop."

"Don't you fucking dare." I grabbed him around the back of his head and kissed him hard as I rode his cock up and down, grinding my hips into him.

"Hold on one second." He stopped me and turned around to push a button. "Found her boys. On the roof. You better hurry, because I'm about to fuck her right."

I was smiling when he popped me off him and lifted me across the hot tub so we were closer to the door.

"I'm going to bend you over the edge of this hot tub and fuck you so hard the whole town will know you came."

He pressed my body down on the decking with one hand on my neck, the cool air stingy my nipples as they pressed into the hard surface, while the other pinned my arms behind my back. His fingers swiped through my soaking wet pussy up to my forbidden spot.

"So fucking wet," he groaned before he pressed two fingers into me.

I whimpered out, almost ready to come at just his brief touch. My orgasm was like a yo-yo that'd been spun up all day and he was about to let me fall. I felt myself clinch around him, as my hips jerked forward. I was a dam ready to break, and I was terrified he was going to stop again.

I pressed back into him, needing more. Wanting more. But as I was about to crest, he dropped my hands and pulled out. "No. Please Jax. Please," I cried out.

"I want you to come around my cock and not until it's in you, will you come."

"Jax," I whined.

"The cries for my cock sound almost as good as your moans."

"Fuck you Ja-" I couldn't finish getting his name out because his wet tongue flicked across my clit, before slipping deep inside. "Fuckkkk Jax." I rose on my toes and tried to grab onto anything, but there was nothing but hard decking.

His own moans of pleasure sounded above the bubbles from the jets. He pulled back and sucked on my clit before diving back in. I let out something between a scream and a moan as my entire body was tensing. I was trying not to show how close I was getting to the edge because I didn't want him to stop.

He pulled back again. "Let it out Everlee. When you quiver, I know you're getting close."

"You said not to come unless it's around your cock and they're watching."

"I did say that, but I'm starving and I love the taste of your fucking pussy."

He pressed his face back in and I felt my body spooling up, my legs, my arms, my stomach- every part of me was shaking and I was about to explode.

"Jax. I'm about to fucking come so hard."

"I want you to come around my tongue before you come around my cock. Squirt for me."

He pressed his tongue as deep as he could go and then pulled out, sucking my clit as he pushed two fingers in. His moves were wild, erratic.

"Fuck!" I reared off the decking just as the door burst open and all three men were standing there watching me as I unleashed the most powerful orgasm I had ever had. I felt myself bursting at the seams as I exploded into the hot tub, pleasure pulsing through every inch, every fiber of my being. I panted heavily, trying to catch my breath, unable to form words.

Jax dove back in, lapping up all my sweet juices and sucking my clit, slower this time, draining every ounce of pleasure out of me.

"What took you guys so long?" Jax said, standing out of the water, wiping the back of his hand across his mouth.

"How did you find her so quick?" Emmett growled, stepping into the hot tub.

"That's for me to know and you to find out, brother. Don't you say anything, squirt." He poked playfully at my side.

I chuckled, turning around. "Squirt?"

"Well." He cocked his head to the side. "Everyone else has a nickname for you."

"And you thought squirt was the best one?"

"It's cute. It fits after what you just did."

I buried my face in my hands. I had never done that before.

He pulled my hands down. "Don't be shy or ashamed or anything less than proud. That was absolutely amazing and exactly what I wanted." He gave me a delicate kiss on the tip of my nose.

"Who knew the SEAL had a soft side?" Knox said, climbing in.

"It's on my belly. Want to rub?" he teased.

"There's nothing soft about your belly," I rubbed my hands up his rippled edges.

He pulled me to him and murmured against my ear. "I hope you're ready for tonight."

"You mean this morning?"

He shrugged. "You've come around my tongue and now you're going to come around my cock."

"I'm going to fix us some drinks and watch our girl get fucked," Callum said.

Knox climbed back out. "Not you." I pointed to the edge of the hot tub.

I grabbed his hardening cock in my hand, wrapping my fingers around the base. I ran my tongue up the underside of it from bottom to top and swirled it around the head. I took just the tip in, sucking it gently like a lollipop, then sucked the entire cock in, hollowing out my cheeks until he hit the back of my throat.

"Goddamn Ali."

"She looks so good with a cock in her mouth," Jax said, lifting my ass out of the water so I was standing on the two benches. "If you want me to fuck you, squirt, we got to get out."

I held my finger up in the air as I continued to suck Knox's cock into my mouth. I could taste the precum at the tip and didn't want to stop, but I also wanted Jax fucking me.

I gave a few more pumps, then stopped.

"I want to try something," I said climbing out of the hot tub, "but we need a bed. Can we go to the sex room?"

All the boys looked at one another, so I added, "According to your contract, this is our last time together. I want you all inside of me. At the same time."

They all quietly looked around the space at each other, so I continued. "I want to take Emmett and Knox at the same time while Jax fucks my ass and I suck off Callum. I know how much he likes to watch." I tossed a wink at him.

"You had me at I," Knox joked.

"You surprise me Trouble," Emmett said.

Callum scooped me up and started walking through the door, back downstairs. "I don't want you to slip and fall."

"My hero."

"I don't know about that."

I laid my head against his chest and listened to his steady breathing. I had never in one hundred years thought I would be about to take four guys at one time. I had read it in one of the books when I was doing research and I figured this may be the last time I ever get to try it.

So long Vanillaville

CALLUM STOOD IN THE room, holding me in his arms for a moment before standing me up. I wish I knew what he was thinking behind those beautiful blue eyes. Hell, I wish I knew what I was thinking. Four guys? I was always ambitious, but this was borderline scandalous.

No. It was. No doubt about it. I had leapt over the edge, leaving Vanillaville behind. I don't know if I was nervous or shy before, but with these men, I felt like I could say, do, or ask anything with no judgement. It was liberating.

Go big, before you go home, I suppose. And never see them again. Well, sexually anyway. Could I do that? See them and not want to fuck them? Not want to daydream about the could be's and should be's?

I needed to stop dwelling about the future and focus on the now. Focus on the delicious men standing in front of me that wanted to help me live out the craziest thought I've ever had. I pointed my finger at Knox and motioned for him to come over with the sexy stare and bent index finger. Again, I felt like I could be as cliche or cheesy with them and it was ok.

I wrapped my arms around his neck and started kissing him softly. He seemed to be the cinnamon roll of the bunch- the pleaser. His hands rubbed up my back and then down.

I pushed away, peppering kisses down his body until I was on my knees in front of him. His hands gently rubbed through my hair and waited as I slowly took him into my mouth. I wrapped my hand around the base of his cock and swallowed him down. He let out a stuttered breath as his hands massaged my scalp and his hips rocked back and forth slowly. My gentle giant. My little cinnamon roll. After a few more strokes, I pulled off. I didn't want him to finish yet. I grabbed his hand and walked over to grab Emmett's, who was slowly stroking himself while he watched us, and I led them over to the bed.

I pushed Knox onto his back, but his feet were still on the floor. I climbed on top of him and sank down without warning or discussion. His hands found my hips as I gyrated against him slowly.

I turned around and looked at Emmett. "Your turn."

He nodded, biting his bottom lip.

I lifted off Knox. "I'll be back. We need to let Emmet wet his whistle."

Emmett walked over and straddled Knox's leg. He lined up at my opening and pressed in, causing me to gasp with excited anticipation. Knox took my breast in his mouth and sucked, while his other hand rubbed the bud of my nipple between his fingers.

"Harder Emmett."

"She's a little sex demon," Jax teased.

I shot him a dirty glance.

"I'm coming for that ass in a minute," He growled back.

"I can't wait."I blew a kiss at him.

He sighed, shaking his head, and his eyes had fuck me written all over them.

Emmett grabbed my hips and pulled me back onto his cock. "Yes!" I yelled out.

"I think she's wet enough now." Callum called out. His eyes looked hungry, like he wanted to get in on the action, but knew he had to wait. He was the last piece of the puzzle, the crème de la crème, the cherry on top. He continued to stroke himself, eager to plant his cock in my mouth, and I was eager to have him there. I wanted them to always remember tonight and remember me.

Emmett pulled out and waited while I climbed on Knox's cock, gyrating my hips a few times.

"Are you ready, Emmett?"

He nodded without speaking.

"Good. Join your friend in my pussy." I bent over, my nipples brushing Knox's chest, and waited.

"I can't wait to punish your filthy mouth," Callum said.

I peeked over my shoulder and saw Emmett grab the base of his cock, and felt his head pressing right at my entrance. I rocked forward on Knox slowly, while Emmett pushed in just a little.

"Oh fuck," Knox groaned as Emmett slid his cock in further.

My eyes rolled into the back of my head as I continued to stretch around them. I slowly slid forward, then pressed back, and they both let out a sigh at the same time.

"I think I'm going to come watching you take two cocks," Jax said with a heady breath.

"Fuck me, Emmett," I commanded.

He pulled out before pushing in again, moving faster and faster. Knox started to slowly rock his hips at the same time.

"Fuck. Fuck. Oh. My." The sensation was mind blowing.

"You feel so good," Emmett moaned, but I didn't know who he was talking about.

I rocked my hips back and forth, moving faster and faster as the wet slaps spurred me on.

"You better get in here fast, boys, if we want to give her all four of us at once, because I'm about to explode inside of her. This feeling is unfuckingbelievable." Knox bellowed.

I heard movement around me when both the boys stopped. I could feel Jax close behind. In front of me, Callum climbed on the bed and watched Jax, patiently waiting, his teeth wreaking havoc on his bottom lip.

The king and his men.

Emmett and Knox slowly rocked into me just as a hand slid down my back, pausing on my naughty area. Jax pressed his thumb in and a jolt of excitement shot through my entire body and I could feel a slickness seep out of me, if that was even possible.

"Let me get in her first and then you can feed her your cock," Jax said, shifting to the other side of Emmett.

I wanted to savor this, take my time, but pure lust and carnal desire were driving me. I wanted the fullness of them all inside of me. I wanted to claim them, as much as I wanted them to claim me.

Fortunately, Jax had used lube or something, because he was sliding in easily, all things considered. He took his time getting past the ring of muscle, then waited for a second while I adjusted. I rocked back slowly and heard a deep growl of approval hum from his chest. I leaned forward, in control, and then pressed back.

A small whimper escaped, and I felt the room pause, but I didn't. It wasn't a whimper of pain, but of... fullness. I moved a little faster, pressing back further, so I was fully seated on their cocks.

"Holy shit. I can feel you both," Jax exclaimed.

He rocked his hips faster and faster, moving at the same time as Emmett, while Knox laid there thrusting his hips just a little. I looked down at him and he winked at me before his hands grabbed my breast.

"Callum," I called, tilting my head up.

"I'll use your tits to hold you up, love," Knox called from below, making me chuckle.

Callum slipped his hand around the back of my head as he guided his cock into my mouth, matching the thrusts of the others. I sucked him in hard, my cheeks hollowing. I gagged and tears stung my eyes, but I had them all. I don't know what this was called, but it was glorious.

The room was filled with wet slaps, grunts, and moans. Nobody speaking, only enjoying the sound of our sex. It was erotic. If you could bottle up this sound and sell it, it would be worth billions.

"You are magnificent." Callum ran his fingers through my hair as he continued to pump his cock into my throat. "You were made for our cocks."

"Yes, she was," Jax grunted.

The words hit me just the right way, and I felt an emotion welling inside of me. What did that mean? I didn't want to think about it right now. I needed to just focus and enjoy this moment.

I balanced on one hand and wrapped my hand around the base of his cock, squeezing as I sucked harder.

"You want more? I'll give you more." Callum's hands clamped to the side of my head as he began to fuck my face. I gagged, and the tears were streaming down my face, but I loved it. I have never felt so wanted, so alive, as I do right now.

Knox bellowed out. "Oh, shit. I'm..."

My hips rocked just a bit.

"Don't you dare come before her," Jax commanded.

"I'm trying, but goddamn."

I felt Jax's rough fingers brush across my clit and I let out a moan around Callum's cock.

"Just a little further, boys, hold it." Jax's thrusts were getting sloppy as he was focusing on making me come first. My clit was throbbing and slick as butter. His finger kept slipping off, but he didn't give up.

Never give up, never surrender!

I moaned again. I was getting closer. This time differed from every other orgasm I'd ever had. It was like my body was so full, so tight, that it didn't know what to do. But it was there in the shadows building. Only Jax was coaxing it out into the light and my God, when it fully stepped into the light, it was going to rip me apart. I have never had an oncoming orgasm scare me as much as this one did, but it was more than just a tsunami. This was going to wipe me the fuck out.

Oh no! What if I pass out? What if I die? Death by orgasm. Who would tell Lizzy? My parents? What would they say at my funeral? I shook my head. Why the fuck was I thinking about this right now?

I stiff armed Callum, pushing him back. "You need to come now, because when I do... I don't know what's going to happen and I don't want to bite your penis off."

A dark chuckle sounded as his eyes locked with mine. His fingers tilted my chin up. "Give me your mouth, darling, so that I may fill it with cum."

A fucking king.

I smiled, just before he thrust it back in, his moves erratic, needy. Jax continued to work my clit, and I felt my hips gyrating, moving up and down without control.

"Callum," Jax called, worried.

"I'm close."

Jax removed his finger from my clit, leaving me aching for his touch. He knew I was a live wire. A bomb ready to explode and that was my detonation switch.

I grabbed Callum's balls, massaging them in my hand as he pounded into my face.

"Fuck. Here I..."

His back stiffened as his hands clutched to my hair, holding me in place. A warm saltiness shot down my throat as I continued to suck him off. Callum pulled his cock from my mouth and I raised up like a hellbeast, who's had its fill. Jax rubbed my clit and within seconds, I felt it. She was there. Lady Orgasm had arrived.

A noise, so low, so guttural, vibrated out of my chest and kept getting louder and louder. My entire body froze, muscles seized, my pussy clenched, and the world moved in slow motion and sounds began to fade, but not before I heard a collective 'Fuck', from the guys behind me and seconds later they were all releasing into me slowly pumping. My orgasm was still riding me, because there was no way I was riding it. It was euphoric, magical, mystical. It transcended... everything. It was so intense I was literally seeing stars and was having a problem breathing and then all the sudden sounds returned, as well as normal time. I collapsed on Knox, panting.

I was jello. My limbs were mush.

"Everlee?" Knox nudged my shoulder.

"I'm alive," I mumbled against his chest.

I felt Jax, then Emmett, pull out, and then I think someone pulled Knox out of me, but I wasn't quite sure and I really didn't care.

"Come here squirt." Jax lifted me off Knox, cradling me in his arms.

"We're going to take care of you." He brushed a kiss across my forehead. Not because we were in a lust filled haze, but because he wanted to. Jax cared for me.

Callum was standing in the bathtub waiting when Jax walked in. Jax gently handed me off and grabbed a towel to wipe himself down before he stepped into the bath. I laid my head against Callum's chest.

Would this be my last time here, with them, like this? It was a Valentine's contract, and their rules stated two... whatever they called it. I didn't pay attention, which I know goes against all the rules known to man. Never sign a sex contract without looking at the deets, but I didn't care. I wanted Callum. I wanted the fun. I wanted the guys.

I tried to keep my eyes open, but I was so exhausted and satiated that I was having problems. I feel like it was just the three of us in the bath, but I kept lolling off. On top of the lavender scent, the gentle hands washing me and the massages over my feet, legs and back, I was out.

I was jostled awake when they laid me on the bed and I felt several warm bodies nestled in next to me. I took a deep breath, and I was out.

Good ol' Betty for the ♥ win

IT WAS STILL IN the early morning. I wasn't sure what time exactly, because this room had no windows, but my eyes still burned and I felt the heavy sedation of much needed sleep still pulling on me, begging me to follow it down into the dark abyss.

I swiveled my head to see who was in bed with me and had Knox on my left, Callum on my right, with Jax and Emmett above me, all of our heads meeting in the middle of this enormous round bed. I noticed the sheets had been changed to a deep purple color, which must have happened when Jax and Callum were in the bath with me.

I did a few kegels to get an idea of how sore I was going to be and was relieved to find it wasn't as bad as expected. I think the aftercare the men were so keen on helped a lot and was definitely welcome.

Last night was epic. Out of this world. It was our last hoorah together and while part of me believed they had changed their minds, the other part of me, the bigger part, believed that even if they all wanted to, they wouldn't allow it. Rules were rules. I laughed at myself since I was notorious for breaking them, but after my conversation last night with Sophie, I understood why they had them. One, or several of us, would get hurt. It was inevitable. Society was not ready for a relationship like ours.

I looked down at my feet and saw an opening between legs. I could slide out, leave them a note, thanking them and be gone.

Damn it!

I felt my eyes stinging and this time it wasn't from the sleep. I tried to hold back the tear, but it trickled out of the corner of my eye, down my cheek, onto the pillow.

Why did I have to let myself get attached? This was for fun. There were never any promises that it was going to be anything other than that. A montage played in my head, Callum at the bar, Callum taking care of me, Bo's restaurant, Valentine's party, WendyDick's face, ice skating, all the delicious sex, the bathtub, the hot tub, Callum holding me in his arms for no reason, Jax kissing my forehead for no reason.

Fuck!

I was in love with the attention and the feeling they gave me. The feeling of invincibility and companionship. The feeling of power and control and vulnerability.

I was in love with everything about them... Which I know is stupid to say because I haven't known them for that long. But it's like those stories you read about where a look, or a scent, or a moment frozen in time and they knew. They knew they were meant to be together. The yin to the yang. Only we weren't two... we were five.

Maybe I had these feelings because they were my first group experience. It's like that first love thing... maybe that's what this was... my first fivesome love. Maybe it was the fact I had a complete dick of an ex who treated me like shit and I hadn't been with anyone else in so long.

I needed to get out of here before they woke up. I didn't need them to see me crying at something that was always a temporary thing. I didn't want to see the fight or the hurt

in their eyes when I left because that would give me hope...
hope that this wasn't over.

I wiggled slowly, pressing the heels of my feet into the
bed, letting it help pull me down to the edge. I felt someone
shift, but I was too scared to look. I froze for a minute and
then continued.

I oozed on to the floor like the pile of mush I was, and then
stood up. I stared at the tangle of beautiful arms and torsos
for longer than I should have, but I wanted to remember
them. My men.

I wiped the tears that were slowly streaming out of my
eyes and hurried towards the door. Once it was closed, I
tore off down the hall towards the kitchen. I slipped into the
office, grabbed a piece of paper and a pen, and scribbled a
quick note.

What do you say? Thanks, it's been real? Thanks for the
fivesome? Honoring the contract? I settled with

Thanks for the memories. You all have given me life! Goodbye.
-E

I had a tear fall on the bottom right corner and tried to
wipe it away, but it was too late. The paper had wrinkled up.
I thought about tearing the corner off or rewriting it, but
I didn't want them to notice I was gone and come looking
for me.

I grabbed my dress and phone and slipped on my shoes,
thankful they'd been relocated to the kitchen at some point.
I prayed to God their alarm wasn't set, because that would
make my sneaky getaway super awkward.

The cool morning air made the tears on my face feel like
ice. I still kept forgetting we were in the dead of winter and
here I was standing outside a mini mansion in a t-shirt and
dress shoes. Hello walk of shame.

I walked down the sidewalk, away from their house, and
tucked into a small alleyway, out of sight of anyone who
would be up at this freaking hour. I pulled my phone out
and looked at it.

4:53. I'd only been asleep for maybe three hours.

I thought about calling Lizzy, but she'd have a hundred questions I couldn't answer right now, or maybe ever. Instead, I landed on Betty.

Us non-hookers had to stick together.

Fifteen minutes later, she was pulling up at the curb wearing a shirt with ducks on it and had dyed her hair a bright pink color. She bent her head down and gave me a look that I couldn't even begin to describe. It was a cross between excited and surprised to see me in my attire.

She waved me in the car. "Get in! What are you waiting for? You're going to catch a cold out there dressed like that."

"Hey Betty." I said, sliding into her back seat.

She threw her arm on the back of the passenger side headrest and turned around. "Everlee." She smacked her lips. "What have you gotten yourself into? You look well fucked and sad."

I let out a snicker. "Well, Betty, your observation is spot on."

She nodded, not speaking for a minute, then pulled onto the road.

"What's got you so gloom and sneaking out of that mansion back there?"

"Mansion?"

"Oh child. This isn't my first rodeo."

I sighed. "I just needed to get away. I'm scared of getting my heart broken."

"Oh, I see. Tricky thing, the heart. You break your own heart it seems to avoid them breaking it, maybe."

She didn't understand, and it was ok. No one could.

My phone dinged like I'd been sent a message from fate or serendipity.

Sophie.

Sophie: *Had a great time last night! Headed to the airport so I'm sure you won't get this until later, but if you ever need to talk, I'm only a phone call away!*

I looked out of the window for a second, gathering my thoughts, then started typing.

Everlee: *Had a blast as well. I would love to chat.*

Sophie: *Oh! Good morning! I didn't wake you, did I?*

Everlee: *No.*

I started typing a long explanation and then deleted it all.

Everlee: *I was already awake. I just left them.*

Sophie: *They don't know?*

Everlee: *No. I thought it'd be better this way.*

Sophie: *Better for who?*

Everlee: *I don't know. I guess me. Last night, per the contract, was my last night with them. Rules and all.*

Sophie: *I see. You are attached?*

Everlee: *I don't know how or why I let it happen. I know it's stupid. I knew this was temporary. And the conversation with you last night made it clear why it has to be this way.*

Sophie: *Oh. I'm sorry.*

Everlee: *No. It was a good talk.*

Everlee: *I needed to hear it because I was trying to talk myself into how this could work, but you're right. We don't live in that kind of world yet.*

Everlee: Family dinners, friends, dates, events... So many things I have to think about. I've been lying to my best friend in the world and that's killing me. I couldn't do that forever.

Everlee: She thinks I'm with Callum, but she's noticed the way the others are around me. The way Jax looks at me, the way we hold a hug for longer than normal. The lingering gazes and brush of the hands.

Sophie: This is for the best. I didn't think so when I decided to leave, but it gets better.

Everlee: You decided? You didn't have a contract?

Three dots appeared, then stopped.

"Everything ok back there?"
"What? Huh? Yea. Just talking to a friend."
"At this hour? You young kids."
"She's catching a flight."
"You should give her my number when she gets back. Trying to build my portfolio."
I laughed. "I will, but she lives in France."
"Oh," She sighed.
My phone buzzed. I looked at her message and had to read it twice.

Sophie: I think I'm the reason they have a contract. We thought we could all be happy together and were for months, but then things started getting more serious. Christmas was coming up and my parents wanted to meet the man who'd been occupying so much of my time. I brought Knox home with me and the others said they were fine with it, but I knew they weren't. And then, like parents do, they started talking about marriage and kids and it just put everything into perspective. I had always wanted those things, and I wasn't going to get it with them. It took another month for me to realize I had to make an impossible decision. So I left. While I loved them, and they loved me, it just couldn't work.

They didn't fight very hard, because they understood and they didn't want to keep those things from me.

Betty stopped outside of my address. "Home sweet home, darling."

"Home sweet home." I looked up at the apartment building. If this was home, then why did I feel like that's what I just left?

"Fares on me this time."

"I can't do that. I probably woke you up to come get me."

"Darling. I get up before the birds every morning. I was just sitting at the kitchen table working on my book of crosswords. You've gotta keep a mind active to keep it young."

"I'll remember that."

Betty tapped her nose. "You get on up there and get you some good sleep. See if it fixes your problems."

"Thanks Betty." I grabbed the fifty out of my purse as I was getting out of the car. I tapped on her window and when she rolled it down, I tossed it in before hurrying away.

I heard her yelling at me as I was walking in the door, but I didn't turn around.

I climbed the stairs, unlocked the door, threw my stuff on the floor and fell into my bed. It still smelled like Jax.

Fuck!

I ripped my sheets off, throwing them into a pile on the floor, grabbed the blanket off the couch in the living room, then fell onto my mattress, wrapping myself in the velvety softness of my reading blanket.

This was for the better, I repeated to myself as I drifted off into the dark abyss.

NDA for an NDA

I LOOKED AT THE clock on the wall.

Ten minutes.

Lizzy was on her way over. It had been a week since I'd seen her after I holed myself up in the apartment and she was getting antsy, and an antsy Lizzy was not a good Lizzy.

I had spent most of yesterday scouring the internet for a non-descriptive NDA. I was going to make her sign it, then tell her everything. I needed to talk to someone that was local to me, and my best friend. Sophie and I had grown pretty close over the last several days as she was there to tell me the reasons this was good for me, while also playing go between with the boys.

They had all showed up on my doorstep the afternoon I'd left, wondering what was going on. We talked about it and I repeated a lot of the things Sophie said. They'd heard it before, but also knew it to be true.

They didn't try to persuade me to come back or try to convince me this would work because they knew. It's why they had the contract. They told me not to be a stranger and said they'd expected to see me at Vixen and offered a standing reservation at Bo's on Mondays at eight. I told them I'd see them, but we both knew that was a lie. At least for now.

They didn't call me out, but they weren't blind. They could see I was hurting and if I let myself look at them, like really look at them, I'd see them hurting too.

They'd given me so much more than they would ever know. After Dick, I didn't feel like the same person. I felt like a fraction of myself. I felt less than worthy. Dick was a... well, dick, an asshole, and if someone like that didn't think I was good enough, then it made me second guess myself. At one point near the end, when I asked him why he never complimented me, he said it was because he didn't want me getting a big head and leaving him. I should have known then, but I didn't. I think by that point he had already pushed all my friends away so that he was my life, my breath. I'd broken up with him several times, but he would always apologize and I always went back because I was an optimist. I wanted to believe he had changed, or at the very worst, could and would change for me. I always got my answer a month or so later though.

He hadn't changed, and I was left feeling worthless and unlovable again.

The last time Lizzy stepped in. She didn't let me go back, and I have thanked her a thousand times since then, but there was still a hole. No matter how hard she tried to fill it, she couldn't. My confidence was less than non-existent.

That was until Callum stared at me in a bar. The look in his eyes, the way he watched me... the way Emmett flirted with me. It was like it reignited a fire within me. A fire that they continued to add fuel to minute by minute, hour by hour.

I felt like my old self. I felt attractive. I felt worthy of love. I felt confident.

That is what they gave me. That and the most orgasms I think I've ever had.

My doorbell rang.

I raced over to the door and saw Lizzy standing there with a box of discounted Valentine's chocolate, a bottle of moscato, a new vibrator, a movie and a large clothing box. I laughed out loud, pulling her in.

"You don't have to always buy me a vibrator."

"Is that weird? I was in the store getting me a little some-thing something and this caught my eye."

"You could have bought it for yourself."

She batted the air. "I did, and then I bought you one. Twinsies."

"You're too much." I smiled.

"But you love me." She touched the tip of my nose. "Now go plug him in next to your other boyfriends while I get us some wine glasses."

"I love you," I said, grabbing the vibrator from her and giving her a hug.

"I love you too."

"Before we watch the movie though, there's something I need to tell you."

"Are you a lesbian? Because that would explain a lot."

"What? No. At least I don't think so." I grabbed the NDA and a pen off the counter and handed them to her.

"What's this?"

"An NDA?"

"A what?"

"Non- Disc-"

"I know what is it... are you a spy? Do you work for the government?" Her face drew very long as shock spread over her. "Oh my God. Is Everlee really your name?"

"Will you shut up! No, I'm not a spy. No, I don't work for the government, and you have known me forever. Unless I was a spy when I was in elementary school..."

"So it is Everlee?" she teased.

"Lizzy!"

"Fine. Fine. I'll bite."

"I'm going to put this up and I'll be right back."

When I came back in the room, she was propped on the couch with two straws in the wine bottle, sitting with her legs crossed.

"Straws?"

"You're making me sign an NDA. Shits about to get real. Straws were needed."

I rolled my eyes, smiling. I should have done this sooner, because my heart already felt happier just being around her for less than two minutes.

"Oh, also, Jax got you something." She handed me the large box.

I looked at her, confused.

"Also, why is Jax buying you things?"

I grabbed the NDA from her and saw it was signed. I took a deep breath and peeked in the box. It was my favorite shirt. The one he had ripped off me when he came to visit the day Dick showed up on my doorstep.

I sighed.

"What is it?" Lizzy grabbed the box from me and tore the lid off. "Don't you already have this shirt?"

"Funny story..."

Ten minutes later...

"SHUT THE FRONT AND BACK DOOR! YOU WHAT?!" Lizzy shouted, climbing on top of me.

I didn't say anything as I let her pace the room now.

"I can't believe you didn't say anything to me."

"I couldn't."

Her eyes grew wide. "But still. I'm your bitch."

"You are my bitch. But... I don't know." I took a big gulp of wine. "I think I was just scared... scared you'd not approve... or maybe you would. I wanted to do it on my own, see where it went. I think I needed to work through some things from Dick."

"Fuck yeah, you worked through things... on things... in things."

"Stop." I smiled.

"I didn't know you were a little kink factory."

"Me either." I chuckled.

She sat down on the couch. "You're definitely not a lesbian. You love that dicky dick too much."

"I do love the dicky dick."

"Good thing I brought you another vibrator. If you're going to start taking four at a time..." She cut her eyes at me with a sly smile spread across her face.

"Will you stop?"

"I will for now, but I don't want you thinking I'm anywhere close to done giving you shit for this. Four..." She was holding her fingers in the air, trying to visualize everything, and I just batted her hand down.

"What movie did you get us?"

"Oh, it's just an empty box that looks like a movie. I felt it went with the whole theme. But I did rent us the most classic breakup movie of all time. Legally Blonde."

"Bend and Snap."

"Yes, Queen."

"I need to connect to my account so we can stream."

I rested my head on her shoulder and shoved a piece of chocolate in my mouth. "I miss them, but I also feel better than I have in a long time. They've given me my confidence back. Made me feel worthy of love. Made me feel like I was enough."

Lizzy rested her head on mine and pressed play.

TO BE CONTINUED..... Bunnies and Bowties (Book 2)

The Ending

PLEASE DON'T HATE ME :/ So the ending... I like to think of it as a happy for now (don't worry, we haven't seen the last of Everlee with her men. I love them too much!). Everlee was in a bad place after dickface. These men showed her love and gave her the confidence to get her spark back, her fire. So while it may not be the ending you wanted or expected, all I can say is I'm sorry, but never fret. Shaking my magic eight ball and it tells me you will get what you want. But they need to figure out how to live in a world that may not accept them. They may get to a point were they say fuck it and do whatever they want. I don't want them to think all is ok and then get too deep in and hurt Everlee first. They have to know what they are missing :)

However, I have added the first four chapters of the next book. Bunnies and Bowties! So you can see they are back together again :)

Bunnies and Bowties

COMING OUT MARCH 14TH! Pre-order here!

Continue reading for the first four chapters

Coming Spring 2023!

It's hard finding good help, or a charged vibrator

"NOW SLIP YOUR FINGERS into your glistening pussy. I want to watch you make yourself come." The man's deep voice commanded through my headphones with a thick accent. He could read the phone book with that voice and I'd probably come. I adjusted the speed of the vibrator and plunged it back in. "That's right. Good girl."

The words hit differently than they did before, but they still caused a flutter in my stomach.

I was getting close.

I hadn't planned on coming home to masturbate in my living room after work, but sometimes you read a good book and the next thing you know you're finger fucking yourself on the couch with one leg propped over the arm, hoping your little peeping tom neighbor in the apartment building beside you isn't chomping down on a handful of freshly popped popcorn watching the show. And then perhaps the other part of you is like fuck it, let them watch and you don't know what turns you on more.

Because you're fucked in the head.

Because I'm fucked in the head.

"Move faster." He commanded.

I started pulsing my bright pink and purple boyfriend in and out. It was the new one Lizzy bought me after... you know. It wasn't the biggest size cock on the market, but it would do the job for now. My other boyfriends were on life support plugged in, as usual, and this one was the only one up to the challenge, although I didn't know how much life he had left in him. I called him BOB because he was my battery operated boyfriend. I only needed him just a little longer because I was getting so close.

My back arched and then...

Silence.

No. No, no, no, no, no. I pulled BOB out and looked at him. He started buzzing again, filling me with hope, and then stopped. He was on the fritz. "Come on BOB, you've been so good to me all these months. The one I could always count on."

Another quick buzz, then nothing.

"You're dead to me, BOB!" I yelled out in frustration, tossing him to the ground. "I guess manual it is."

The girl was now moaning in my ear as she was coming undone.

At least one of us can girlfriend.

I slipped my fingers down to my clit and began circling, the wetness making it slick.

KNOCK! KNOCK!

I froze, staring at the door.

KNOCK! KNOCK!

Who was at my door? It was a Thursday night at nine o'clock. I glanced out of my window and saw my neighbors' living room lights were on.

Probably your neighbor looking to help you finish. Bertha said, sipping tea out of a fine porcelain cup sitting by the window. She was the elephant in the room that followed me around, so I decided to give her a name.

Was I crazy? Maybe a little. I mean, it wasn't, but two months ago I walked away from four insanely hot men who wanted me, because I was trying to protect myself.

KNOCK! KNOCK! KNOCK!

"Open up this door, bitch. I know you're inside."

Lizzy. I chuckled, standing from the couch, and slipped my pajama pants back on.

KNO-

I opened the door, mid knock.

She stood there with bunny ears on her head, wearing a light brown trench coat, eyeing me up and down with a large box in her hand.

"No." I said simply. Whatever she was trying to sell would not be good.

"Oh stop. You don't even know why I'm here."

I backed around from the door and let her in. "You're here to convince me to go to some crazy holiday party, probably at Vixen, if I had to guess."

She narrowed her gaze on me. "Ok. Well, maybe you do then. But come on." She pleaded, dropping the box to the ground.

"Lizzy. I can't."

"You can. You're just choosing not to. It's been two months since you have gone out. You can't hide away forever."

"I'm not hid-"

The buzz of the vibrator reverberated against the floor, pulling our attention.

She looked over and found him laying by the couch. "Well, I'm glad you're using the one I bought you." She smirked.

I rolled my eyes.

"Let's go! This is an intervention. They probably don't even remember you."

"Lizzy!" I snapped.

"You're right. That was mean and I'm sorry. They definitely remember you, because who wouldn't? You're a bad bitch who is gorgeous and stupid. I can't believe you walked away from them."

"Lizzy!" I snapped again.

She held her hands up. "I know, I know. I suck right now. I'm in unfamiliar territory. At least with dickface, he was a douche, so it was easy. It made sense. But these guys..."

"You aren't helping your case at all."

She puckered out her bottom lip. "Ok. Look. For real. I'm worried about you. You need to get back out there. How do you plan on meeting someone if you never put yourself out there?"

"I don't."

She huffed.

"Vixen is having a bunnies and bowties party tonight. I'm going and really want you to come with me, but I won't force you." She dropped to her knees and opened the large box. "I got you an outfit in case you said yes. I thought we could be twinsies."

I looked at the outfit and back to her and could feel myself changing my mind. I wanted to go. I wanted to see them, but I was scared. What would it be like? Would they ignore me? Would they not? Would it be awkward? I mean, it was their rules, after all. I was just following along, even though they seemed to be up for changing them. *But you didn't give them the chance.* Bertha reminded, now wearing bunny ears, looking at me.

Lizzy could sense my mind changing and started getting all jittery. She held up the white satin corset, bunny ears and little cotton tail.

"Fine."

She stood up and wrapped her arms around me. "Oh thank you, thank you, thank you!"

"I don't understand why you're so excited."

"No reason."

"Lizzy." I groaned.

"What? Can't a girl be excited about having her best friend in the world come to a nightclub with her?"

"Yes. But I don't trust you."

She batted the air. "Now, go get dressed!" She checked her watch, which made me a little apprehensive.

I grabbed the box and went into the bedroom and tossed it on my bed. I heard her moving around the kitchen, clinking glasses together, and assumed she was making us some cocktails.

I slipped the corset and tail on and looked at myself in the mirror. I pulled my boobs up a little to give them some more lift. If I was going to do this, then damn it, I wanted to look good. Before sliding the ears on, I ran the curler through my hair, gave a few twists, and touched up my makeup. I rifled through my closet and found a pair of low heels. I had a flashback to the last time I wore them on Valentine's Day. Memories started flooding my mind of that night at the guy's house and all the naked fun we had.

"What's taking so long?" Lizzy knocked on the bedroom door.

"Coming."

"I hope you do."

I opened the door and glared at her.

"Too soon?"

I pushed past her, not answering her question, and grabbed the drink she'd made off the counter in the kitchen.

"Cheers!" I said, holding up the glass to hers.

Lizzy smiled, clinking my glass. "To an unforgettable night."

"Yay." I said deadpan, tipping the drink back.

"Ok. Let's go. Our car is waiting downstairs."

"Waiting? Was it waiting this whole time?"

Lizzy smiled.

"You should have told me."

"It's fine. I gave them a big tip to wait."

"I hope they're still there."

"I'm sure she is."

"Give me one sec." I grabbed my vibrator off the floor and ran into the bedroom, plugging it in.

I looked at my wall of boyfriends and bid them all a good night. I really hoped I didn't regret going.

Don't be a bridezilla or a cunt bag

WE WERE DOWNSTAIRS A few minutes later walking to the car, and I recognized the four-door blue sedan. I crawled into the back seat and Betty turned around, looking at us.

"So you got her to come?" Betty smiled.

"Betty, that is a personal question." Lizzy teased, handing her ten bucks.

I looked curiously at Lizzy. She said a big tip. I was expecting over ten dollars.

"I'm not going to take your money." Betty batted her hand away and started pulling onto the road.

"Betty. A bet is a bet, and I lost." Lizzy insisted.

"Oh, fine!" She huffed, reaching her hand back when we got to the stoplight. I saw her place it on the hundred-dollar bill, which I assume was the tip Lizzy gave her for waiting.

"How are you doing, darling?" Betty asked, looking at me in her rearview mirror.

"I'm doing good."

"She's not. She was masturbating in her living room when I got there."

"Fuck, Lizzy!" I smacked her arm.

"What? Betty's part of the team."

"What team?"

"Team Everlee."

"I don't have a team."

Lizzy laughed. "Oh, darling."

"Had I known you two were going to team up against me, I would have never connected you."

"Don't say that, Everlee." Betty laughed. "Lizzy has been keeping me busy." She turned to Lizzy. "Did Tony win the bid?"

"He did." Lizzy bounced up and down in her seat.

"That's great to hear. I know he was really nervous about it falling through at the end."

"It was touch and go there for a bit. They made some last minute changes, but everything worked out."

"So good to hear! Is he still taking you to Bo La Vie to celebrate?"

Lizzy glanced at me, and I raised my eyebrows. "He is. We're going on Saturday night. They have a special Easter menu."

I sighed, remembering my night with Lizzy at Bo's. It was Emmett's baby he had recently opened up, and the food was divine. I missed it greatly and even though Emmett said I had a standing reservation every Monday at eight; I hadn't gone. I couldn't. I knew they'd all be there, because that's when they had their weekly meeting discussing all their business ideas and such. Which I still wasn't sure what all they had their hands in.

I could feel my stomach tighten into knots the closer we got to Vixen. I was not ready to see them. It's been two months, but I don't know if that was long enough. I mean, we weren't together for that long, but the sex. God, the sex.

I let myself get caught up in their world, and I loved it. They made me feel alive. Wanted. Confident. All the things I needed to help me get back to who I was after dickface. I had hoped I would have been able to go out after them, but every time I tried, I couldn't do it.

"Here we are, girls." Betty said, pulling up to the front. There were several other ride shares dropping people off, so she had to pull further down the curb, close to the road that led to the back of the club.

I looked down the dimly lit alleyway and saw Callum's black Audi parked at the door, with Brady standing beside the car. He looked up at me and after a second, he waved, so I waved back.

Shit.

My stomach twisted in knots.

I was going to see him tonight. My heart was pounding a hole through my chest.

"Lizzy." I started.

She looked at me and her smile dropped as she saw the terror on my face. "You got this, and if you don't. We'll leave." Her words were sincere as she interlaced her fingers in mine.

I nodded. "Ok." I could do this. I could go see three, maybe four, deliciously hot men who I let sexually ravage and delight me. Who I couldn't get off my mind, even though it's been months. Who I let myself get attached to. I could do this.

"Let's go find you a cock to ride, because I know you didn't finish earlier."

"You're like the sex whisperer."

She threw her head back and laughed while we walked past the very long line of people waiting to get in. "It was nicer when you were fucking them. At least we didn't have to wait in this line."

"That's the truth."

The weather was still cool, but not as bad as it was at Valentine's. We left our jackets in Betty's trunk because she was planning on coming back to pick us up.

We found the last spot, which was about fifty, maybe sixty, people from the door and waited, pressing up against the brick wall.

"I'm glad their business is doing so well." I said, looking down the long line and then turning to see a large group of about twenty people walking up behind us. It looked to be a bachelorette party, because all the girls were wearing pink corsets except for the one rambling in the middle, wearing a white corset with a crown on her head.

"OMG, this line is so long, guys." The bride-to-be whined, walking up. "You should have called and told them we were coming. Gotten us VIP access or something."

One girl clasped her hands together. "We tried. We called, and they said their VIP section was already booked for the night."

"On a Thursday before Easter Sunday? Who would be here then?" She whined again, grating on my nerves.

I looked at Lizzy, whose eyes got big. We were both thinking it. Who would be here? She was here. Why was she special?

I felt the girl shuffling behind me, looking over my shoulder. "Ugh, this line is not moving."

"You're going to love it." The one girl who spoke earlier said.

"I hope so. If not, you're no longer my maid of honor."

I heard the girl gasp.

I signed to Lizzy. *If you act like that, I will dump your ass.*

So no bridezilla?

Hell to the no.

Lizzy laughed.

"Oh girls, look, they're deaf."

I hated this girl. The way she said it was as if we were some sort of attraction at the zoo. I wanted to punch her in the face.

She mumbled something about my shoes not looking right with my outfit and how she would have gone with a different heel and then mentioned something about my age.

I took in a deep breath and Lizzy grabbed my hand. I don't know if it was to calm me down or prevent me from punching her.

"Oh. Are they together?" She sighed. "Is this a gay bar?"

I bit my bottom lip, trying to hold my words in.

"No. No. God no. We would never." The maid of honor sighed.

The bride-to-be just moaned and then looked over my shoulder again. "Oh good. Someone from the club is coming this way. Maybe they'll let us in because I'm getting married." She peeped.

"You think they'll let us all in?" Another girl asked.

"I don't know," she snapped back.

Seriously, why did these girls stay around her? She was horrible.

I looked down the line and saw a man dressed in all black walking up the sidewalk, getting closer and closer to us. At first, when she mentioned someone from the club, my heart leapt, thinking it was Callum. But I didn't recognize this man.

The bride-to-be was squealing behind me. "Girls, were you tricking me? He's coming over here."

I heard the maid of honor nervously laugh.

The man stopped beside us. "Everlee?"

I looked at him. "Yes."

"Can you and your friend come with me?"

I muttered something, so Lizzy answered for us. "Yes. Yes, we can."

We stepped out of line and before we started walking, I heard the bride-to-be huff and then call out, "What about me? I'm getting married Saturday!"

The man in black turned to look at her. "No."

"But." She stomped her foot, mumbling something about us.

I turned to look at her.

"Ev, don't." Lizzy pleaded, grabbing for my arm.

"I'm good." I said, then turned around. "I feel bad for the man you're marrying. He's going to be miserable, because you are miserable."

"You don't know me."

"You're right. I don't. I only know the five minutes of you I've had to endure, and I can't imagine why these girls hang around you. You are a self-centered cunt bag and your maid of honor, whoever she is, deserves someone who actually appreciates her. And for the record, we aren't deaf. Surprise. Nor are we a couple, although if we were, I'd be one lucky girl. She was holding my hand, so I didn't turn around and punch you in the face for saying stupid shit."

She gasped, and I turned and started walking away.

The man in black looked at me with a smile tugging at his lips. "Are you ready?"

"Now, I am."

We got to the door, and the bouncer looked at us, then unhooked the rope.

"Why did you get us?" Lizzy asked.

"Callum heard you were here and didn't want you both waiting outside."

I licked my lips, expecting to see him waiting for us when we walked in, but he wasn't there.

"You two have a good night." The man walked away, leaving Lizzy and me standing in the hall.

"Ok then." She said, looking around. "Bar or dance floor?"

"Bar."

You should never kiss a stranger in the dark

I COULD FEEL THE nerves coursing through me. I'd forgotten about them for a second when we were waiting outside because I was focused on that bridal hussy, but now it was just us, the music and my thoughts. Callum knew I was here. What did that mean? Why did he pull me out of line?

I could feel myself being sucked down the hole.

We walked to the bar, and I looked for Emmett and had mixed feelings when I didn't see him. I wanted to see him, but at the same time, I didn't.

"This wasn't a good idea." I mumbled to Lizzy.

"Let's just have a few drinks, then we will leave. What time is your flight tomorrow?"

"Three in the afternoon."

"Perfect. You can get wasted and then come home with me and stay."

"Lizzy..."

"What?" She pushed her way through the crowd, to the bar. "Two lemon drop shots-"

"And two pineapple martinis?" The bartender finished. She was cute and edgy. She had a pixie haircut, with a fade on one side, and streaks of purple and blue colored throughout. She had her eyebrow, nose and lip pierced, with several small tattoos scattered around her arms, neck and chest. "Haven't seen you here in a few weeks."

I thought she was talking to me, then I realized she was talking to Lizzy. "Yea. It's been crazy at work."

"Where's Tony tonight?"

"He's with his brother and sister."

"You should have told them to come here." She handed us the shots, then started on the martinis. "Well, is his sister as attractive as he is?"

"Low, I thought you were seeing that other chick."

She sighed. "Yea. It fizzled out last week." She looked at me. "Who's your friend?"

"This is Everlee, but she loves cock. Everlee, this is Harlow."

"Bummer. Well, nice to meet you Everlee. I've heard so much about you."

I panicked for a moment, and Lizzy put her hand on my arm. "Guilty. I may have told her all about you."

"Hopefully not everything." I smiled. Like the part where I used to fuck all the owners of this club.

"No. Just the embarrassing parts."

"Perfect." I laughed. "Nice to meet you, Harlow."

"You can call me Low."

I smiled as she handed us our drinks.

"Tab?"

"Yes, please." Lizzy said before we walked away.

I had already glanced up to the second floor three times, looking for any sign of Jax, Knox, or Callum, but I hadn't seen them. I grabbed Lizzy's arm. "Let's go sit over there." I pointed to the far corner of the room. From those seats, it would make it difficult to see anyone on the top floor.

The air was warm, and the lights were dancing all around us as the bass pumped through the air. A woman walked by in a black corset and black bunny ears and asked if we wanted a shot. It was some sort of liquid in a chocolate Easter egg. I, of course, had to try it.

"It's our special recipe. One of the owners created it." Emmett.

"I'll take two then." I said, grabbing another off the tray. If Emmett made them, I knew they were going to be dangerously good.

I tilted the first back and let out a moan. It was heaven. Some sort of vanilla vodka paired with the milk chocolate egg.

"Damn. Emmett knows what he's doing." Lizzy said, biting a piece off the egg.

"He does." There was a long silence between us. "Have you seen them?"

"Not tonight."

"But you have other nights?"

She nodded slowly.

I wanted to ask her if they ever asked about me, but I couldn't get the words out. I wanted to know, but also didn't. I knocked back the other shot and ate the chocolate. "Want to go dance?"

"Would love to." She smiled.

We walked onto the dance floor, and I fought the urge to look up. Instead, I let the music flow through me, closing my eyes, letting all the worry and pain go. I could feel the buzz from the drinks and paired with the music thumping through my body, I felt great. I had watched a show once that talked about the beat of the music extremely important to ensuring the dancer was having the best experience. I never realized how much science went into EDM music.

"Hey girls." I heard a voice and opened my eyes to see a shirtless man, wearing black satin boxers, a bowtie and some bunny ears. He had golden blond shaggy locks and green eyes.

"Hey there." I smiled.

"My buddy is having a party up in VIP and wants some hot girls up there. You want to go up? There are free drinks."

"Yea!" Lizzy said, pumping her fist in the air.

I looked at her cautiously.

"Cool. My name is Mark."

"Hi, Mark. I'm Lizzy and this is Everlee." She leaned over and yelled into his ear.

"Everlee. That's a cool name."

"Thanks!" I smiled, cautiously. It always felt so weird having guys just walk up to you at the bar. I always felt guarded, which was probably why I haven't found anyone since dickface. It could also be because I was looking in the wrong places.

"This will be fun!" Lizzy said.

Yeah. Fun for who? I was trying to avoid seeing them and now I was going to the place they would likely be. *Are you really trying to avoid them, though? You came to the club they own, to not see them??* Bertha asked, dancing in one of the cages with her trunk around a pole.

"Let's do this!" I should just go find them, say hello and get this over with. We could still be friends. Be civil. It's not like we dated for very long.

Long.

I had a memory of taking Callum's long cock in my mouth while the other guys watched. Get it together Everlee!

We followed Mark to the set of stairs, where he thumbed over his shoulder, letting the bouncer know we were with him.

Once we were upstairs, there were streamers and balloons all over the place with two enormous balloons with the numbers three and five. I quickly scanned the floor, but still didn't see any sign of the Callum, Jax, or Knox.

Lizzy grabbed my hand and gave it a gentle squeeze.

"Come to the dance floor. I'll introduce you to the birthday boy!" Mark called out.

We followed him through the crowd to a man who was dancing with two other women. Mark tapped him on the shoulder. "Hey Rich. I brought two more up."

I felt my stomach drop.

Rich turned around and standing in front of me was Dick.

Lizzy looked from me to Dick, back to me.

"Everlee?" He smiled, leaning forward to give me a hug.

I awkwardly accepted it, but didn't return it. He moved to give Lizzy a hug, but she stiff armed him. "No, thanks."

"You know them? Crazy!" Mark said, turning to go back downstairs.

"We can leave." I offered.

"No. Don't be silly. Stay! Drinks are free up here!" Dick said, smiling and dancing still.

I studied him for a minute, then turned to look at Lizzy.

She looked at him. "I will stay for the free drinks, but I'm not singing happy birthday to you."

Dick chuckled. "That's fair." He turned to look at me. "You look good, Everlee."

"She's knows." Lizzy barked back.

He laughed, "I see you're protective as ever." He winked at me, then turned back to the girls and continued dancing.

"Let's go get a drink." Lizzy mumbled.

I walked with her to the bar, glancing over my shoulder to look at Dick. Of all the things I thought would happen tonight, ending up at Dick's birthday party never made the list. The last time I had seen him was a few days after the Valentine's Day gala when he showed up at my doorstep and tried to get me to give him another chance. He said he was going to win me back, but it's been radio silence. It was probably a good thing, because I would have slipped. Not because I wanted to get back with him, but because I was sad and horny and he was someone I knew. It would only be to fuck him, but that would open the door and I didn't feel like dealing with that baggage.

I heard a squeal that caught my attention and turned to find bridezilla was up here now dancing with Dick. I guess flies are attracted to shit, so it makes sense they would find each other. They were grinding and dancing, their hands moving in places they probably shouldn't be.

"I guess some things never change." Lizzy said, staring at Dick.

"Good luck to that woman's groom." I mumbled.

"Want to go dance? On the opposite side of the floor from him?"

"Sure."

We sat our empty glasses on the bar and walked, hand in hand, to the other side of the dance floor. All the other times I'd been up here, it had just been a few of us. It was weird to see it so busy, but I was happy for them. The club looked like it was doing really well.

The song changed, just as we got on the floor, and it must have been a popular song, because suddenly the floor was packed. A man pushed his way in between Lizzy and me and started dancing with us. I tried not to think too much and just moved my body, letting the beat take control.

A moment later, I felt a hand on my side. I leaned back and closed my eyes, dancing with this stranger, moving my hips, rubbing against him. I just wanted to have fun and let go of everything. Callum, Jax, Knox, Emmett, Dick.

The man's hand slipped up to my waist, then back down to my hip. My body felt electrified right now. It was humming. The vibration from the bass and the drinks probably helped. I felt his head drop beside my face as he continued to grind into me. Our bodies moving together in rhythm. It felt so right. So perfect. I snaked my hand around his neck, holding him in place. His lips began to gently kiss my neck, and a moan escaped my lips. I felt him smile against my throat as he continued to nibble and suck on my fevered skin.

I turned my head to find his lips just as the lights went out. The kiss started off soft, cautious, and then quickly turned into something more. His tongue brushed across my lips and I opened, letting our tongues dance. I turned around, so I was facing him chest to chest.

I wanted more. I needed more.

I heard the crowd sing happy birthday, but I didn't care about anything but these lips on mine right now. It had been months since I had kissed anyone and these were delicious. I felt my insides tighten as I melted into him.

The song finished, and the lights clicked back on. I pulled away and looked at the man I'd been kissing.

His bright blue eyes were on my face with a smile tugging on his lips as his hand rested on my cheek.

Making up... for lost time

- -

"Everlee." His thumb brushed over my cheekbone.

"Callum." I breathed, reflexively pressing into his hand. "I should have known..."

He chuckled as his eyes settled on my face. "You kissed me first." He defended.

I pushed against his chest, his hard muscles twitching under my palm. "I don't think so, buddy. You were kissing my neck."

He let out a low hum. "I suppose that's true."

I couldn't help but smile looking at him. He was just as sexy as the last time I saw him, with maybe a few more strands of silver threaded through his dark hair.

"Are you here with Rich?" The infliction in his voice when he said Rich made me smile.

"No. Some guy brought us up for his friend's birthday. Turned out to be Dick's, and he invited us to stay for the drinks."

He hummed, grabbing my hand and guiding me over to a booth in the corner. I caught Lizzy's eye, so she knew where I was going. Her face was glowing with a shit eating grin.

"How have you been?" He asked, sitting beside me, with his hand on my thigh.

"Good." I answered, breathlessly. "You?"

His eyes were boring holes into me. The skin under the touch of his hand was on fire. I felt my core spooling and butterflies dancing in my stomach. "I've been better." He admitted and I couldn't help but wonder if I had something to do with that.

I shrugged. "I guess I've been better as well, also."

His hand slid up my leg, and a wanting breath escaped from between my lips, but he stopped.

"Callum." I cried softly, begging him to continue. I wanted to feel his touch. Feel his lips.

"Everlee." His voice was broken.

I was searching his eyes, and they looked torn. I placed my hand on the side of his cheek and his eyes closed slowly, savoring my touch on him. He turned his lips to press them into the palm of my hand. "God, I miss the taste of you." He mumbled.

"So... fix it." I encouraged.

His eyes shot to mine as he held my gaze for a moment.

"Come with me." He stood from the couch and walked over to a door in the corner of the room. He pulled his retractable ID from his clip and swiped it against the pad, then pushed the door open. He pulled me inside and pressed my back against the door, closing it, as his lips took mine and his hands tangled in my hair.

I let out a moan as my hands feverishly raked across his body, sliding his jacket off, and then fumbled with the buttons on his shirt.

"Everlee." He warned, his hands holding my wrists.

"Please. Just this once. I need you."

He swallowed and then moved his hands back to my corset and began to untie the ribbons in the front before unhooking each of the clasps. I slipped his shirt off and pulled away from our kiss so I could admire his beautifully tattooed torso. I kissed his chest and heard him suck in a breath between his teeth.

His hands continued with the hooks. So many fucking hooks! I unhooked the ones between my legs and pulled the corset the rest of the way down. I was standing in front of him, completely naked, seconds later.

"Fuck Everlee. You're a goddamn vision." He moved in quickly and took a breast in his mouth, while his hand grabbed the other. "And I see no panties again." He said in between switching breasts.

"Didn't really go with the outfit."

"No. I guess they didn't," he said, dropping to his knees and throwing my leg over his shoulder. A second later, his tongue was swiping up my wet folds from back to front, before he plunged his tongue in.

"Callum." I moaned out, pressing my back against the door.

"I've missed your moans too."

"I've missed your mouth on my pussy." I said, tangling my fingers in his hair.

He wrapped his arms around me and stood up, sliding me up the door. I threw my other leg over his shoulder and held his head tightly as he carried me over to the couch and laid back so I was sitting on his face.

"Fuck my face Everlee."

A wave passed through my stomach as I rocked my hips back and forth as his tongue pressed further into me. His groans of delight urged me on faster and faster. His hand reached around my leg as his fingers found my clit and began working in gentle circles.

"Fuck Callum." I was so close. My hands gripped into his hair as I continued to gyrate on his face.

BEEP!

We froze.

The door was unlocking.

Shit! Shit! Shit!

My clothes were across the room and there was nothing I could use to cover myself.

"Callum? Have you seen Ever-"

Jax.

Fuck me. He looked as hot as ever.

He closed the door and just looked at us, a smile tugging on his lips. "I guess that answers my question. Enjoying yourself, love?"

"Yes." I nodded, removing my hands from my chest.

His teeth scraped across his bottom lip as his eyes raked across my body.

Feeling extra bold, I asked. "Do you want to watch or do you want to join?"

"What do you want?" He asked, cocking his head to the side.

I smiled at him. "I want your cock in my mouth while Callum fucks my pussy."

"I see your mouth isn't any less filthy." Jax said, running his hand over the growing bulge in his pants.

"No." I started rocking on Callum's face again as he started rubbing my clit. I moaned out as I looked to the ceiling, running my hands over my breasts. "I'm going to come, Callum." I was almost there before the door opened, and now having Jax watch me was like adding fuel to the fire.

I turned my head to look at Jax watch us, his eyes almost animalistic.

"Oh, fuck." I cried out.

Callum grabbed both of my legs, pulling me down on his face, holding me there while the wet sounds of my juices caused desire to flood through me like a dam released. I exploded in an orgasm as I rode the waves of ecstasy on his face. He was holding me there, eagerly lapping up all he could as my body pulsed around his tongue. That was so hot and erotic.

"I've fucking missed you." I growled, pushing off his face.

"Samesies." Jax said, walking over with his hand, stroking his cock.

"Ass." I climbed off Callum and met Jax in the middle of the room. I shoved against his chest, but he grabbed me by the throat, his eyes locked on mine, before he claimed my mouth with his. He pushed us towards Callum, who was now waiting on the couch, stroking himself.

Jax pulled away from our kiss, his hand still clamped under my jaw. "I can't wait to feel your lips around my cock. It's missed you." He kissed me one more time, then dropped his hand.

"Do you have a condom?" I turned to Callum. "I don't need your cum dripping down my leg the rest of the night."

It's been two months without them and yet it feels like it's been days... hours even. Slipping in right where we left off. Everything just felt so right... so natural with them. Even from the second I felt Callum's hand on me on the dance floor before I knew it was him.

He smiled. "I guess." He flicked his hand up with a condom pressed between his index and middle finger. "Though I would love to see my release all over you, and for everyone to know, I just fucked you."

He slipped the condom on and, without hesitation, I climbed on top of him and sank down, letting him fill me. It had been months since I had an actual dick inside of me, so it took a minute for me to stretch around him. But he felt like heaven. I had a tingle move up my spine as my body appreciated the feeling.

"Goddamn you're so tight."

"I've not had sex in a while." I looked at him and his chin tilted up.

"Well then, let's give you all we have tonight." His hands clamped around my hips and I rocked into him slowly, letting my body appreciate the full size of his cock. I could feel my skin tingling with excitement as desire pulsed through me.

"You feel so good." I moaned, grabbing my breasts, looking at Jax and smiling.

He walked over and wrapped his hand around the back of my head and guided me towards his cock. No words, just lust and need filled the air. I grabbed around the base, wrapping my fingers one at a time as I ran my tongue up the underside before swirling it around his head, running my tongue through his slit, licking the precum off the tip. I sucked just the head into my mouth, letting my tongue play while I continued to rock on Callum.

This was definitely not how I pictured my night going when I left work this afternoon.

"You're teasing me." Jax moaned.

I looked up at him as I sucked him into my mouth, taking him in as deep as I could. A nonverbal dare for him to say something else. His eyes rolled back into his head before he looked at me. I pumped my hand up and down his cock, cheeks hallowed, never diverting my eyes. I wanted to watch him watch me. I wanted to see the fire in his eyes. The longing to have my lips around him.

"Damn Everlee." His hand gripped tighter in my hair as his hips rocked into me, hitting the back of my throat.

He was perfection. His teeth were clamped tight on his bottom lip as his eyes locked on mine.

Callum's finger began to rub on my clit. I moaned around Jax's cock as I continued to rock back and forth. I raised off him some, because I wanted to feel him fuck me from underneath. I wanted him to claim me.

"Do you want it hard, Everlee?"

I hummed a yes.

"Hold up Jax. Let's change." Callum said.

Jax sighed and pulled away, wiping his finger across my lip before taking my mouth in a kiss.

"Jax." Callum warned.

"Sorry. I just missed her lips." He said, winking at me.

I felt my insides melt. I was a pile of mush. Put a pin in me, I'm done.

Callum pointed for Jax to stand at the end of the couch. I got up on all fours and Callum moved around behind me. "There. Now I can fuck you the way you deserve to be fucked." Callum said, lining his cock up at my entrance before plunging inside.

A grunt escaped and a trickle of pain radiated as he pushed deep inside. But I didn't care. I loved the feel of him. His hands rested on my hips as I pushed back, my body needing more. "Harder." I moaned. I didn't wait for him to speak before I grabbed Jax and brought him to my mouth. A deep swell of passion, of fire, raced through me. I missed these boys with every fiber of my being, and I was stupid for walking away.

It took a couple of thrusts, but we got into a rhythm where Jax and Callum were fucking both ends of me.

"That's my good girl." Callum said, running his hand down my spine.

I bucked my hips up and moaned around Jax's cock.

"Our good girl." Jax corrected.

My eyes fluttered as my stomach clenched. Their words were going to make me come before their cocks did. Why did I ever leave them? We could find a way to make this work. They were worth it, and so were their cocks.

I could feel Jax's hands clamp tighter in my hair, holding me in place. He was getting close and so was I.

"Callum?" Jax asked.

"Almost."

Callum's hand slipped around my hip and began circling my clit. "She's so fucking wet, I keep slipping."

"You're out of practice, brother."

Out of practice? Does that mean they haven't slept with anyone either? No. That can't be. No. I was thinking too much and needed to just focus on them. On right now.

"Come on, baby. Come for me." Callum changed the angle of his thrusts, rubbing on all the right spots as his speed picked up.

"Give her what she wants." Jax hummed.

I felt something wet hit my back and felt Callum's finger swipe over my tight hole.

Fuck.

"Oh, she's getting excited." Jax said.

I moaned at the same time Callum pressed his thumb in. I clenched around Callum's cock and squeezed onto Jax's.

"Shit!" Jax shouted before a warm saltiness exploded in my mouth, but I didn't let up on the thrusts as I swallowed him down. "Damn, Everlee."

A second later, I released Jax, and he rubbed his hand over his cock, watching us finish. Callum's other hand moved around to my clit and he began circling. Was I holding myself back from my orgasm because I didn't want this to end?

"Your tits look so perfect." Jax said, watching them swing.

"Here brother." Callum said sitting back, bringing me with him so I was on his lap with my back pressed to his chest.

"Yes." Jax groaned, walking over and getting on the couch in front of us. Callum paused, letting me sink on him while Jax took my neck in his mouth, biting and sucking. His one hand played with my nipple, while the other slid down and began rubbing my clit. Soft, slow.

I moaned and slowly rocked my hips on Callum.

"You like that?" Jax asked.

"Mmhmm." I let my neck fall to the side, giving him more access.

"You want more of this?"

"Yes."

He pinched my nipple between his fingers, causing a ripple to move down my body to between my legs. I started rocking harder and faster as Jax's finger pressed harder on my clit.

He leaned down and took my breast in his mouth, sucking my nipple.

"You should have never left us Everlee." Callum murmured into my hair.

"I know. I'm sorry." I was sorry. I walked away from them for fear of getting hurt, but that fixed nothing. I still got hurt, but with no sex. Stupid me.

"She's getting close." Callum said, pressing his hands to my legs, holding me down so he could grind into me.

Jax's finger moved faster as he sucked my breast, rubbing his teeth over my nipple.

"Fuck!" I cried out. My orgasm hit me hard. A low grumble echoed from deep inside as Jax's mouth slid over mine, swallowing my moans. I felt Callum pump two more times before he stopped. I felt like a limp noddle. Jax's kiss went from hard and fast to slower and more passionate.

I whimpered out one more time and Jax pulled back and swiped his thumb across my bottom lip. "Beautiful." He gave me a quick peck on the end of my nose.

I climbed off Callum and walked across the room to grab the tissue from Jax.

"Well, Knox and Emmett are going to be pissed." Jax said matter-of-factly.

I scrunched my face. "How are they?"

"They miss you. They kept hoping you would stop by Bo's on Mondays."

"We all missed you." Callum corrected, walking over, grabbing another tissue.

"I missed you guys, too." I grabbed my outfit near the door and slid it back on. "I just... I knew you had your rules, and we were technically done."

"Technically?"

"What happened to rules are meant to be broken?" Jax asked.

"I wanted the rules to be broken..." I adjusted the bunny ears on my head. "I was scared you all didn't and... that was going to hurt. And then the other part of me was scared you wanted to change the rules, but even then wouldn't because of societal pressures."

Jax and Callum were both tucking their shirts back in. "Sounds like you made a lot of assumptions." Callum said, running his fingers through his hair.

"I know." I whined.

I walked over to the mirror in the room and rubbed my lips a little. They were swollen, just fucked lips. There was no way I was going to hide that from Lizzy. Hopefully, she just didn't make a huge deal about it in front of everyone.

I looked between the both of them. What was I thinking when I walked away?

"Are you drooling?" Jax asked.

"Shut up." I laughed. "I was just trying to figure how mental I was to walk away from you all."

Jax chuckled. "We were all fighting each other, trying not to knock down your door and bring you back to us. There were a few times we were close."

"You were outside of my office a couple of weeks ago, weren't you?"

"No." Callum spat quickly, looking guilty.

"Callum?" Jax warned.

"Fine. I wasn't going to kidnap her... I think. I just wanted to see you. It's not like you weren't camped out in front of her apartment for several nights." Callum tattled.

Jax's lips puckered.

"Well, I visited Lizzy a couple of times and showed up early and waited outside, in hopes you would drive down the road at the same time and see me." I pointed. "You didn't, so I sat there freezing my ass off." I laughed.

"You could have always come down to Vixen, like you did tonight."

"I could have, but I was scared. I almost didn't come tonight."

"Glad we could help." They winked.

I smiled. "Well, that kind of come... yes, thank you... but..."

"Does Lizzy know about us?"

I scrunched my nose. I don't know what prompted the question. Perhaps she had said or done something one of the times she was here?

"We couldn't be mad at you if we wanted to."

"After everything happened, I needed to talk to someone. I made her sign an NDA though, if that makes it better."

Callum shook his head, smiling. "Well, that's something."

"Speak of the devil..." Jax said, looking at the cameras just before a knock thumped on the door.

"Lizzy?" I asked Jax before walking over.

He nodded.

I opened the door, and she peeked her head in before stepping in. "Wanted to make sure you dirty fuckers were all dressed. Although I wouldn't hate to see what you hide under those shirts." She pointed at Jax and Callum with a devious smile.

"Lizzy..." I said, blushing.

"Hello Lizzy." Jax droned.

"Guys." She nodded to them both before running her hand from my cheek to chin. "Thank you for taking care of her. She needed a good fuck."

"Lizzy!" I snapped.

"She really does have a gift." Jax smiled, impressed.

"It can be a pain in the ass sometimes."

"Oh, but you love me."

"Yes. I do."

"Are you ready to go?" She asked, then looked at the boys. "Am I allowed to take her?"

"Yes." I answered, looking longingly at Jax and Callum. What did I say? Where did we go from here?

Callum walked over and slipped his arm around me, giving me a kiss on top of my head. "We need to talk, but the next couple of days aren't good. Are you free next week?"

I looked at Jax, who was leaning forward in the chair, his forearms resting on the desk.

"Yes. I'm free."

"Perfect. We'll call to set up a time." Callum said, putting his hands in his pockets.

"So formal." I teased.

"We could just kidnap you if you prefer?" Jax smiled.

"Kinky."

He shook his head.

"You girls have a good rest of the night. Your tab from downstairs has been comped." Callum interjected.

"You didn't have to do that." Lizzy said, batting her hand in the air.

Callum winked at me. "Have a good night."

Lizzy and I walked out of their office and down the stairs. I ignored the glance from dickface as he watched us leave their office, no doubt wondering what was going on in there.

"Queen." Lizzy said, grabbing my arm when we got outside.

I blushed again, laughing awkwardly.

"Quueeenn."

"Stop."

"Well, I'm glad you got some dick tonight."

"It was so good, Lizzy."

"I take it you got both?"

I smiled.

"I try not to be a jealous woman, but damn girl. You got me in my feels."

Betty pulled up before I could respond. As I stepped into the car, I looked back at Vixen.

"Did you both have a lovely night?"

"Yes, we did." Lizzy answered for both of us, fortunately not elaborating.

I decided to stay at my house tonight since I wasn't drunk and it would give me time to think about our meeting next week. Fortunately, I was headed home for the long weekend to spend some time with my family. Time by the lake always seemed to help set my mind right, and I needed it after tonight. No Vixen, no Lizzy, and no guys.

Thanks so much for reading! Don't forget to leave a review and share with your friends! That is the best and most efficient way to get our books out to others!

Printed in Great Britain
by Amazon

23212981R00148